I was at my desk  ring through to the answering machine. The machine whirred to life and Carmen's voice filled the room.

"Mr. Dahms," she began, *"I know we just met and that I've no reason to trust you, but…But I've got to trust someone. I really don't have anywhere else to turn."*

Although her voice was steady, alarm edged her words. I picked up the phone. "Carmen," I said. "What can I do for you?"

"Oh, Lyle," she sighed, her composure dissolving. "Thank God you're there. I'm so frightened. I think they're outside waiting for me. You've got to come over here. You've got to come over right away. I'm at my apartment." She gave me an address on Eighth Street Southeast. "It's on the bottom floor. I've got some things to tell you about how Ted died. Please Lyle. You've got to come over right away."

"Calm down, Carmen," I said. "What's so urgent?"

"I can't tell you right now," she sobbed. "I can't tell you on the phone. Please, just come right away."

I didn't like it. I don't get a lot of calls from mob-connected damsels in distress and my instincts told me to err on the side of caution. But I'd been carrying around a mental picture of Carmen since we'd met and I couldn't shake the memory of that knife-edge of fear I'd seen flash in her eyes.

"Are you in some kind of danger?" I asked, trying to sound businesslike.

She didn't answer. There was a clicking sound; then the phone went dead.

The great big nothing coming from the receiver was corrosive. It ate at my insides. I pushed back from my desk and headed immediately down to my car.

Praise for The Shiver in Her Eyes

"…This tale mines the gritty underbelly of Minneapolis and turns up gems: a soulless hit man, a heart-stealing woman, a mob-controlled pornographer, and a tattered but loyal PI. Suspenseful, heart-warming, and wonderfully written, just try to put it down…"

~Roxanne Dunn, award winning author

The Shiver in Her Eyes

by

Brian Anderson

The Shiver in Her Eyes

Cover Art by *Kim Mendoza*

The Wild Rose Press, Inc.
PO Box 708
Adams Basin, NY 14410-0708
Visit us at www.thewildrosepress.com

Publishing History
First Edition, 2022
Trade Paperback ISBN 978-1-5092-4280-1
Digital ISBN 978-1-5092-4281-8

Published in the United States of America

Dedication

In memory of Richard Gatten

Acknowledgments

I am deeply grateful to my editor Kaycee John and the entire team at The Wild Rose Press for giving me the opportunity to bring this novel to print.

It may not have come together at all without the advice and support of my critique group of the last twenty plus years—Jessie Irene Fernandes, Diane Spahr, Roger Schwarz, Mark Knoke, Meredith Fane, and Nik Joshi—fine writers all. My thanks also go out to "Burnsville Boys" Eric Lindbom and Nic Santiago for their inspiration and long friendship. Thanks are also due to the staff and regular customers of the late, lamented Valli Restaurant, now merely a dimming memory of my days in Dinkytown U.S.A.

But most of all I am thankful to my family—my much better half Sue, and daughters Nicole, Sydney, and Miranda. You are my light.

Chapter One

The day had started off so nicely, I reminded myself, dipping my sponge into the bucket of warm water and taking another swipe at the blood-smeared wall. Standing some three feet away, holding a clipboard and making little clicky noises with his tongue, cleaning crew supervisor Brad Decker squinted disapprovingly at my work.

"Use a little more degreaser on that stuff over there."

That "stuff," as Brad put it, was a grayish-white blob of brain encircled with dried blood and anchored to the wall like an infected pimple. I sprayed on additional solvent, swallowed hard against the nausea that was creeping up my throat, and recalled how only an hour earlier I had made my triumphal return to my old employer, Personnel Service Industries.

I didn't have many happy memories of the days, years before, that I'd worked at PSI—a Minneapolis temporary help agency that specializes in placing day laborers. The pay was lousy, the hours worse, and a sense of hopelessness and despair hung over the place like the aroma of discounted scrod at an outdoor fish market. I'd been positively giddy when I'd finally found a real job and had walked out of the small redbrick building, I'd hoped, for the last time. But earlier that morning, despite mid-December temperatures that had plunged to the double digits below zero, when I entered, kicked the

1

snow off my shoes, and looked up across the room into the face of PSI owner, and Brad's father, Luther Decker, I flushed with a warmly nostalgic glow. Luther, resplendent in a red plaid shirt and a pair of blue jeans two sizes too big, seemed to feel it too. He smiled when he saw me come in. More accurately, the corners of his mouth stiffened, pushing back his jowls to form something that resembled a smile. It was, I quickly realized, a smile more condescending, than welcoming. Nostalgia is too often more than just the fond recollection of things past; it's also the force that prompts unquiet spirits to linger at the sites of their suicides.

There were a dozen or so men waiting in the cramped lobby facing the assignment desk. Luther was still showing his teeth as I approached. When I reached him, he took a half step back. "Well, if it ain't Lyle Dahms." He then leaned forward and announced loudly, "We must be living right, boys. Christmas is still two weeks away and the fat man's already here."

I managed a weak chuckle. My mom taught me it's important not to be too sensitive about these things. Besides, I wouldn't say that I'm fat. There always seem to be plenty of people around to say that for me.

"Golly, Luther," I replied, "I can't tell you how tickled I am that you remember me. I was worried when I didn't see a candle burning in the window."

Luther's smile faded. He coughed, then flipped a clipboard across the desk to me. "Sign in if you want to."

"What you got today?"

"Assignments aren't out yet." Luther wiped a splash of coffee from the counter with a spit-moistened finger. "You're late. Don't know if I can help you today."

2

I shrugged, signed the clipboard, and took a seat with the others.

Despite his warning that I was late, Luther assigned me to a cleaning crew with his son, Brad, and two guys of indeterminate age with wild hair and grime-encrusted, thrift shop overcoats. Brad didn't work very hard at hiding his contempt as he sized us up. He was in his early twenties, tall, trim, and certainly better dressed than either my co-workers or me. He had on a pair of tight fitting, white denim pants and a striped dress shirt, left unbuttoned enough to expose a tanned, hairless chest. His jaw was firm; his teeth were white and perfect. I looked closely at my confederates. Neither of them had perfect teeth.

As we were about to leave, Brad paused. Puffing himself up, he said, "Today we will be cleaning a residence on Garfield Avenue. The owner will not be home. It seems that there has been some unpleasantness at this address. It is important that I impress upon you that this job requires not only our diligence, but also our discretion. In other words, gentlemen, I wish us to be on our best behavior today."

The three of us manual labor types glanced inquiringly at one another. Brad pointed at the back door with his clipboard. "Come, our van awaits us."

The conversation during the drive over was not what I'd describe as scintillating. Brad was silent the entire trip. My two new colleagues exchanged a significant look before introducing themselves as Phil and Don. One of them—Don, I think—grunted unfavorably when I told them to call me Lyle. They both then proceeded to ignore me, preferring instead to whisper between themselves in voices so soft I couldn't even be certain what language they were speaking.

Our assignment was a well-kept bungalow that dated from the mid-1920s. A walkway of gray and rose paving stones led from the street to a wide front porch, hugged by green shrubbery. The walkways had been shoveled entirely free of snow and the house itself appeared recently painted. It stood in some contrast to many of the surrounding houses, whose state of ill repair testified to a neighborhood that had gone considerably to seed since the houses were originally built.

It had been bitterly cold all week. To make matters worse, the wind had picked up that morning and when we climbed out of our toasty van, the frigid air seemed to bristle with needles. We reached the porch, I stomped my feet, vainly trying to keep circulation flowing, as Brad fumbled with the door key. When he finally managed to work the lock, I rushed gratefully into the house. But despite the warmth, the scene inside made the blood in my veins go to instant slush.

The door opened directly into a living room. Off to the right, a blue sofa with wood trim took up most of the wall. A four-foot Christmas tree in the farthest corner was a riot of tinsel and glass ornaments. Kitty-corner from the sofa sat a television stand, but, oddly, the set was missing. Nearest the door, directly opposite the TV stand, was a brown leather recliner with an afghan draped over one arm. The chair was a mess. Someone had bled all over it.

A thick, red stain soaked through the leather and stuffing glared out from a large hole in the back of the chair. Bits of gray matter rested in the clotted blood which had oozed down to the mustard-colored carpet. Behind the recliner, an arc of blood and brains splattered a crazy mural on the wall.

Something too small to be seen buzzed past my ear, followed by a lot of somethings, swarming invisibly around us. The room was stale and musty, edged with a vaguely offensive tang that lingered like the dim memory of a childhood nightmare. Phil and Don both stood with their heads bowed—like penitents before a grim deity. I drew a deep breath and closed my eyes. I opened them when Brad let go a dramatic sigh.

"As you can see, gentlemen," he said, "there has been much unpleasantness here of late."

"Who bought it?" I asked.

Brad stared at me with distrust. "What was your name again?"

"Dahms," I told him. "Lyle Dahms."

Brad shifted his weight from side to side, ran a finger through his long blond hair, and flashed a prideful smile. "Well, Dahms," he began, stressing my name as though he found it unpalatable, "the owner was one Theodore Rovig. Ted, to his friends, of which there were several, despite the rather unsavory clientele for whom he worked. Rovig was an accountant who numbered among his clients a certain Mr. Alexander Farnum, this town's only truly well-known purveyor of pornographic material."

I'd heard about it, of course. Rovig's death had been big news for nearly a week. Minneapolis was on a record-setting pace for murders that year, but even with the glut, the Rovig murder stood out from the crowd. The tie-in with Farnum was what brought real juice to the story and the TV and newspapers were playing it up with the enthusiasm of a sailor who'd just bought himself a ten-dollar hooker.

Farnum had first come to prominence decades before as the owner of a large chain of adult bookstores in the Twin Cities area. Unlike most sex merchants, Farnum seemed to love the spotlight, and the local media had made his the face of porn in the Twin Cities. When his bookstores became unprofitable, Farnum moved to mail order, 900 numbers, and the Internet, finding that he could reach far more people if he made his product available to his patrons without requiring them to appear in a public place to purchase it. In recent interviews, Farnum had gleefully bragged that his porn profits were greater than ever. He was fond of saying that there was a lot of money to be made in the dark.

It was no surprise that the reports of Rovig's death concentrated on the dead man's connection to Farnum. Casual mention was made that he had other clients, but the image being pushed was that of the smiling porn king. It was widely speculated that Farnum, if not directly responsible for Rovig's death, had at least led the accountant down the path that eventually led to his murder. For their part, the police said what they always said—they were following up several promising leads and an arrest was expected at any time.

Brad cast a weary glance over the scene. "Well, gentlemen, it would be pleasant to stand here and chat about this all day, but we have the dubious honor of cleaning up what remains of our Mr. Rovig, and we must get on with the work. If you would kindly go back out to the van and retrieve the implements of our trade, I will stay here and map out our strategy."

By this I decided that he wanted us to go out and get the cleaning supplies, so my buddies and I each made two trips out to the van bringing in buckets, sponges, solvents, rubber gloves, and a two-ton carpet shampooer. Meanwhile, Brad walked around the house occasionally making a note on his clipboard.

Finally, surrounded by our "implements," we turned to Brad so he could outline our strategy. He took a deep breath and offered us a look rife with disagreement. "Gentlemen, it is important that you realize our position here. This home has been under a great deal of scrutiny, and PSI is nothing if not a reputable company. As my father is the owner of PSI, it is frankly a matter of family pride to me that we afford this job our utmost care."

We stared blankly back at him.

Brad's eyes narrowed. "By this I mean that I do not want it said that anything turned up missing after we have concluded our business here." He paused. "I trust that I make myself understood."

"Yes, sir, Mr. Decker," I told him. "We darn sure wouldn't want to do anything to muddy your reputation."

Brad raised an eyebrow before turning away.

As Phil, Don and I went to work, I did my best to keep an eye on Brad. He hung around for a few minutes, but soon began to make his way down a hallway that led to the rear of the house. He paused to glance into the adjacent kitchen but was moving on when a knock at the front door stopped him. He didn't have time to answer it before the door swung open and two men entered.

The first guy through the door was a large, well-muscled, young man who, despite the cold, wore no overcoat. He was dressed in a crisp, blue suit, white shirt, and blue paisley tie. As he entered, he stepped to one side, keeping his eyes on us while allowing the second man to enter.

Man number two was short, overweight, and wore a

shabby, olive raincoat. Having stepped through the door, he carefully pushed it closed with his heel. Slowly and silently, he unbuttoned the coat, under which he wore a rumpled, charcoal gray suit that, from the looks of it, he'd purchased sometime back in the Clinton administration. He put his hands on his hips, pushing back his suit coat to reveal his ample stomach, a pair of black suspenders, and a shoulder holster. I shielded my face, hoping he wouldn't recognize me.

My morning had taken another potentially bad turn.

The short man quickly surveyed the room, then fixed his eyes on Brad. "Okay, pal," he snarled, "who the hell are you?"

Phil and Don dropped their spray bottles and lowered their eyes. Brad, who had stopped at the end of the hallway, held his clipboard across his chest and shivered slightly. "We're from PSI," he said in an even voice. "You know, Personnel Service Industries. We've been contracted to clean this place up." Then he looked down his nose at the man and in a voice just this side of arrogant, asked, "Who, might I ask, are you?"

The short guy didn't answer. Instead, he wheeled on his partner. "Christ, Mickey. Who was the jackass that authorized this cleanup?"

"Um...Ah, I guess I did, Augie," the younger man replied, careful not to make eye contact. "I mean we've been over and over this place, and I uh...I thought...I released the crime scene. I told you yesterday that I'd take care of it. You didn't really give me an answer. I didn't know you wanted to look around again."

Without bothering to reply, the short man nodded a couple of times, then turned away. The younger man sighed and stiffly posted himself at the door.

Brad took a step forward and cleared his throat loudly. "Am I to understand that you gentlemen are from the police?"

"No flies on you, pal," the short man said as he approached and didn't stop until he stood practically nose to nose with the kid. Brad hugged his clipboard even tighter.

The cop reached into the inside pocket of his suit coat and produced a badge. "Name's Tarkof. Homicide." He smiled thinly. "I'm not disturbing you, am I?"

Brad folded completely. "Uh, not at all, sir. I mean…I mean, we're sorry if we're in your way, sir. We were told you were all done here. You know, with your investigation and stuff?" He lowered his eyes and his face tightened visibly, as if at any moment he might burst into tears. "You are done?" he asked. "Aren't you?"

"You mean with our investigation *and stuff?*" Tarkof replied sharply. "Oh, hell yes. We're all done with that. No, we just stopped by to see if you guys needed anything. You know, maybe we could get you some lemonade, or something."

The younger cop by the door chuckled. Brad stared at his shoes.

After a moment, Tarkof declared, "Well, if you're gonna clean, then get on with it. Just stay out of my way."

Brad took several very small, quick steps backward and sighed audibly. I was turning back to the wall that I'd been working on when Tarkof noticed me. A smirky grin spread over his pudgy face. Coming closer, he said, "Dahms? What the hell are you doing here? This part of your campaign against crime? Mopping up dead guys?"

Brad stiffened. He jerked his head; his lips began to quiver. "Officer, I swear," he insisted, "I've never worked with this man before. Really, if he is some kind of criminal, I had no way of knowing. I've been watching him and I—"

"It's Detective," Tarkof interrupted. "Relax, junior. Dahms here ain't a criminal. In fact, he's a—"

I cut him off. "I'm just an acquaintance of the detective's," I sputtered, my eyes mutely pleading with Tarkof not to say anymore to Brad. Tarkof stared at me a moment before giving me a slight nod. Brad continued to eye me suspiciously. "Really, Mr. Decker," I assured him, "I ain't never been arrested."

Tarkof laughed. "Like I said, relax, junior. You boys just get back to work."

Grateful, I turned around and had just enough time to put the sponge to the wall when Tarkof piped up again. "On second thought," he said, "you other guys can get back to work, but if Mr. Dahms has the time, perhaps he could help me out with a little something."

Tarkof took me by the arm and led me back toward the door, away from Brad and the others. He leaned in close and whispered, "What gives?"

"I'll tell you later, Augie."

"Damn right you will."

Tarkof stepped back. "Now, we've already got a pretty good idea of what went on in here. But there are one or two points that we need to be sure of. What I need is someone to help me reenact the crime." He grinned. "You know, like on TV."

"How 'bout your boy, Mickey?" I asked, pointing to Tarkof's partner, who was still stationed by the door, arms crossed over his chest. "Does he get to do anything besides stand around and look pretty?"

Tarkof smiled, reached up, and rubbed at his unruly

mustache. "Well, I tell ya," he said, shaking his head in amusement, "Mickey just ain't dressed right for the kinda work I had in mind."

Mickey glared at me. I considered blowing him a kiss but thought better of it.

"Here's what we need, Dahms," Tarkof continued. "Rovig got it in the face with a shotgun. His assailant seems to have come in through the front door. The back door, the one back there in the kitchen, was locked. The front door was found wide open. There are no signs of forced entry, so either he let the killer in, or the killer let himself in through the unlocked door. Anyway, he's in the chair and our guy comes in, circles around in front of him, levels the shotgun right at his baby blues, and lets him have it. You with me so far, Dahms?"

I nodded.

"Now, say you're Rovig, and I'll be our bad guy. You take a seat in the chair there and I'll—"

"Hold on, Augie," I interrupted.

Tarkof's brow furrowed slightly, but he was otherwise expressionless. His gaze held mine as he nodded toward the chair. I followed the nod, letting my eyes travel to the shredded upholstery, the chaotically twisting springs, and the clumps of stuffing lacquered in place with the burnt umber of dried blood.

"You're not serious," I said.

"Be a good citizen, Dahms," Tarkof drawled, his eyes glinting. "You wouldn't want your boss over there...What's his name? Decker? You wouldn't want Mr. Decker over there to wonder why you wouldn't help the police conduct a little official business."

I looked over at Brad. He was studying my face in case he'd have to pick me out of a lineup later.

11

"No way," I told Tarkof.

Tarkof answered with a broad smile. Brad narrowed his eyes, checked his watch, and made a note on his clipboard.

"You got your job," Tarkof said, "I got mine." He gestured toward Brad. "You help me with mine, I don't have to interfere with yours."

Tarkof extended a large hand and gently pushed me down into the chair. I closed my eyes as the back of my head came to rest in what used to be Theodore Rovig.

When I opened them, Tarkof was standing over me, drawing a bead on my head with an imaginary shotgun. Behind him, Mickey wore a wide and goofy grin.

"Yes, sir," Tarkof said, "the killer shot him point blank. I hope he was wearing a raincoat 'cause he'd have got splashed good."

Tarkof chuckled to himself, but slowly the humor drained from his face and he seemed to become lost in thought. After some seconds, he turned back to face me. He seemed a little surprised that I was still there. "Oh, that's all, Mr. Dahms," he said. "You can get up now. A grateful public thanks you for your help."

I rose, running a palm across the back of my head. The murder had taken place days before, so the chair was no longer gooey, but I wasn't exactly feeling minty fresh.

Tarkof took out a small notebook and Brad started across the room toward me. "Excuse me, Mr. Dahms, but I think you've had enough of a break," he said. "Please get back to work." He pointed to the wall and my scrub bucket.

"Whatever you say, boss," I said, an angry little quaver in my voice.

Tarkof's partner, Mickey, actually laughed out loud.

Tarkof made a couple of final notes before closing his notebook. "Okay, Mickey," he said, "let's hit it."

Mickey uncrossed his arms and loped toward the door.

"Sorry if we caused you any trouble, Mr. Decker," Tarkof said brightly, though a menacing glint remained in his eyes. "Just doing our job, you understand."

Brad broke into a smile. "Oh, yes, Detective," he oozed. "Certainly, I understand. And I hope we were able to be of some help to you." He fumbled for something more to say and finally came up with, "Service is our motto, Detective. That's what we do."

"That's very gratifying, Mr. Decker."

On his way to the door, Tarkof leaned in close to me and whispered, "When you're done here, come see me. My office. This afternoon."

****

With the cops gone, Phil and Don each moved to one side of the dead man's chair, lifted it, and like two shabby pallbearers, carried it out into the kitchen. Then we fired up the shampooer and got to work deep cleaning the carpet. Phil manned the nozzle while Don and I stood poised to move furniture for him, leaving us very little to do. Don made a great show of busy work every time Brad passed through the room, which wasn't very often.

Our leader seemed preoccupied with the other parts of the house—those not sullied by the shotgun blast. He disappeared into the kitchen, and I could hear him opening cupboards and moving things on the counters. I kept an ear on his movements and began to look around myself.

I examined the front door and confirmed that the doorframe was intact and that the killer had not forced his way in. The deadbolt lock had a key in it so that the owner could open it from the inside. For no particular reason, I took the key from the lock, replaced it, and quietly turned the mechanism.

Brad came out of the kitchen, glared at me, and ordered me to get back to work. I picked up an empty bottle of cleaning solvent and told my co-workers that I would start tidying up our mess. Brad took off down the hall toward Rovig's bedroom.

I went into the kitchen, opened the cupboard under the sink and found a garbage pail. Tossing the bottle away, I glanced at the back door. It was fitted with the same brand of lock as the front door but had no key in it. My guess was that the front and back door keys were identical, designed to stay in the locks when the owner was home, and to be removed and hidden away when he was gone. If that were true, there should have been a key in the back door as well.

This speculation, while surely more interesting than the watching carpets get shampooed, was not helping me accomplish what I was being paid to do. As quietly as I could, I slipped out of the kitchen and into the hall. Don and Phil were too busy to see me as I made my way toward the back bedroom.

Through the open door, I watched Brad as he poked through the dead man's things. He had started in the closet and had moved on to the dresser. There were a couple of small wooden boxes along with a paperback book and a stack of what looked like receipts. Brad opened one of the boxes and carefully began to take out the contents. He lined up several tie clips—most studded with what appeared to be semi-precious stones. He shook his head slightly, then looked back at the open door.

I ducked back along the outside wall before he could spot me. I gave him a few seconds, expecting him to at least close the door, but when he didn't, I peered back into the room. The tie clips were no longer on the dresser and Brad was looking through the other box. I heard him inhale sharply as he pulled something out. He smiled a thin, almost feline smile as he held up a ring to the light that was streaming in through a crack in the curtains.

It was a diamond. I didn't get much of a look at it, but I figured it to weigh at least half a carat. Even if he had passed on the tie clips, I knew he wouldn't pass this up. He held the ring appreciatively in his hand, buffed it lightly on the sleeve of his shirt, then slipped it into the pocket of his jeans.

"What ya doing, Bradley?" I asked.

His whole body shook from the start I gave him. At first his eyes were like a frightened doe's, but slowly his alarm turned to challenge. "Dahms!" he barked. "What the hell are you doing? Get back to work before I bounce you outta here."

I smiled—a friendly, understanding smile. "I don't think so."

He blustered some more, but I interrupted him. "Now, Brad," I said. "I don't want you to worry too much about this. You and I can come to some kind of arrangement. I'm not a greedy guy. You shouldn't be either. The way I figure it, this kind of opportunity comes your way all the time. You know, here you are cleaning up some guy's house and he's careless enough to leave valuables lying around. Well, in this case he's careless enough to have had his head blown off with valuables lying around, but...Hey, this guy won't even miss the little trinkets you steal. Am I right? Again, Brad, neither of us need be too greedy. Say, how 'bout this? You can have everything. Everything you found on the dresser and anything you've picked up anywhere else in the house. Everything…except that ring."

Brad struck a pose right out of the J. C. Penny catalog—his nose in the air, his hand on one hip, his rear end sticking out. "I don't know what you're talking about, pal. But if you're talking about violating our client's trust…If you're talking about stealing, you're going to find yourself in a great deal of trouble."

"Uh huh," I said. "The thing is, I figure this isn't the first time you've pulled this sort of thing. I wonder what would happen if I asked your father about it."

"He won't believe you."

"But, Brad," I said, putting a measured combination of whine and insistence into my voice, "if you've pulled this before, all he has to do is check for reports of valuables that have gone missing on PSI jobs. He matches them to the crews that were working, and bingo…You go to bed without your supper."

"Anybody working those jobs could be responsible," Brad protested. "It didn't have to be me."

"True, true," I said, nodding my head. "But how about those two cops that were here earlier? How do you think they'll react to you removing items from the scene of a homicide investigation? I don't see them being real thrilled, do you?"

"I, ah…I, um…"

Brad was starting to squirm. The thought of his dad finding out about his little criminal pastime was one thing, but the idea of the cops finding out was another.

"You wouldn't really go to the police, would you, Lyle?" he asked almost sweetly

I grinned at him. Suddenly I was like a little boy who's pulled the wings off a housefly and watches it twitch in desperate attempt at flight.

"Hand over the ring, Bradley," I demanded.

He reached into the pocket of his tight jeans, produced the ring, and stood for a moment with his hand outstretched. "But it's like you said, right?" he asked. "We can be like partners."

Nodding, I took the ring from him. Then, quickly, I grabbed him by the wrist, spun him around into a neat hammerlock, and rammed him face first into the wall. I was surprised at how much I liked the sound it made.

"Oops," I whispered into his ear, "I just thought of something." I pushed up hard on his pinned arm and tripped his feet out from under him, letting him fall to the floor.

He rolled over, looking up at me with hurt, anxious eyes. I reached into my back pocket and pulled out one of my business cards. I flipped it down to Brad who looked too scared to get up. The card landed on his belly, and he reached for it, like he was picking a tarantula off his chest.

"I just remembered," I continued, "I'm going to have to tell your daddy. You see, he hired me."

Brad stared at the card. Then the tears started, a myriad of emotions passing over his face. He was scared, sad, angry, and ashamed to be crying in front of me. He turned away, wiping at his tear-stained face. Then he murmured, "My dad hired you? You're a private investigator?"

"Uh huh."

"You bastards."

"Uh huh," I repeated. "Merry Christmas."

Chapter Two

Homicide Detective Augustus Tarkof worked on the fifth floor of City Hall. To visit him you had to walk down a long aisle that ran between rows of gray metal desks separated from one another by low partitions that were covered with an off-white, vinyl fabric that was textured to resemble plaster. He was at the end of the aisle, his nameplate the only thing that distinguished his desk from the others.

When I arrived, Tarkof was finishing a phone call, an unlit cigarette hanging from the corner of his mouth. He looked up at me. "What were you doing there?"

I smiled. "That's right, Augie, I forgot you aren't much for small talk. What was I doing there? I was cleaning someone named Theodore Rovig off the wall in his living room."

"Dahms," he said slowly, "I don't want to hear that you're fucking around with the Rovig murder. If I hear you are…" He paused to stare at the cold end of the cigarette he was rolling between his fingers.

"*Moi?*" I replied. "Interfering in an ongoing police investigation?" I feigned shock. "You don't think that I enjoy your company so much that I'd do anything like that? Now, that yummy Mickey you were with this morning…Um, boy. Him I could spend some time with. But you? I don't think so."

Tarkof put down the cigarette. "You're a funny guy,

Dahms. Why is it you fat guys are always so jolly?"

I smiled at him. Tarkof had probably been something in his youth. Underneath the layer of flab that he'd added over the years was still a healthy amount of muscle. Maybe I did have a couple of pounds on him, but it wasn't like he'd be able to quit the force and find work as an underwear model. Still, I let the remark pass.

"So, what were you doing there, Dahms?"

"I was doing a favor for an old friend," I told him. "That kid? Brad Decker? He's the son of an old guy who gave me a couple of breaks a few years back. Before I got into the P.I. thing. Trouble is, the kid is wrong and my friend knows it. He hired me to get something concrete. Damn near broke the old guy's heart when I handed the kid over to him today, but..." I shrugged. "I guess he'd like to handle this himself. That is, unless you got some objection."

He picked up the cigarette again, holding it under his nose and sniffing at its delicate aroma. Naturally, it had been years since anyone had been allowed to smoke anywhere inside the building, but it was hard on old cases like Augie. The unlit cigarette was a forceful presence in the room with him—so much more forceful from the lack of smoke, the lack of satisfaction and release. It was like promise of sex—more potent in its anticipation than in its sweaty reality.

He tossed the cigarette back onto the desk. "I got enough to keep me busy without sticking my nose into some pathetic little case of yours, Dahms. Besides..." Tarkof looked down and a kind of faraway look passed over his features. "Besides, I always kinda liked old Decker." He smiled. "I do hope that he can beat some sense into that kid of his, though."

"Not much he can do," I said. "His biggest problem is that he loves the little shit. When Luther's wife Marie died, the kid was all he had. He loses the kid, he doesn't have anything."

Tarkof nodded but seemed to be thinking about something else. We sat in silence for some moments until at last he looked up. "You got nothing better to do than sit around here all day. Go out and spend some of Decker's money. He paid you for this, didn't he?"

"He paid me."

"Then get out of here."

I rose and stepped into the aisle. Having dismissed me, Tarkof began shuffling through some papers on his desk. I got maybe five feet before something made me turn around. "Augie?" I asked. "Who took out Rovig?"

Tarkof screwed up his face unpleasantly. "Now, you're not gonna go messing around with that, are you?"

I sighed. "No, but you know, a guy gets a little curious after having spent the morning cleaning up someone's brains. I kinda got to wondering who's responsible." I paused. "Who killed Rovig?"

"Don't know," he replied. "But it was a hit, that's for sure. No forced entry. Two hundred and fifty bucks in Rovig's wallet and the wallet untouched in the guy's back pocket. Shooter used a pillow to muffle the sound of the shotgun blast. Not many pros use a shotgun, but…" He reached up and smoothed his mustache. "Funny thing, though," he continued. "The TV is missing. It don't fit, the shooter taking that. Nope, it don't fit."

I nodded and turned to leave. I was nearly to the elevator when Tarkof called to me. "Say, Dahms. You know Farnum, don't you?"

I managed to get out of there without having to answer him.

****

When I got to the street, I couldn't help but think about how Tarkof had needled me about spending Luther Decker's money. In the old days, Luther had been there with a job at a time when I really needed one. And other than a nettlesome IRS problem that had developed when I neglected to set aside a portion of my income to share with the government, his generosity was one of the few things from that time that I could look fondly back on. It wasn't just that Luther had made sure that I had work even when there wasn't much to go around. In addition, without ever coming out and saying it, Decker had let me know that he liked looking out for me—like I was someone he cared about. Of course, he'd rather be gutted with a rusty railroad spike than admit it and this fact too secured the old guy in my affections. I owed the old man, and maybe I should have just helped him out for friendship's sake. But I really needed the five bills he'd paid me.

I also needed to eat, so I decided to hoof it over to nearby Hennepin Avenue.

The Great Steak House was part of a local chain of some eight restaurants—all apparently owned by a single, large, Mediterranean family. At each location you'd be met by a swarthy guy in a messy apron who first asked, "What do you want, please?" Then, after taking the order, he'd invariably say, "Thank you very much, please." I'd long subscribed to a theory that all of these look-alike, sound-alike, aproned guys were actually just one guy who'd somehow learned to get around the time and space continuum, but I'd never been able to prove it.

The place was pretty quiet and there wasn't anyone else in line when I approached the swarthy guy and asked him for the filet dinner. I helped myself to a beer from the cooler at the end of the counter—delighted to find a bottle of Bass Ale hiding behind several bottles of Michelob Golden Light—and watched as the man who took my order tossed a steak on the broiler and brushed melted butter on both sides of a thick piece of white bread. He slid the bread onto a flat metal grill next to the broiler and stirred at some mushrooms already sautéing in a square, stainless-steel pan. The sizzle of my steak on the grill had me squirming with anticipation.

The full meal included the steak, Texas toast, a baked potato and salad bar. I went over to the salad bar and grabbed a brown, plastic bowl from a listing stack and filled it with iceberg lettuce, cucumbers, onions, and shredded cheddar. I ladled too much thick, blue cheese dressing over the salad, and returned to find the swarthy guy setting my meal on a red, plastic serving tray. Thank you very much, please.

I took my meal over to a corner booth and sat with my back to the wall under a framed poster of the Acropolis. I spotted most of a newspaper lying on an unused table across the room and I went over to get it. I settled back heavily into the booth.

I was tired. Despite my earlier anticipation, when the food was in front of me, I found that I'd lost my enthusiasm and ate it without much appreciation. I kept thinking about Augie Tarkof and that damned death chair. I ran my fingers through the hair at the back of my head, and although I'd combed through it a number of times, what I really needed was a shower.

I also thought about Theodore Rovig. One day the poor sap is living a quiet life in a cute little house in South Minneapolis, and the next day some guy he never met is sitting in a restaurant wondering whether any of his corporeal essence might be stuck in his hair. The newspaper said that the killing had taken place between 9:00 and 11:00 p.m. It also said that the police had found the front door unlocked, open, with the key in the lock on the inside. The back door was secure; I had checked that myself. The killer got in through the front door somehow and had either found Rovig watching the tube or had asked him to take a seat in the armchair. Either way, he picked up a throw pillow from the sofa, maybe gave Rovig a conk on the head to make sure he'd sit still, put the pillow against Rovig's face and the barrel of the gun against the pillow. Bang. Rovig's dead and the killer lets himself out, neglecting to close the door behind him.

It all seemed pretty clear to me. Of course, there were a few loose ends that the cops would have to clear up, like the identity of the killer and why the television had been taken. But I didn't have to busy myself with that. No. All I had to do was to keep my mind occupied during dinner so I wouldn't have to think about how, for a moment, in that bedroom with Brad Decker, I'd wanted more than anything else to kill him slow.

Chapter Three

The next morning, I woke up early, a jumble of dreams I'd had in the night swirling vaguely in my mind. I needed coffee badly.

Home for me was a rooming house on Seventh Street in the Southeast Minneapolis neighborhood of Dinkytown, near the university. Living near the U hadn't been my first choice when I moved to the city from the south suburbs where I'd grown up. Back then I was living in a delightful little piss hole on Chicago Avenue just at the edge of downtown. It was a lovely place, especially at night when the cool of the evening was filled with cries for help, the occasional gunshot, and the pulsating whirl of sirens. A friend of mine, Stephen Edgerton, came to visit me there a couple of times after the sun went down.

On one of these occasions, he swore that on his way to my place he was solicited for drugs no less than five times, for sex twice, and for help once. The guy who needed help stumbled out from where he had been hiding behind some bushes. He was bleeding pretty good from a knife wound in the belly, but he didn't want Edgerton to call an ambulance. Instead, he asked for a cigarette, then wondered if maybe Edgerton had a handkerchief or something he could use to sop up some of the blood. Poor guy, nobody carries handkerchiefs anymore.

Shortly after that, Edgerton invited me to move into

an empty room next to him. It was hard to see a downside, so I agreed.

The new place, though once elegant, had lost all of its former grandeur from years of rental abuse. It was typical of the rest of the houses in the area. Blue paint peeling from the weathered siding and the front walk had buckled in several places—with wedges of cement rising upward like the heads of breaching whales. The front porch had been reconstructed at the suggestion of the city inspector and was surfaced in green, treated lumber. The yard along both sides of the house was overtaken with all manner of weeds and a couple of near-dead junipers. The backyard had been sacrificed for parking, and at night, if you listened closely, you could hear the cars rusting out back. The once spacious interior of the house had been sliced up into several bedrooms forming a maze of little cubbyholes—few with an adequate escape route in case of fire. All in all, it was surprising that the place hadn't been condemned. But if our house had to go, half the neighborhood would have to go, and the city really couldn't afford to tick off all those absentee landlords. Besides, the neighborhood had history. Our place in particular.

Long ago, someone had hung a hand-lettered sign over the front door that read, "The Bijou." No one who lived there now knew why the name "Bijou" had been chosen, but we all felt that it singled the house out somehow. It was better living in "The Bijou" than in some place that had to make do only with a street number.

That morning I had the common areas of the house to myself, and I was undisturbed as I emerged from my room to make a pot of coffee on the communal stove in the kitchen. The kitchen stood in an alcove just off the hall on the second floor of the house and consisted of a single sink, the stove, and a refrigerator. Since my room had a small sink and I'd bought one of those tiny refrigerators designed for dorm rooms, I rarely needed to use the kitchen. If I'd have bought an electric coffee maker, I wouldn't have had to use the kitchen at all, nor have had to put up with the smell of the rarely emptied garbage pail that squatted in there. But I'd been making coffee on a stovetop for years, and besides, my morning trip to the kitchen was one of the only activities that forced me to join into the communal life of the Bijou.

I set the percolator on the stove, lit a fire under it, and went down to the basement to take a shower. Having washed any remaining traces of Theodore Rovig out of my hair, I returned to the kitchen, poured my coffee into a thermos, rinsed the pot, and returned to my room. I turned on my TV and watched one of the more popular morning shows over coffee and a bran muffin that I had squirreled away in the cupboard.

During the break for local news, a young woman with dark hair wearing a red blazer and an enormous ruffled bow tie came on to say that although there had been no arrest in the Rovig murder, Homicide Detective Augustus Tarkof of the Minneapolis Police Department assured her that they were running down several promising leads. But, Tarkof added, as this was an on-going police investigation that was all he could tell her at this time. The newscaster related this information over videotape of Augie standing outside City Hall mouthing words at a camera with a microphone shoved in his face. He looked properly professional throughout, until his mouth stopped moving and he decided to smile. He probably didn't know that he had something in his teeth.

After breakfast, I locked up, paused briefly at Edgerton's door, but hearing no sounds within, I left the house and headed for my office. It was located only two blocks from the Bijou in the Minneapolis Technology Center, which had once been a high school. The building had stood vacant for a couple of years after the powers that be decided to consolidate some of the local schools and the elderly Dinkytown high school lost out to a newer facility a couple of miles away. A group of investors talked the city out of some money to help renovate the old building in the hope of drawing some new high-tech firms to the city during the entrepreneurial boom of the 1980s. It hadn't been a rousing success, but the building did boast the offices of a couple of software companies, a small publishing house, the Malvina Thomas dance company—which operated out of the old gym—and one private investigator.

The management company that rented me the place insisted on calling it a "suite" though it was only one small room on the third floor. Inside, past the door where "Lyle Dahms Investigations" was stenciled on the windowpane, I had a couple of high-backed chairs covered in brown vinyl that was supposed to look like leather, a large steel desk with a wooden swivel chair behind it, and two gray metal filing cabinets.

On the wall behind my desk, I'd hung a framed copy of my investigator's license to impress the clients with my professional credentials. On another wall I'd hung a large map of the greater Twin Cities metro area. I hoped that people would think I'd put the map there so I could immediately track down the location of any skullduggery I was asked to investigate, but actually it was there because I'd got it cheap and took up a lot of wall space.

I picked my mail up off the floor as I entered the office and sorted it as I walked to my desk. The message light was blinking on my answering machine. I hit the play button, but instead of a message, I got silence followed by the sound of a phone hanging up. The machine had recorded the same thing happening three times the previous day. There had been no other calls.

I knew that Edgerton had to work later that morning and he'd made it a habit of stopping by my office on the way to his job, ostensibly to spend a moment or two chatting, but really to fill a thermos with my coffee. Not wanting to disappoint him, I made a fresh pot on the office machine, then sat down behind my desk and did what I did most mornings when I didn't have a case. I drank the coffee and looked out the window. After about forty-five minutes, a man stepped noiselessly into the office. It wasn't Edgerton.

Michael Angelino was in his mid-forties, wearing an expertly tailored, charcoal-gray suit with a discreet pinstripe. His overcoat was slung over his arm. He was a large man with a dark complexion and shoulders as broad as a city bus. He closed the door behind him, and when he turned to face me, his jacket opened just enough to reveal the gun that rested in a shoulder holster under his left arm.

I poured the last of the coffee into my cup, turned to my visitor and asked, "Care for some coffee, Mr. Angelino?"

He crossed the room to take a seat in one of the chairs across the desk from me. There was no expression in his slate blue eyes as he sat there, not looking at anything in particular, but, I thought, minutely aware of everything in the room. "I'd like to talk with you."

Angelino and I had met briefly several times in the past, but as far as I recall this was the first time that he'd actually spoken to me. He'd worked for Alexander Farnum for the last twenty years or so and Farnum was rarely seen in public without him. I'd first seen him in one of Farnum's bookstores. It was several years earlier when I was working through a kind of fascination with the quarter movie booths that stood in the back of the stores. At the time, I was quite impressed that the technology enabled a patron to enjoy only his favorite scenes from a number of different adult films simply by moving from booth to booth armed with a roll of quarters.

For a while I was something of a fixture in Farnum's store at the corner of University and Central—enough of a fixture that even though Farnum himself made only infrequent appearances at that particular operation, he came to recognize me. Once, when I was at the counter changing a ten spot for a roll of quarters, Farnum came in, Angelino at his side, and he called me over.

"I've been seeing you around," he said. "What's your name?" I told him and he smiled at me—a gentle, vaguely whimsical smile, like that of a father who finds that his son has discovered his secret stash of *Playboy* magazines and tells the kid that it's okay for him to look at them as long as Mom doesn't find out.

"Lyle," Farnum said, "You look like a guy who can handle himself. How would you like to work for me? You know, minding the counter, keeping an eye on things. You take the job, you get all the free movies you can watch."

The offer filled me with dread. Not only didn't I

think of myself as the kind of guy that would work for someone like Farnum, I didn't even think of myself as the kind of guy who would ever be caught in one of his stores. I politely declined Farnum's offer and left the store with that roll of quarters weighing heavily in my pocket. Later, after I'd become a private investigator, I ran into Farnum and Angelino from time to time. Farnum would always nod at me, that same whimsical smile on his face, as if we shared some powerful secret.

Angelino shifted in the chair across from me. I wondered what he thought of me or if he thought about anything at all. I had never seen him smile or look angry. He never made more than a few perfunctory remarks and his face never seemed to betray any emotion—neither humor, nor anger, not disinterest, nor desire.

"Mr. Farnum would like to see you," he repeated.

"Oh joy," I said.

Angelino made a barely audible humming sound.

"Just what does Al want to see me about?" I asked.

"This afternoon Mr. Farnum can be found at his condo on Main Street." He eyed me coldly. "On the river. I'll give you the exact address. You are to be there at two o'clock."

He reached into the breast pocket of his jacket and removed a business card that had nothing more than an address printed on it. He handed it to me, stood, and silently left the room, closing the door behind him.

I turned back to the window and looked down into the parking lot. But all I could see was some poor, fat kid hurrying down the street, a roll of quarters bulging in his pants pocket.

****

I was making yet another pot of coffee when

Edgerton's rail-thin frame appeared at the office door, an empty thermos dangling from his fingertips. "Missed you at McCauley's last night."

"Couldn't make it," I told him. "I had a job yesterday and I was pretty whacked by the time I got home."

"You didn't miss much. Although this guy they call the Dancer had a little too much to drink and ended up standing on the bar and threatening to relieve himself on the cash register.

"You gotta figure that kind of thing's gonna effect food sales."

"Thankfully, it didn't come to that. As I happened to be sitting nearby, I mentioned to Dancer that since the cash machine was plugged in and that urine was a pretty fair conductor of electricity..." Edgerton let his voice trail off.

"You told him that unless he wanted his johnson served up extra crispy he might like to rethink that plan?"

"Something along those lines. Yes."

"It's good to have a man of science on hand at these critical junctures."

"I do what I can."

Stephen took a seat in the same chair that Angelino had been in an hour before. "Was it interesting?" he asked, checking to see if I had a full pot of coffee. "The job, I mean."

"It seems to be turning into something. A gunman named Angelino who works for Al Farnum was just in here. He invited me over to Al's for a little conversation this afternoon."

"The guy whose accountant got murdered last week?" he asked.

"Yeah."

"Hmm. What do you think he wants?"

I sat back down in my chair. "Maybe he wants me to do a photo layout for a new magazine he's working on called *Private Dicks*."

Edgerton smiled wanly. "Uh huh. So, how scared are you anyway?"

"I can take care of myself. Thanks anyway, Mom."

"Yeah, maybe. But you gotta admit that this Farnum guy is one scary character."

"It's not Farnum who's scary," I told him. "It's the guys around Farnum. It's Angelino and a half dozen other made guys that Farnum thinks are working for him but are actually there to keep an eye on him and his operation. Those are the scary guys."

Edgerton shifted in the chair and ran a hand through his thick mop of red hair. "What do you mean those guys aren't working for him?"

"Farnum's whole operation is financed by the mob. Farnum fronts it, but the real decisions are made by others. Those heavy hitters, like Angelino, that surround Farnum…Well, let's just say that their loyalties lie elsewhere."

"Sounds lovely," Edgerton noted with a wry grin. The grin very nearly masked what appeared to be genuine apprehension in his eyes. "So, what do you think Farnum wants?"

I spent the next half-hour telling Edgerton about the Decker business the day before, about the Rovig murder, the missing television, and Tarkof's warning to stay clear of the whole thing. I left out the part about how Tarkof made me sit in the death chair, but other than that, I gave him the complete story. Stephen listened thoughtfully

32

and without interrupting me.

When I finished, he smiled. "So, what does Farnum want from you?" he repeated.

"He was probably having Rovig's house watched. If that's so, then his people saw me there yesterday. He knows who I am. He's probably wondering what I was doing there. I think the most likely reason for Farnum's invitation is to see if I know anything about the Rovig murder."

Edgerton nodded his head and thought for a moment before saying anything. "It's a bit bothersome," he observed at last. "You don't know if Farnum wants information about his accountant's death or if he wants to find out if you know anything that might implicate him in the murder. You know, there is every possibility that Farnum is responsible."

"I know, Stephen. And I agree, that is a bit bothersome."

"So, are you gonna go?"

I smiled and raised my hands in a gesture of helplessness. "The fact is, they're not really giving me any choice."

Chapter Four

Angelino's business card directed me to a high-rise condominium complex along the Mississippi in a neighborhood known as St. Anthony. It was there that the city was born when the first flour mills were built to operate on the power that was wrested from St. Anthony Falls. The old mills were now little more than crumbling foundations secreted along the overgrown banks of the river and the sandstone riverbed from where once plunged the mighty St. Anthony Falls had been so smoothed by the flow of water that long ago it had been shored up with concrete to keep it from disappearing altogether.

Farnum's condo overlooked both the river and downtown Minneapolis rising above on the opposite bank, the kind of view reserved only for the moneyed few. I knew that he didn't actually live there. Anyone who watched the TV news and saw the frequent pickets that various moral watchdog groups organized outside his stately, suburban home knew that he didn't live in the city where he had set up his businesses. But it didn't surprise me to find that he kept a place in the city. It might not do to have some of his business associates visiting him in his exclusive neighborhood. Too much mob activity can really screw up real estate values.

I was buzzed through the security door at the main entrance and took the elevator up to Farnum's condo.

The moment I reached the door, it was opened by a young man in a blue suit wearing a pair of wraparound sunglasses with neon orange frames. I stepped into a huge living room and had to squint against the light that streamed in from the sliding glass door that led to the balcony.

Once inside, the light seemed to grow even more brilliant as it reflected off the white, leather sofa, loveseat, and Scandinavian styled recliner that furnished the room. I turned to the man who was closing the door behind me, pointed to his sunglasses, and asked, "Can I borrow those?"

He didn't say anything.

When my eyes finally adjusted to the brightness, I looked around the room. Angelino sat in the recliner looking out onto the balcony. There were two other rather large gentlemen sitting on the loveseat wearing what appeared to be the same exact suit as the guy with the sunglasses. I figured they'd got them at a volume discount. Either that or their mommies enjoyed dressing them alike. I, on the other hand, found myself sartorially embarrassed. I was dressed in a green down jacket over a black T-shirt with Billie Holiday's face on it and a pair of blue jeans that rode a little too far below my waist. I took off my coat, handed it to the doorman with the sunglasses, and walked into the room.

The guy with the glasses wordlessly dropped my coat on the floor next to the door and circled around to stand behind the pair on the loveseat. Behind them, a six-foot Christmas tree was ablaze with light. Spilling out from beneath the tree was a pile of wrapped presents. Someone had been awfully good. There were a heck of a lot of presents. I stared at Farnum's tough guys—stone-faced in front of the merrily blinking tree. I didn't think the presents were for them. I couldn't say for sure, but my guess was that Santa had entered these guys under the heading *Naughty* rather than *Nice*.

I pointed to each of them, one after another, and smiled. "Don't tell me. Let me guess. You're Casper, you're Melchior, and you must be Balthazar. The three wise guys."

Nobody laughed.

I turned to Angelino. "Where's Farnum?"

"Mr. Farnum will join us in a moment," he said, still looking out onto the balcony.

That seemed to settle it for him, and since nobody asked me to sit, I just stood there for a few minutes feeling foolish and wondering what to do with my hands. Finally, Farnum emerged from a hallway that I assumed led back to the bedrooms. He was a short man in pretty good shape for a guy in his early sixties. He had a square jaw and a healthy head of curly, white hair that he kept cropped in a modified flattop. He was casually dressed in a black and white jogging suit and wore a pair of high-top sneakers with the laces untied. He came into the room with an air of utter confidence, a man at home in his surroundings, who was so sure of everything that he found it unnecessary to even look at the other people in the room. He was carrying a tall glass filled with ice and an amber liquid.

As he sipped at his drink, he said to no one in particular, "All right, you guys can leave. I'll let you know if I need anything."

With that, Sunglasses and the other two guys in blue suits left the room—silently, like a marine drill team. Angelino remained seated in his chair.

Farnum strolled about the living room for a few moments, straightening porcelain knickknacks and running his finger along the shelves as if checking for dust. Then he spent a moment apparently examining his distorted reflection in one of the glass bulbs on the Christmas tree. At last, he sat in the middle of the sofa, took another sip from his drink, and looked up at me. Since Angelino had the recliner and Farnum didn't look like he was going to ask me to share the sofa, I took the loveseat.

"Lyle," Farnum began, "you're probably wondering why I asked to see you. You see, I've recently lost a friend. This loss saddens me all the more as I am a man who has few true friends."

"Say it ain't so, Al."

"I'm quite interested in bringing Ted Rovig's killer to justice," Farnum continued, ignoring me. "Unfortunately, the police are unwilling to share what they know with me. I'm forced to rely on the newspapers and an occasional conversation with acquaintances who are following the case. One of these acquaintances mentioned that you might be able to shed some light on this dark affair."

"Whatever could you mean?" I asked.

"It seems that you were in Ted's home yesterday. Shortly afterward, you visited the officer in charge of the investigation."

Farnum paused, waiting for me to answer. I let him wait. "I would be most grateful for anything you could share with me."

I looked around the room for a couple of seconds, before turning back to Farnum. "Well, Al, you might not believe this, but I really don't care. My visit to Rovig's had nothing to do with his murder. I was working on something involving the cleaning service that was hired to take care of the place. I didn't even know it was Rovig's house until I got a look at the mess. Again, I don't care if you believe this or not, but while I was there, Augie Tarkof wandered in, saw me at the scene, and not unlike you, asked me to come around to explain myself. I don't know anything about Rovig's murder."

Farnum exchanged a glance with Angelino, and after a second or two of thought, he turned back to me. "Despite your protests to the contrary, Lyle, you might not be wholly disinterested to find out that I do believe you. If you say that you don't know anything about the murder, then you don't. But you have visited the crime scene. Perhaps you saw something that might point the way toward the killer. Perhaps something that seemed unrelated at the time."

"There are those that would point the blame at you," I reminded him.

He gave me that same smile. "My arrest would make some people very happy. I've never really understood that, you know. I provide a service that is enjoyed by people from all walks of life. From the rich to the poor, from the cultured to the profane. And yet, many of the same people who take advantage of the entertainment that I provide insist on condemning me for providing it. Perhaps, Lyle…Perhaps you understand why they are like this. I do not."

"I don't know, Al. Maybe that's just the nature of temptation. Maybe just because something is fun doesn't preclude it from being harmful. Maybe it's just natural to want to seek the ruin of the tempter."

"I didn't know you were such a philosopher. It

seems that your taste in reading material has become somewhat less…uh, *elemental* since we first met. But we have strayed from the subject at hand. Is there anything you can tell me about Ted Rovig's murder?"

"You know, Al," I said, "I could use some coffee. Would you have any made up? You know, if it's not too much trouble."

"No trouble at all." Turning to Angelino, Farnum said, "Michael, would you get Mr. Dahms a cup of coffee? I think you will find some brewed in the kitchen."

Angelino went into the kitchen without a word, without even a glance at either of us.

"I don't know if I can help you or not," I told Farnum. "I don't know for sure that you honestly want my help. But if you do, maybe you could answer a couple of questions."

"What would you like to know, Lyle?"

"For starters, is there any reason that you would like to have seen Rovig dead? He was your accountant. Have there been any irregularities with the books lately?"

"You saw how Rovig lived. I'm a generous employer. His salary would have enabled him to live in a style much more opulent than he enjoyed in his quaint, little home in that rather down-at-the-heels neighborhood. Ted was not particularly motivated by money. If he was, I'd have increased his salary. He had but to ask. But Ted was interested in other things. He lived in his boyhood home—the home in which he was brought up. After his parents died, he told me that living there gave him a connection to the past. He was deeply interested in maintaining a sense of what, for lack of a better term, I will call old-fashioned values. He was a man with a strong moral center."

"And yet, he worked for you."

"You find that ironic. I do not. It may surprise you
to learn that I think of myself as having a strong moral
center as well. My business does not deprive me of this
sense. My business, to use a time worn phrase, is to give
the people what they want. And, I would add, what they
are guaranteed by the Constitution. My business hurts no
one and gives pleasure to many. And it puts me in a
position to help in the struggle to safeguard our First
Amendment rights against an out-of-touch and
overreaching government."

"Yeah, Al," I sneered. "You're the friggin' Tom
Jefferson of the porn industry. So, you're saying that
Rovig wasn't skimming?"

"That is correct."

Angelino returned with my coffee. It was poured
into a delicate cup and saucer—a pearly, lustrous, white
china with tiny blue flowers encircling the cup and a
matching pattern on the saucer.

"Thank you, Mr. Angelino," I said.

Angelino bowed slightly and returned to his chair.

"Okay," I said to Farnum. "You didn't want Rovig
dead. If not you, it could have been anyone. Someone
else in your organization, a jealous husband, a moral
crusader, anyone. I really think you ought to let the cops
do their job. Frankly, leaving this alone is gonna make
you look a lot less guilty."

"Why do you say that, Lyle?" Farnum asked,
leaning forward.

"Let's look at this thing the way the cops will. First,
if you go poking around trying to scare up a suspect, the
cops are gonna figure that you're just looking for

someone other than yourself to pin it on. Second, the cops want to scratch this thing off the books as much as you do. Even more since they're the ones that gotta prove to the public that they're doing their jobs. And if they do their job, and you didn't do it, they're not gonna prove that you did. Third…Ah, I can't think of a third right now, but you get the idea."

I took a sip of coffee.

Farnum sat back and settled into the sofa. He tugged gently at a loose thread on one of the cushions. "I understand your point. But I think it likely that the police will be under some pressure to bring me into it even though I was not involved. The only way that I know of to keep them from bringing me into it, is to bring myself into it."

I thought about that. I didn't understand it, but I thought about it. At last, I said, "I think Rovig knew the killer. I think it was somebody he knew and somebody that had been to his house before. I can't prove it, but that's what I think."

"Go on, Lyle" Farnum prompted, settling back into the sofa.

"The key to Rovig's back door was missing. Rovig had the kind of setup where your keys are all ground to a single shape so any one of them will unlock the deadbolts on each of the outside doors. When you're home, you keep the keys in the locks in case of fire or something. When you're gone, if you're careful about these things, you pull the keys and hide them so if a burglar climbs in a window or something, he can't just open the door and carry the big stuff out. He'd have to break down the door and make a whole lot of noise. Burglars hate noise. Anyway, Rovig was home when he got killed, so I figure the keys would be in all the locks. When the cops found Rovig's body, the front door was unlocked and open. The back door was locked up tight. A key was in the lock of the front door. The back door, the locked door, had no key."

"How does that prove that Ted knew the killer?"

"It doesn't prove anything. But suppose that someone Rovig knew came to his house some time before the murder. Maybe even earlier the night of the murder. Rovig would unlock the front door and let that someone in. Suppose it was someone that was familiar with the house. Someone that Rovig trusted. They sit in the living room and talk or watch TV or something, then the killer asks Rovig if he's got a beer in the fridge, or he goes to get a cup of coffee like Angelino did just now. When he's in the kitchen, he takes the key from the back door. Now, he can get in anytime he wants. He comes back later and whacks Rovig."

"What do you make of that TV being missing?"

"I don't make anything out of it. It's not like I'm working the case."

Farnum reached into the pocket of his jogging suit and pulled out a pack of cigarettes. He inhaled deeply, like a man who had not had one for a while. He blew a lungful of smoke into the air, and I watched it swirl in the rays of the sunlight that streamed into the room.

"I want you to look into this for me, Lyle."

Before I could say anything, he added, "I'll give you five hundred dollars a day and will cover any expenses that you might incur. If you are able to find the man that killed Ted, I will give you an additional $10,000 bonus. You will have my complete cooperation and the cooperation of all the members of my staff."

There was a note pad and a pen in a brass holder on the end table next to the sofa where Farnum sat. He picked up the pen and wrote something on a piece of notepaper, then handed the paper out to me without rising. "This is my cell phone number," he said. "You can call me at any time."

I stood, walked across the room, and took the phone number from him. I returned to my seat, staring at the small, neat handwriting.

I didn't want to work for Farnum. I didn't like the man, and Angelino scared the shit out of me. But I didn't want to say no to him. There's no sense in pissing off a guy with his connections. Besides, at five hundred dollars a day I could afford to mess around for a couple of days while the cops solved the thing.

"Okay, Al," I said. "You got yourself a P.I."

Farnum was writing me out a check to serve as a retainer when I heard a door open in the back of the apartment. I turned around just as a woman entered the room.

As she appeared, Angelino stood but otherwise remained as expressionless as a slab of basalt. Farnum remained seated, but his face broke into a smile that I can only describe as one of pure joy. He held out both arms to her, as if to hug her, but she did not rush to his embrace. Instead, she nodded to Angelino and leveled her eyes on me. I fumbled in my seat for some confused seconds, but finally stood, and my eyes met hers.

She was young, in her early twenties, and I was immediately struck by the youthful, almost luminous glow of her creamy, dark skin. She was tiny, about five foot two, and her stature suggested a vulnerability that was belied by the firmness of her body and the strength that showed in her brown, tranquil eyes. She was dressed in a pair of acid-washed blue jeans and a silky, purple blouse. The color of the fabric accentuated the deep beauty of her milk chocolate complexion.

It felt like something had reached out to clench at my insides. This was a lovely woman. Gifted with a beauty so deep that at once I wanted to be lost within it. She reminded me of twilight, of the last moments of the day when the sun slips behind the horizon and dusk comes on to cool the soul before enveloping the world in the sleepy darkness of night.

She smiled and the whiteness of that smile broke across the room like heat lightning across a midsummer sky. The sight of this woman didn't just cause me to drift into uncharacteristic, poetic rhapsody. She actually made me ache. Totally unused to the effect she had on me, I felt ridiculous standing there and staring at her. I lowered my gaze and shuffled my feet like an embarrassed schoolboy.

"Carmen!" Farnum exclaimed. "There you are, my princess. We were just concluding our business. But here you are and I-I-I." He stuttered, unable to finish his thought. He turned to me, and regaining his composure, said, "I think we're done here, Lyle. Keep me informed."

The sight of a befuddled Farnum made me forget that she had just had the same effect on me. I smiled at him. "I can see you have other things on your mind now, Al," I said. "I'll just be going."

"Alexander," Carmen said. "Please introduce me to your business associate."

Hers was a voice of silk and sandpaper—low and steady, yet somehow breathless, with a catch like the tiny growl of woman on the brink of ecstasy. It was a voice that demanded attention.

The smile disappeared from Farnum's face, and he looked at her quizzically for a moment, but finally he sputtered out, "This is Mr. Dahms. He will be working for me for the next few days. Mr. Dahms, this is...uh, this is Carmen."

She stepped forward and extended her hand. "Mr. Dahms? That's a bit formal, isn't it?"

I wiped my hand on my pants and placed my hand in hers. "Lyle, ma'am," I said. "Lyle Dahms."

Her hand was soft and dry, and her handshake was firm. I realized that I was grinning like a maniac.

She let go of my hand and I took a step back, but she did not turn away. "What will you be doing for Alexander, Lyle?"

I wasn't sure what I was supposed to say, so I just smiled and looked to Farnum for help.

"Dahms will be looking into the Rovig matter for us, sweetheart," he told her. "He is a confidential investigator."

Carmen lowered her eyes, then looked up at me. "Ted's death was such a shock to all of us. He was such a fine man. He was involved in so many worthy causes. He used to say that it was not enough for a person to simply live his life, but rather that we should share our lives with others. And he did share his life. He was a volunteer. He taught people to read and to do math. But not just those things. He wanted to help others learn to become better. And he was always working to become better himself. He was a good man. Not the type of man who should be cut down by some killer in the night."

"Nobody deserves to die like that," I said.

She looked at me with an expression of great

patience, as if to say that we both knew that she didn't mean to imply otherwise. This expression of patience struck me all the more, because as she talked about the dead man, her eyes had moistened. But she hadn't cried, nor had her steady voice quavered. This was not a woman given to theatrics. Instead, it was clear that she was genuinely grieved by the loss of Rovig and that her only motive for telling me this was to share her sorrow. Once again, I felt foolish.

"I don't know if I'm making myself clear," she said. "I didn't know him well, but he had such a good heart, I think it must have touched mine."

"I understand completely," I assured her. "Al has already told me something of Mr. Rovig. I believe he described him as having a strong moral center." I looked at Farnum. His eyes were fixed on me.

"I do hope, Lyle," Carmen continued, "that you will be able to help the police find Ted's killer. It seems vicious, but I don't want his killer to go unpunished."

"It's not viciousness," I said. "We all have a need for justice. Catching Ted's killer would only be just."

She nodded.

While we were talking, I'd glanced over at Farnum a couple of times. He was obviously not happy about something. He kept staring at us, absently turning his wedding band around and around his finger. Then he'd glance at Angelino, who stood motionless throughout the exchange. Angelino didn't return these looks. Instead, he kept his eyes fixed on Carmen, his eyes and face set in that damned expressionless manner of his. I hated that I didn't know what he was thinking.

Suddenly, Farnum cleared his throat loudly and rose from the sofa. "You have my retainer, Mr. Dahms."

There was something about his tone. I turned to face Farnum and realized with shock that he had become suddenly enraged. He held his hands at his sides, clenching them convulsively into fists. He strode toward me purposefully. His face flushed red and his features were monstrously contorted. This storm of anger had come on so suddenly and with such strength that my whole body shuddered as I instinctively prepared myself for an assault.

I took my eyes off Farnum long enough to glance at Carmen. She hadn't moved at all, but I saw a flash of fear flicker in her dark eyes. Her fear cut through me like a straight razor. The effect was immediate. I turned, ready to bash Farnum's head in.

I'd forgotten Angelino. With a fluid grace, he stepped in, took Farnum by the arm, and led him to the other side of the room. He stared at Farnum, watching as the rage slowly went out of Farnum's body. At last, Farnum smiled, and as though nothing at all had happened, said, "Well, Lyle, Carmen and I have early dinner plans this evening and I'm sure that you are anxious to begin your inquiries. If you'll excuse us."

Angelino let go of Farnum's arm.

Taking that as my cue, I walked to the door and picked my jacket up off the floor. "I'll let you know what I find out," I said.

Farnum nodded.

Angelino turned his back on me and sat back down in the recliner. I heard Carmen say, "Good luck, Lyle," as I closed the door.

Driving home, I thought about Farnum, Angelino, and Carmen. But mostly I thought about Carmen. I was way too old for schoolboy crushes. But Christ, I couldn't get her out of my mind. I honestly thought that she was the most beautiful woman I had ever seen.

A guy on a bicycle ahead of me maneuvered to avoid some chunks of ice and snow that were strewn like rubble along the edge of the road. He drifted into the lane directly in front of my car. I swerved to miss him and cursed as I watched him fade away in my rear-view mirror. I turned on the car radio and listened for a moment to a news report. But I couldn't stop thinking about Carmen. I kept seeing her smile. Her smile and the fear that I'd seen flash through her eyes.

I shook my head. I told myself that she was nothing to me. Nothing more than the girl Al Farnum was sleeping with. But I couldn't make her image go away. At last, a loud voice rang out, startling me. "Just knock it off!" it said. I was even more startled to discover that the voice was my own. I swallowed and turned up the volume on the radio.

I was nearly home when I heard the announcement on the radio that there had been an arrest in the Rovig murder.

Tarkof, it seemed, had found the missing TV set.

Chapter Five

By five o'clock in the afternoon I was sitting at the bar in front of the television set at McCauley's Pub. Every day at that time there was something of a shift change involving the patrons who showed up to drink coffee and eat free popcorn in front of the TV. *Rachael* was over and the talk show and soap opera crowd ceded the space to the smaller TV news crowd. The same faces gave way to the same faces at the same time each day and I had long ago raised my banner alongside those of the news crowd. I was nearly finished with my first beer and was about to signal Skip, the bartender, for another, when Edgerton came in.

He took the barstool next to me, nodded, and shook his head as he stared at the TV screen. We had a long-standing disagreement over which of the local newscasts was the one to watch. Edgerton was in favor of the local NBC affiliate because it featured a blonde bombshell named Inga as one of the anchors.

I, on the other hand, would only watch the local CBS affiliate out of respect for the network's long history of excellence and integrity going back to Murrow and Cronkite. Also, I was quite enamored of a cute, little, brunette anchorwoman named Amy.

I held up two fingers and Skip brought us each a glass of dark beer.

"Murrow's dead, you know," Edgerton muttered.

"Shut up," I said.

The brunette on the television finished up a story on how an impending rail strike would affect shipments of Minnesota grain to market then yielded to her male counterpart for a story on the arrest in the Rovig murder.

"Police today arrested a nineteen-year-old, Minneapolis man in connection with the brutal slaying of Theodore Rovig," he began. *"As you will remember, Rovig, a Minneapolis accountant and associate of porn king, Alexander Farnum, was murdered in his home last Wednesday night. The man arrested today is Thomas Ehlers, who, police say, was an acquaintance of Rovig's through the murdered man's volunteer work at Gateway House—a local program that teaches basic literacy and math skills to the city's underprivileged youth. Ehlers was a student in a class taught by Rovig and he allegedly turned on the man who had tried to help him. Police reportedly found Rovig's television set, which had been missing since the murder, in Ehlers' apartment on Garfield Avenue which he shares with his mother and is located only a few houses away from Rovig's South Minneapolis home."*

"So," Edgerton said as the report concluded, "I guess that lets you off the hook with Farnum."

"Not hardly. He hired me."

Edgerton furrowed his brow. "What's he want you to do?"

"He wants me to find out who killed Rovig."

Edgerton took a sip of his beer. "Well, that shouldn't be hard. Looks like they caught this Ehlers guy dead to rights. The cops didn't leave much for you to do."

"That's okay with me. Working for Farnum makes me feel dirty. If this guy, Ehlers, really did kill Rovig, all

I gotta do is poke around a bit, then tell Farnum the killer's in custody and I can go on my merry way."

"What do you mean, *if* the guy killed Rovig? The cops think he did. Don't you?"

I shrugged. "How should I know? But I'll tell you, just because the guy knew Rovig, and just because he was found with the guy's television set, doesn't necessarily mean that he's the murderer."

He arched an eyebrow. "Maybe you'd like to explain that a little more fully for the benefit of us poor, uneducated types," he said. "The kid knew Rovig. He had Rovig's TV in his apartment, so you can figure that he had to be in Rovig's house. The kid probably had some kind of grudge against him. So, he goes over, blows the guy's head off, and using all the raw intellect that kids like this are known for, decides to make off with the TV. Case closed."

I shrugged and took a long, cool draught of beer. "Sure. Why not? It could have happened that way. And I'm not saying that it didn't. But there are a couple of problems."

"What problems?"

"If the kid killed Rovig, why did he just take the television? There was a stereo, jewelry, Rovig's wallet wasn't touched. Why not make off with all that as well?"

Edgerton thought for a moment, running a hand over his mustache and beard. He wore the beard just a shade long. Fiery red, it came to a point giving him a vaguely devilish aspect.

"Okay," he said at last. "The kid lived less than a block away. That means he was probably on foot. He had to carry whatever he was going to steal back to his apartment. He's just killed Rovig in a loud nasty way in front of the TV. The kid's afraid someone heard the noise. He thinks about ripping off the wallet, but he doesn't want to get all messy rummaging through the dead man's pockets. He doesn't think he has much time, so he decides not to go through the rest of the house. The one thing he sees is the television. He picks up the TV and hustles home."

"He carried both the television set and the shotgun home with him?"

"Sure. Why not?"

I shook my head. "Could have happened that way. But if you just made that much noise, and you thought that the neighbors would call the cops any minute, or at least look out their windows to see what was going on, would you stagger past those same neighbors, on foot, carrying a great big old TV set in your arms while balancing a shotgun under your chin? The whole neighborhood would've watched you walk right into your house. You wouldn't have enough time to plug the damn set in before the cops would be at your door."

"Maybe that's what happened," Edgerton said. "The cops picked him up. Maybe the neighbors did see it and that's why he's in jail right now."

"Nobody saw that kid take that TV set," I said.

"What makes you say that?"

"Because if they had, the cops would have picked him up that night. They wouldn't have waited a week."

"So, nobody saw the kid take the set. Does that mean he didn't take it? Does that mean he didn't kill Rovig?"

I sighed and drained the last of the beer from my glass. "No. The kid took the set," I said. "Either that or someone planted it in his house, and I don't think that's very likely. I just think it's odd that nobody saw him do it. If somebody blew off a shotgun in the house next to mine, I'd damn sure look out the window. I may not call the cops right away, but my curtains would be twitching. No. I think this Ehlers kid took the set sometime after the shotgun blast. Long enough afterwards that everyone had dismissed the noise as an engine backfire or something. Long enough later so that the good citizens of Garfield Avenue had gone back to sleep."

"So, he killed Rovig and then waited until he thought it was safe," Edgerton suggested.

"He waited? He waited in that house with the dead body and the threat that the cops would show up any minute? He waited there until the neighbors were sawing logs and everything was all safe and wonderful outside? A guy with the balls and the presence of mind to do that isn't going to leave money in Rovig's wallet or jewelry in Rovig's bedroom and content himself with a fifty-five-inch Vizio."

"So, you think something else is going on?"

"Maybe."

"So, you're going to look into it for Farnum?"

"Yeah."

Edgerton cocked an eyebrow. "He paying you well?"

"Very well."

"Then I guess you can afford to poke around for a couple of days."

I chuckled. "Who told you?"

When the news broadcast was over, I had Skip refresh our beers and we moved away from the bar to a booth in the corner near the jukebox.

Once there, Edgerton began excitedly to tell me all about a new project he'd begun. I don't know where he found the time. In addition to working the night shift at a copy center and in the afternoons for a metal smith who fashioned authentic replicas of medieval suits of armor, Edgerton seemed to be able to pursue whatever captured his fancy at any moment.

His latest sideline was writing and drawing his own self-published comic books. Over our beers, he began describing the one that he was currently working on—a retelling of the ancient Sumerian epic of Gilgamesh, who, following the death of his friend Enkidu, traveled the world vainly searching for an escape from death. In Edgerton's version, this quest was secondarily, though significantly, concerned with the coining of the timeless question, "Why did the chicken cross the road?"

I tried to listen, but eventually my mind wandered. Finally, I became aware of a silence at our table and realized that I hadn't responded to anything that Edgerton had said for several minutes. When I looked up, Edgerton was staring at me patiently.

"What's wrong?" he asked.

"Ah, I'm sorry, Stephen. I was thinking about something else."

I ordered us a couple more beers and Edgerton changed the subject and began talking about his job with the metal smith. Specifically, he began to explain in excruciating detail how they were designing a mold that would replicate the head of a 14th century, Italian war hammer. He even pulled out a notebook to show me. According to Edgerton, the head was the perfect fusion of utility and art. Composed of solid steel, the piece resembled a short, chubby dragon with a spiked tail for armor penetration and a ragged mouth that would maximize damage to an opponent's skull. A few minutes into his explanation, I checked out again. I don't know how long I'd been staring across the room in silence when Edgerton tapped a pencil against the rim of his empty beer glass to get my attention.

"You want to tell me what's wrong with you tonight or should I just go on talking to myself here?"

"No," I said. "It's really nothing. I mean…I mean it's nothing that should be bothering me. You see, well…There was this woman…ah, at Farnum's condo. It's the damnedest thing. I can't stop thinking about her."

Edgerton smiled, but not with his eyes. After a pause, he said, "You know, any woman that you met at Farnum's is probably not someone you want to get involved with."

"I know. I know. I'm not completely stupid. But…"

"But you can't stop thinking about her."

"No. I can't."

"You should try."

"I know," I agreed. "But it's not going to be easy."

Chapter Six

The next morning, I stood outside the Franklin Community Center in South Minneapolis, looking quite dapper in a pair of gray slacks, a white dress shirt, a maroon tie, and my lime green sports jacket. The jacket brings out the green highlights in my eyes. At least that's what my mom tells me.

The community center, like my office building, was another converted school, the former Elgard Elementary and was home to several neighborhood-based social programs. It was a one-story building constructed as a square around an open, central courtyard. Inside the main entrance, a board listed the room numbers of the various programs operating out of the center. I wanted Room 140. I must have started down the wrong direction because I seemed to go around forever until I finally stood in front of a sign that read, "Gateway House. Please Come In."

I heard a noise farther down the hall and turned to see a middle-aged guy swirling a mop on the floor several feet away. He was big. Really big. So big that the mop handle looked like a swizzle stick in his meaty hands. He wore a red plaid shirt with the sleeves rolled up and a pair of overalls so large they looked like they could have been made from a half dozen or so regular-sized pairs sewn together. He was almost perfectly square. His huge head, topped with a thick thatch of reddish-blond hair, sat directly atop shoulders so broad that I wondered if he had to go through doors sideways. He had no neck and no waist. His barrel chest melded seamlessly into his thick middle and his thighs were like prize-winning hams. He glanced briefly at me, then back down at his mop. Then he took a break in his mopping altogether to watch me with wide, guileless eyes, scratching at one end of his bushy mustache with a short, thick finger. He kept looking at me as I stepped through the door.

I entered a spacious, open room furnished with several large, round tables encircled by metal folding chairs. The walls were covered with posters that condemned drug abuse, spousal abuse, and child abuse and others that extolled the merits of literacy, mentoring programs, and finally getting that GED. There was no one else in the room, so I spent a moment walking around looking at the posters.

I lingered in front of one of them. There, the image of a little girl—maybe six years old, holding a teddy bear—peered out at me with large, innocent eyes. They were the same huge, soulful eyes that I remember from a couple of pictures that hung in my room when I was a child. Pictures of a little boy and a little girl in harlequin outfits. Those eyes used to watch over me at night. Sometimes they kept me awake. Eventually my mom replaced them with a print of dogs playing poker.

After a moment, I heard someone moving around in a little office through a door in the back of the room. I moved toward the office and on the open door spotted a plastic plaque that read "Lorraine Rovig. Program Administrator."

A tall, blonde woman in her late thirties stood inside

with her back to the door scanning the titles of books that were lined up on shelves that covered nearly the entire wall. As I watched unnoticed, she bent down to remove one of the books from a lower shelf. She looked pretty good from the back.

"Mrs. Rovig?" I asked.

The woman straightened and turned to face me. She looked good from the front too. She wore a cream-colored dress of heavy cotton fabric with a high neckline, cut to reveal a pair of shapely, athletic legs. She hadn't been the least startled by my unexpected entrance. Instead, her face was coolly impassive. She neither smiled, nor frowned, but rather looked at me with an air of patience that was not altogether uninviting. She had high cheekbones that gave her face a strong, even regal air, and her green eyes sparkled like diamonds on a moonlit sea.

She stepped toward a large, metal desk that took up most of the small office and picked up a pair of wire-rimmed eyeglasses that lay there. She put the glasses on and said, "Yes. Can I help you?"

I entered the room, smoothing imaginary wrinkles out of my sports jacket. "My name's Lyle Dahms. I'm a private investigator looking into the murder of Theodore Rovig. I'm hoping I might ask you a few questions."

"I was under the impression that Ted's murderer was already in custody, Mr…Dahms, is it?"

"That's right, ma'am. The police have arrested a suspect. But there are still one or two questions that need to be answered."

Her eyes narrowed. "You said you were a private investigator? May I ask for whom you are working?"

I gave her my used car salesman grin. The one that

says, no matter what you might think, I'm not hiding anything. "Al Farnum," I said. "Ted's former employer. He asked me to look into this, ma'am."

She didn't like my answer. I'm a trained observer; I pick up on stuff like that. When she heard Farnum's name, she looked at me as though I were the remains of a bug that had been squashed against the windshield of her car on the interstate—not with pity, nor disgust, but with a kind of fascination that so much goo can come out of something so small.

"With all due respect, Mr. Dahms," she said, "I have spoken with the proper authorities several times over the last few days. The police have asked many questions and I have done my best to answer them. I see no need to answer any more. At least not to some self-described private detective."

I smiled at her again, this time resignedly, as if I ran into this kind of resistance all the time and understood perfectly what she meant. I reached into my back pocket and pulled out my wallet to show her the little laminated card the state had issued me to prove that I was licensed to ask these kinds of questions. She didn't seem very impressed when I held it out to her.

"Again," she said, "I prefer to deal only with the official authorities. Now, if you'll please excuse me, I am quite busy at the moment."

The smile didn't seem to be getting me anywhere, but I kept it in place anyway. "Mrs. Rovig, there isn't a soul here besides the two of us. I don't think you're too busy to talk with me. I know that you may not be used to the idea of speaking with private investigators, but hey…you're probably not used to having your husband's brains blown all over his living room either. You are his wife, are you not?"

"His ex-wife," she said.

I nodded. The fact was that until I'd walked into that office, I hadn't known that Rovig had ever been married.

"Do you mind if I take a seat?" I asked, moving to a chair that sat in front of the desk.

"Yes. I do mind. I think I've made it clear that I do not wish to speak with you."

"Why not? Is there something about your husband's murder that you don't want me to know? Is there something you haven't told the police?"

She shuddered but recovered almost immediately. "I'm hiding nothing. I would simply prefer that you leave."

I shook my head. "Well, that ain't gonna happen. Not before I find out a few things. I can't help solve this thing without your cooperation and—"

I was interrupted before I could finish. Behind me, a low, even voice sounded. "The lady asked you to leave," someone said. Startled, I wheeled around to find the man with the mop standing in the doorway. "Time for you to go," he added.

"Listen, pal," I hissed at him. "This isn't any of your business. You're the one who should—"

I didn't get to finish my sentence. Before I got the words out, the big man dropped the mop and closed in quickly. I didn't even have time to move before he had a big mitt wrapped around my throat. He smiled ever so slightly as he backed me against a wall and lifted me, by the neck, a couple of inches off the floor. Some kind of framed certificate that had been hanging on the wall clattered to the floor beside me.

"Stop that, Irv!" I heard Lorraine Rovig say. I

couldn't tell if she was ordering him to put me down or to just quit knocking things off the wall. In either case, the big man didn't let go.

My arms were thrashing uselessly at my sides. I began to flail at him with my legs, but he was too close for me to really connect. Squirming, I must have looked like I was trying to dog paddle my way out of his grasp. My head started to swim as well. I tried to suck in some air, but instead all I managed was an eerie, creaking sound. As I felt myself going limp, I looked into my attacker's eyes. Surprisingly, there was no real menace there. Actually, he looked a little dippy. He had an open, innocent face and vacant eyes, slightly crossed, and set too close together. But while it is doubtful that those eyes ever simmered with intellect, at that moment they were splashed with pride. Not malice, just innocent pride.

I'd be pretty proud myself, I thought, if I could hoist a guy my size with one hand and pin him to a wall. The thought made me smile just a bit, even as Irv's face began to ooze out of focus. Then something hidden in a dusty corner of my memory began to press against what remained of my consciousness. There was something familiar about Irv. I'd seen him before, I thought. I'd seen him do this before. I struggled to remember, but everything was getting so dark.

"Milkman," I muttered, as a warm gray cloud enveloped me, and my mind shut down.

I was unable to see the expression on his face when it came to me, but I must have been right because he let go of my throat and I crumpled to the floor. I sucked in air, coughing, sputtering, and spitting between gasps. The world started to come back; the gray cloud slowly dissipated. When I was able to see again, I looked up at the big man, who was standing over me but appeared to be concentrating not on me, but rather on the strands of spittle that I'd been hacking onto the floor. Then he glanced ruefully over at the mop that he had dropped. Great, I thought, now I've created even more work for the guy. How's he going to react to that?

When his gaze returned to me, I forced myself to smile and, wheezing, managed to say, "You *are* the Milkman, aren't you? Irving, 'the Milkman' Mulligan? I remember you from the old days of the AWA."

Mulligan nodded and broke in a grin. "Yeah. I used to wrestle under that name. You a wrestling fan?"

"Hell, yeah!" I said heartily, though my voice was still a harsh croak. "I was a fan back when you wrestled, anyway. I've kind of drifted from the sport since then."

Mulligan shrugged and looked around the room. "Yeah, me too."

I rose slowly, rubbed my neck, and coughed a couple more times. "Well, let me tell ya, Milkman. You still got it. You could climb back into the ring anytime."

"I try to stay in shape," he said, his grin widening into a prideful beam.

There is something overwhelmingly weird about being a sports fan, or, I suppose, a fan of any kind of celebrity. In the presence of someone you greatly admire, or who at least you've seen lots of times on TV, you tend to stop acting rationally. I found that this was true of myself, anyway, because as I looked into the smiling face of this former professional wrestler—a man who had disappeared from the limelight nearly three decades before—I forgot all about his having just ushered me into near unconsciousness; I forgot the reason I was in the room; I forgot about my own safety. No, all I could think of were all those Saturday mornings that I'd watched wrestling on TV waiting for the Milkman to enter the ring.

Milkman Mulligan had been a crowd favorite, but not for his ring prowess. Instead, he was our beloved underdog—a man with a huge smile and enormous enthusiasm, who for the life of him, couldn't seem to ever win a match. There were lots of headliners—wrestlers whose personas and interview styles and whose slick and devastating moves commanded the attention and respect of both fans and foes alike. But although the headliners were responsible for ticket sales, they evoked nothing like the affection that Mulligan did.

The Milkman was a professional wrestler of the old school. He didn't need an outlandish costume or some comic book persona. He also didn't have the sculpted, bodybuilder physique that has since become the standard. Instead, he was just a big, big man who gave every indication of truly loving his job. When he entered the arena, he exchanged high-fives with the crowd on the way to the ring, and once there, he pumped his fists and shouted enthusiastically, a loopy grin on his face and every fiber of his being eager to engage his opponent in battle.

His matches didn't last long, however. Invariably, after briefly gaining the upper hand, he would be dealt some crushing blow and the match would end with his ignominious defeat. But he would return again the next week, ever ready, ever hopeful. He was one of us, a regular guy coming in to work after a couple of days off, rejuvenated and irrationally expecting things to work out better this time.

"You ever think about it?" I asked, shaking my head

to see if all my synapses were still connected. "Returning to the squared circle, I mean. Kenny 'Sodbuster' Jay only hung it up a few years ago. He's much older than you and probably not in anywhere near your shape."

"Don't let the Sodbuster's looks fool you," Mulligan said. "That guy's tougher than a two-dollar steak."

"You'd know," I said.

"Excuse me," Lorraine Rovig interrupted. "I seem to have lost track of just what we're doing here."

I turned to find her looking at us with bemused incredulity. "You just don't know what a thrill this is, ma'am. The Milkman here was part of the glory days of the American Wrestling Association. Anyone who grew up around here has to have a soft spot for the old AWA. Verne Gagne, The Crusher. Mad Dog Vachon. Milkman Mulligan?"

"Ah, hell," Mulligan said, now looking at the floor and shuffling his feet. "I was never in the same league as The Crusher and Mad Dog."

"Well," Lorraine Rovig said, "I grew up around here and I don't know what you're talking about."

"You've got the Milkman working for you and you don't even know about his storied past?"

"He must have left it off his resume."

Mulligan stiffened and the smile melted from his face. "No, ma'am," he said, shaking his head firmly. "I put it all down. You could look it up."

"I'm sure you did, Irv," she said sympathetically. "It must have slipped my mind."

Mulligan relaxed and we all stood around for some seconds in silence. "Well," I said, "since your boss here isn't much of a wrestling fan, maybe we should change the subject back to her former husband's murder. I really do need to ask a couple of questions."

Mulligan looked to her for direction. There was no doubt in my mind that, fan or no fan, Mulligan would toss me out of there if she wanted him to. She turned and looked at me intently. I tried that grin again.

She rolled her eyes. "I don't suppose you're going to leave quietly before I talk to you."

"Not quietly, no ma'am."

"Have a chair, Mr. Dahms."

Mulligan gave a relieved sigh, but remained by the door, hovering. Mrs. Rovig sat down behind her desk, laid her hands in front of her, and waited for me to begin.

"Tell me about Thomas Ehlers," I said. "The young man who was arrested. You know him?"

"Yes," she said exhaling deeply. "I suppose you expect me to tell you that he was a deeply troubled youth who I had always suspected of having violent tendencies. I hate to disappoint you, but the fact is that he never made much of an impression on me. He was just another young man passing through the program. Just another kid who came here looking for a chance, looking for a way out of the circle of poverty, despair, and hopelessness that he was born into. You probably want me to tell you that he was troubled. Well, they're all troubled. Troubled by a society that not only tolerates a permanent underclass, but actually needs to sustain that underclass as a source of cheap labor. An underclass born into wretched poverty from which they feel the only chance of escape is to become a professional sports star or to turn to crime."

She paused for a moment and looked down at her desk calendar. She shook her head almost imperceptibly then continued, a sarcastic edge creeping into her voice.

"Oh, a fortunate few are able to educate themselves, to provide themselves with the ability to read, to fill out a job application so they can go to work in some office or some fast-food place somewhere, to earn a paycheck that isn't enough to pay the rent, let alone put food on the table for their families. Everyone who comes in here looking for help is troubled, Mr. Dahms. And when we try to help them, more often than not, we fail. Thomas Ehlers is just another person who we failed. Just another face that came through that door out there. When I saw his picture in the newspaper this morning, I wasn't even sure I recognized him. That's what I can tell you about Thomas Ehlers."

She finished her speech and I nodded, staring deeply into her lovely green eyes. "I don't give a shit about any of that," I told her.

"What?" she asked in disbelief.

"That's not my problem."

I heard Mulligan moving around behind me, but I kept my eyes on his boss. She stared at me. "That's not your problem?" she asked at last, as if still trying to comprehend what I'd said.

"Nope. My problem is finding out who killed your ex-husband."

She looked at me some more, then looked down at her desk, then back up at me. After a while, a wry smile appeared on her face.

"Well, at least you're an honest son of a bitch."

"I try. Now, what can you tell me specifically about Ehlers and his relationship with your former husband?"

"I really only know what I've read in the papers. That and what little the police have told me. Apparently, Ted befriended the boy. He not only helped him here, in his Thursday night sessions, but when Ted found out they lived within a few houses of one another, he invited the boy over to his home. I don't know how often or if those were also tutoring sessions. Despite his faults, Ted was a concerned man. He took a special interest in his community and in those around him. Most likely he'd developed a special interest in the boy. Ted was always talking about the changes in his neighborhood. Did you know that he lived in the house he grew up in?"

I said that I did.

"Well, most probably that's what drew Ted's interest to the Ehlers boy. Ted often complained about what had happened to his neighborhood since he was a boy growing up there. The crime, the poverty—nobody cared about it anymore. He thought he could change a little piece of it, just a little piece. That's why he started working here. That's probably why he tried to help Thomas Ehlers."

"Did Ted volunteer here back when you were married?" I asked.

"No."

"How long have you worked here?"

"Many years."

"Hmm. But Ted didn't work here until after your divorce?"

"That's correct."

"Maybe he wanted to be near you," I suggested.

"I really wouldn't know, Mr. Dahms."

"Do you think Ehlers killed Ted?"

She threw her head back as if about to laugh. "How should I know?" she asked, without a trace of amusement in her voice. "Ted and I did not share very much these past months. We saw each other here twice a week.

When we talked, we talked only about our work here. We had, long ago, stopped talking with each other about personal matters."

"Wasn't it difficult for you to see him every week and not ask him about how things were going? Didn't you ever just chat about how you were getting along since your divorce?"

She looked me in the eyes and said, "No. No, it was not difficult."

"Not at all difficult," I pressed, "even though you were once married to him? Come on, Mrs. Rovig. Nobody could continue to see their former husband, their former lover, that often and not even inquire innocently about their health or discuss what they watched on TV the night before. Surely, he told you something about his personal life since the divorce."

Her face became a blank. "No," she repeated, "it was not difficult."

I studied her face, her eyes. Her eyes said that she was hiding nothing. They were calm, without a trace of sadness or bitterness. They said that she and Rovig had simply drifted apart, that there had been no desire to know anything more about the man to whom she had been married. They said that their life together had stopped making any difference. I studied her eyes. I knew she was lying.

There was something she didn't want to tell me, maybe lots of things, but I wasn't going to find out what they were. Not right then anyway.

"Do you know of anyone who would have had reason to kill you husband?" I asked.

"No," she said. "No, I do not."

She began shuffling through some papers that were

piled on her desk. She took off her glasses and set them down gently next to her nameplate. Behind me, I heard Mulligan's quiet cough.

"Now, if you will excuse me, Mr. Dahms, I've got work to do," she said. "Perhaps Irv would like to show you out."

The big man stepped forward and laid a hand on my shoulder.

"No thanks, Mrs. Rovig. I'm sure I can find my way out all by myself." I shrugged off Mulligan's hand, rose and stepped past him to the door.

"Mr. Dahms," she said, as I reached the door.

Still sitting, she picked up her glasses, placed them on her nose, and peered at me with a thoughtful look. "Just one thing I have to mention before you leave," she said. "That is, without a single doubt, the ugliest jacket I have ever seen."

Chapter Seven

It was only a few miles from Lorraine Rovig's office to Ted Rovig's former neighborhood. I slowed my car as I passed the white house where the murder had taken place. A young man wearing a dark, woolen overcoat was struggling to drive a "For Sale" sign into the frozen ground. Whoever owned the property now—probably his ex-wife—was moving quickly to sell the place.

On the next block down from Rovig's house, I scanned the street looking for the number of the apartment building where Thomas Ehlers lived. I spotted it, then had to circle around the block twice before finding a parking spot.

Ehlers's apartment building was a turn-of-the-last-century, three-story brownstone. Accents of flowers were carved in relief in the gray stonework that framed the windows that faced the street. The building had probably been pretty nice once, but now the façade was scrawled with graffiti and most of the windows sported sheets and blankets rather than curtains or blinds. The front door was recessed in the center of the building forming a V that ran the length of the structure. The original lobby had also likely been inviting as originally designed, but had been remodeled, the changes prompted by security rather than by aesthetic concerns. It was still pretty wide, but so shallow that when the outer door shut, I was afraid that it would push me, nose first, up against the inner glass security door that barred passage to the front stairway. Banks of mailboxes were bolted to the walls on both sides. I checked the mailboxes, each affixed with a small strip of paper where a nearly illegible hand had scrawled the name of each apartment dweller.

Ehlers lived in apartment 301. To the right of the security door was a panel with a series of buttons. Above them was a speaker with a large tear in the mesh covering. I punched number 301 with faint hope that the decrepit security system would actually work. I hit the button three times before a soft, elderly-sounding, female voice came through the speaker.

"Yes. Who is there, please?"

I cleared my throat loudly. "Mrs. Ehlers, my name is Lyle Dahms; I'm here to see you about getting Thomas out of jail."

There was a silence on the other end of the speaker. At last, the voice came back. "Are you a lawyer, or something? I don't have the money to hire no lawyer."

"This isn't going to cost you anything, Mrs. Ehlers," I replied. "Do you think I could come in and talk to you? It's getting kind of cold out here." I stamped my feet for effect.

The door buzzer rang out sharply and I scraped the security door open just as the buzzer stopped. I ascended the stairs, reaching the second floor, when I heard a door open above me.

The gentle, elderly voice drifted down the open stairwell. "I don't know if I should've let you in. There's a lot of crazies out there, you know."

"I know, Mrs. Ehlers," I said, breathing heavily as I climbed the last few steps. "You can't be too careful."

The woman I met at the top of the stairs didn't look anything like the image I had formed from her voice. Instead of a frail, older woman, she was in her early thirties. Her slim, somewhat hippy figure was encased in a pair of tight blue jeans, and she was wearing a "Metallica" T-shirt. She had dark eyes, a thin, gold ring piercing her left eyebrow, and hair that could be politely described as strawberry blonde but had probably become its present color as the result of too much experimentation with supermarket hair dyes. She had a nice face with pudgy cheeks that suggested she had to work to keep her weight down, but that gave her the kind of little girl cuteness that always makes me smile.

I was smiling as she stood in the doorway, sizing me up. I evidently passed whatever test she was putting me through, because she pushed the door open wider. "Come on in," she invited me. "I think I got some coffee in the kitchen if you want some."

"Thank you, Mrs. Ehlers. Coffee would be great."

She closed the door behind us and said, "And you can forget that Mrs. Ehlers stuff. My name's Francine. What did you say your name was again?"

"My name's Lyle Dahms," I replied.

She led me into the living room and pointed to an armchair covered with a brown, terrycloth bath towel. "You can have a seat there, Mr. Dahms. I'll go get us some of that coffee and then you can tell me how you're going to help get my Tommy out of jail."

I took a seat as Francine went into the kitchen. There were some magazines on an end table next to the armchair and as I was leafing through a copy of *Rolling Stone*, I heard the hum of a microwave oven.

"Are you a private lawyer, or one of those public

defenders?" she asked from the kitchen.

"I'm not actually a lawyer, Francine. I'm a private investigator. I work for a lawyer."

"That so?" she asked, emerging from the kitchen with two cups of coffee.

"Yeah. I work for the law firm of Rabinowitz and Rabinowitz. Down at Rabinowitz and Rabinowitz they hired this new, crackerjack attorney. He's a young guy, but he's got just a ton of experience. Used to be a real hotshot at a firm down in Georgia. That's where he's from. Anyway, Rabinowitz and Rabinowitz hired him as their new, chief litigator for criminal cases. He's been putting in a lot of time in court, but he's yet to find a case that he can use to really make a name for himself."

She handed me one of the cups and I made a yummy face at her after I'd sampled the coffee.

"You want any cream or sugar?" she asked. "I always take mine black, but I got some sugar. I guess I don't really have any cream, but I got some milk in the refrigerator. I keep that for the cat. Oh, by the way, I have a cat, so if you feel something furry rubbing up against your leg, don't think that I'm coming on to you or something."

She laughed softly at her joke

"As I was saying," I continued, "this lawyer that I'm working for saw the story in the paper about your son's arrest and he doesn't think the cops have a case. He says they never should have arrested Tommy. He says that your son may even be entitled to some kind of compensation, and he would like to look into the matter."

I leaned closer to Francine and confided, "You see, this may be just the case that he's been looking for. Something with a lot of local interest that will generate tons of publicity. That's why he's willing to take on the case for nothing. The way he looks at it, it's a win-win. When he gets Tommy off, he'll make a fortune defending folks that can afford what he usually charges."

"Oh, I know that Tommy didn't kill that Mr. Rovig," Francine said. She too leaned forward and glanced from side to side as if worried that we would be overheard. "Now, I'm not saying that my Tommy never got into no trouble, you understand. He's had some trouble with fighting, and there was that time last year when he got caught stealing cigarettes from the grocery down the street. But I'm here to tell you that he didn't kill that Mr. Rovig."

"How exactly did Tommy come to know Rovig?"

"Why, he met him at that school for reading," she said. A wary gleam in her eye chastised me for asking a question to which I should already have had the answer. "Just like they said in the news yesterday."

I leaned back in my chair. "Yes," I said, "but what we need is for you to tell us what isn't being reported on the news. For instance, Mr. Rovig had many students, but as far as we know, Tommy was the only one he invited over to his house. Maybe you could tell us why."

"When Tommy first started going over there, I wondered about that myself," she said. "I don't have to tell you that there's lots of crazies and perverts out there. Tommy starts spending a lot of time with an older fellow, one that lives in his mother's house…Well, at first, I wondered if maybe Mr. Rovig didn't want Tommy around for the wrong reason. If you know what I mean."

I nodded.

She smiled. "Well, I put that right out of my head after I met that nice Mr. Rovig. He wasn't no kind of fairy, no sir. He explained to me that he and Tommy just got to talking one night after class and Tommy tells him that they live in the same neighborhood and all. Then Mr. Rovig says, real polite, that Tommy should drop by his house sometime. Probably not really meaning it, you understand, but just being polite. Well, Tommy, he doesn't drop everything and run over there. No. But a few weeks later, Tommy told me, he was walking home, and he passes by Mr. Rovig's house and Mr. Rovig is out clipping his bushes, and he sees Tommy. One thing led to another, and Mr. Rovig invites Tommy into his house. Tommy don't like to admit it, but he really liked Mr. Rovig. He liked learning how to read better and to do those math problems that Mr. Rovig was teaching him. Now, maybe Tommy should've learned those things in regular school, but back then he just didn't seem to want to spend the time, you know. But with Mr. Rovig…Well, many's the night I seen Tommy sitting over there at that kitchen table, right over there, studying up on that stuff, working so hard to impress Mr. Rovig that I thought his head would burst. That Mr. Rovig was a fine fellow, if you ask me. He didn't have no kids of his own, even though he dearly loved that wife of his. You know, the one that left him. Anyway, Mr. Rovig told me that since he didn't have no kids of his own, he felt that it was incumbent—that's the word he used, 'incumbent'—he said that it was incumbent upon him to do what he could to help other people's kids. Especially neighborhood kids, you know. From this neighborhood. It was especially incumbent upon him to help kids from this neighborhood."

"How often did Tommy visit Mr. Rovig at his house?" I asked.

"Oh, not real often. He was over there once a week or so. I told him not to go bothering Mr. Rovig too often or maybe Mr. Rovig wouldn't want him coming around no more. Do you have children, Mr. Dahms?"

"No, I don't, Francine."

"Well, Tommy's my only child and I raised him the best I knew how. I sure didn't raise him to be no murderer, I'm telling you."

"How do you suppose he got ahold of Mr. Rovig's television set?"

"I know exactly how that happened, Mr. Dahms. But I didn't know it was in the house until the police found it. You should have seen my face when those police showed up here with that search warrant and they go into Tommy's room and there sits that TV. I'll tell you, when I saw that, I mostly freaked. But even then, I never imagined it could be Mr. Rovig's TV. No sir. That came out later." She stopped and took a sip of her coffee.

"Just how did it get into his room?" I prompted.

"Oh, he put it there. I talked to Tommy in the lockup. He told me all about it. You see, he was coming home from a party. Some of the guys he's been hanging with got an apartment over by Loring Park. Well, they had a party that night and Tommy got pretty messed up. So, he catches the bus, and it drops him off down at the corner. He has to walk right past Mr. Rovig's house to get home. Well, he's walking home, and he sees that Mr. Rovig's front door is open. Tommy says that Mr. Rovig always kept his house locked up tight, even when they were both in there together. So, when he sees that door open, he figures he'd better go check it out. Tommy says he was pretty drunk that night, but when he saw what was in that house, he sobered up right quick. Tommy says he was really scared and really drunk and just as he was about to run out of there, this idea comes into his mind. He says it just kind of occurred to him that he could take that TV with him. Now, that ain't the kind of thinking that I raised him to think and maybe folks'll say I'm a bad mother because of it. But I talked to him, and he knows it was wrong for him to have took that TV. He told me so himself. He made a mistake and he knows he'll have to pay for it. But I know it happened like he said. I know he didn't kill that Mr. Rovig."

I drained the last of my coffee. "Sounds like your Tommy was just in the wrong place at the wrong time. Our first priority, of course, is to get him released, but after that we may well find that there are grounds for a civil case against the city."

Francine's eyes momentarily glowed with avarice. Then she lowered her eyes. "I only want this nightmare to end," she said quietly. "I only want Tommy back."

I glanced past Francine to a small bookshelf where I spotted a picture of her posing with her arm around a tall, grim-faced, young man that I assumed was Tommy. Francine was beaming proudly, but the image of her son made me wince. He was a lanky, well-built man with cold, dead eyes and the practiced stony expression of a street punk.

I pointed at the picture. "Nice looking boy."

"I think so too," Francine said.

"Getting back to his arrest, how did the police know to look in Tommy's room for the television?"

"Oh, they weren't looking for the television," she said, shaking her head vigorously. "No one saw Tommy with the TV. No one knew it was here. They were looking for Tommy. You remember those friends of his that I was telling you about? The ones with the apartment near Loring Park? Well, this man says he got robbed in the park the night before Tommy got arrested. He goes down to the police station and he looks through those books they got down there. You know, the ones with the mug shots? Anyway, this man picks out Tommy and a couple of his friends as the ones that robbed him. The police came here to ask Tommy about that man that got robbed. Only Tommy says that they didn't ever rob that man. Tommy says that the man is a fag that got mad when they didn't want to have sex with him. He says they never touched that man."

"Did the police find anything that could tie Tommy to that robbery?" I asked.

"They found some money in Tommy's dresser. They took that when they took Tommy. Now, you tell me, how can they prove that he got that money from that man in the park? Money all looks like money, don't it?"

I said that it did.

"Well then, they can't prove that Tommy robbed that man, and they can't prove that Tommy killed Mr. Rovig either."

I nodded in agreement and stood to take my leave. "Well, Francine," I said, "you've cleared up a lot of things for us and we sure do appreciate your time. Now, I have to go back to the office and tell that Georgia lawyer what you've told me and, hopefully, we'll be getting back to you on how we're going to handle Tommy's defense."

"Well, I sure hope you can help my boy get out of jail, Mr. Dahms," she said, rising to show me to the door. "I don't mind them teaching him a lesson for stealing that TV, but he sure don't deserve to do time for killing that nice Mr. Rovig."

"I'm sure we can do something about that, Francine," I told her.

Francine and I both reached for the door at the same time. We fumbled at it for a moment until I showed the good sense to let her open it. The instant the door opened, from out of nowhere, an enormously fat tabby cat suddenly bounded across the room. Francine slammed the door shut before the cat could escape. The cat looked up at her and hissed menacingly.

"Uh, that's some cat you got there, Francine."

"That's Bosco, Mr. Dahms. Sorry to close the door on you like that, but I sure wouldn't want to lose him. He's all I have until I get Tommy back."

With a malevolent glare, the cat hissed again.

"Animals can be such a comfort," I said.

Francine nodded and reached down to pick up the cat. Balancing Bosco in one arm, she opened the door for me. I stepped through the door but stopped when a thought struck me. "Just one more thing, Francine. You said something about how much Ted Rovig loved his ex-wife. Did he talk to you about their relationship?"

"Oh, no, Mr. Dahms," she answered. "But Tommy did. Tommy says that Mr. Rovig talked about her all the time. Tommy says that Mr. Rovig was just pining away for her. He once told Tommy that the worst day of his life was the day she left him. Tommy says that Mr. Rovig was always hoping that she'd come back to him. Tommy says that's the real reason he did the tutoring, so he could be close to her. Yes sir, Tommy says that was the worst day of his life, the day she left him. Worst day, that is, until the day he died."

Chapter Eight

I left Francine's and had driven about three blocks before I spotted the car behind me. It appeared to be the same navy-blue sedan I'd seen earlier that morning at Gateway House and again later when I was circling the Ehlers' apartment building looking for a parking spot.

I kept going, then took a left onto Thirty-Fifth Street and crossed over the freeway. Two blocks down, I turned into the lot of Ted Robinson's Barbecue and Sports Bar. I popped open the glove compartment, took out my .38, and slipped it barrel first into my belt at the small of my back. I got out of the car, tugging at my jacket to make sure that the gun was completely hidden from sight. When I reached the restaurant, I used the glass of the door as a mirror, watching as the Civic pulled over to the curb across the street. I was pretty sure there was only one guy in the car.

Robinson's was nearly empty—only a couple of stragglers lingered over a late lunch in a booth along the far wall. A man in an apron covered with red, saucy fingerprints was leaning against the counter next to the cash register just inside the door. He was tallying up a guest check. As he turned to greet me, I reached inside the breast pocket of my jacket and pulled out my wallet. I let the wallet drop open just long enough to for him to glimpse my investigator's license. The man came to attention as I snapped the wallet closed and walked briskly past him. "Toops," I announced. "Name's Mort Toops. I'm with the health department." I pointed to the back. "The kitchen's this way, right?"

The guy in the apron followed quietly a few steps behind me, past a couple of uncleared tables, and through a pair of double doors into the kitchen. The chef—an ebony giant chopping on a rack of baby back ribs with a meat cleaver—looked startled by our sudden entrance. He whirled to face me, raised the cleaver, and glared at me with a pair of yellow, bloodshot eyes.

I stared at him narrowly, then turned to the man from the front counter, now standing behind me. "Where's this man's hairnet?" I barked. "This man should be wearing a hairnet."

The counterman stared at me gape-mouthed for a moment, his eyes darting uncertainly from me to the cook. "Elliot!" he wailed at last. "Didn't I tell you to always wear a hairnet?"

I shook my head. "This doesn't look good, pal."

I approached the cook, who had put down the cleaver but was still glaring at me. There was a pair of metal tongs on the counter next to him. I picked up the tongs and strode to the back of the kitchen. Near the rear door, a couple of open aluminum saucepots were bubbling atop a gas stove. I stirred at one of them briefly, then bent down to open the oven door. Using the tongs, I reached inside the oven and pried loose a hunk of baked-on goo. Then I proudly held my prize out in front of me like a bride-to-be showing off the new diamond on her left hand.

"Just as I thought," I said. "When was the last time anyone cleaned this oven?"

Before either man could answer, I pointed to the

counterman. "I'm going back out to get my clipboard. When I get back, I want to see you down there with a sponge and a spray can of Easy-Off. You hear me?"

He glanced nervously at the cook. "I'll get right on it, sir," he assured me. "Believe me. Right away."

I nodded and went quickly out the back door.

Adjacent to the restaurant were an antique shop and a dentist's office. On the far side of the dentist's office an alley led back to the street in front. In the alley, I picked up a fist-sized chunk of concrete that had been nesting in a pile of broken glass. Emerging from the alley about a block behind the Civic, I tried to appear casual, sneaking up on it with the hunk of cement in one hand and my gun in the other. The driver didn't spot me until I was beside him at the car window. He tried to grab for his own gun, but he was too twitchy to reach it in time. I roared as I brought the concrete down hard against the window, sending kernels of shattered safety glass raining down on both of us.

I dropped the concrete and grabbed the driver by the collar, pulling his head through the broken window. I smiled at my reflection in the pair of orange, wraparound sunglasses he was wearing.

I pressed the barrel of my .38 against his temple. "Could you please hand me that gun you've got there?" I asked him. "Just use two fingers. Butt first, please."

Slowly, he reached into his coat and brought out the gun. I let go of his collar and took his gun from him.

The driver settled back into his seat, staring straight ahead, his mouth set in a sullen pout. "Now, don't let it get you down, son," I told him. "This isn't really your fault. I blame Farnum. He had no business sending some flunky to tail me in the first place. It's his lack of trust that bothers me most."

The man still refused to look at me, so I reached down and removed his sunglasses. He managed a sneer, but fear crowded the corners of his eyes.

I smiled again, trying for the same paternal smile that Farnum always used on me. "Maybe you're just in the wrong line of work," I suggested. "I mean, I know how proud your parents must be, but ask yourself, do you find it fulfilling? You know, it's never too late to change career paths. Perhaps you should find something you're more suited to. I'm guessing you're a people person. You know, there are some great opportunities in the hospitality industry."

Pressing the barrel of the gun a little harder against his temple, I continued. "If it's not too much to ask, could you do me a teensy favor? Could you tell Farnum that I don't like being followed? Could you let him know that I'll be happy to report to him when I have something? Golly, I'd appreciate that so much."

The man gave me a minimal nod. I stepped back from the car.

He rubbed his neck and brushed some of the broken glass off from his coat. Then he stuck out his chin defiantly. "I'm gonna kill you for this, man," he said. "I'm gonna kill you."

I grunted. "Yeah, sonny. You keep telling yourself that. But for now, just tell Farnum what happened."

He eyed me as he started the car and pulled away from the curb. But then he stepped down hard on the accelerator, his tires spinning crazily on the icy pavement, spraying shards of sand, snow and ice across the street, over my shoes and halfway up my trousers.

I was back to my car and was wiping at my shoes

with a tissue when the door to the restaurant opened and the last of the lunch patrons emerged. Behind them, I spotted the counterman staring out at me. I waved at him as I drove away.

On the way back to my office, I stopped at a Ukrainian deli on Hennepin Avenue and picked up a takeout order of assorted vareniki and a couple of piroshkis. I was at my desk, slathering the vareniki with sour cream and horseradish sauce, when my phone rang.

I popped one of the dumplings into my mouth and let the call ring through to the answering machine. The machine whirred to life and Carmen's voice filled the room. "*Mr. Dahms,*" she began, "*I know we just met and that I've no reason to trust you, but...But I've got to trust someone. I really don't have anywhere else to turn.*"

Although her voice was steady, alarm edged her words. I dropped my fork and picked up the phone. "Carmen," I said, chewing quickly. "I just came in. What can I do for you?"

"Oh, Lyle," she sighed, her composure dissolving. "Thank God you're there. I'm so frightened. I think they're outside waiting for me. You've got to come over here. You've got to come over right away. I'm at my apartment." She gave me an address on Eighth Street Southeast. "It's on the bottom floor," she said. "I've got some things to tell you about how Ted died. Please Lyle. You've got to come over right away."

"Calm down, Carmen," I said. "What's so urgent?"

"I can't tell you right now," she sobbed. "I can't tell you on the phone. Please, just come right away."

I didn't like it. I don't get a lot of calls from mob-connected damsels in distress and my instincts told me to err on the side of caution. But I'd been carrying around a mental picture of Carmen since we'd met and I couldn't shake the memory of that knife-edge of fear I'd seen flash in her eyes.

"Are you in some kind of danger?" I asked, trying to sound businesslike.

She didn't answer. There was a clicking sound; then the phone went dead.

The great big nothing coming from the receiver was corrosive. It ate at my insides. I pushed back from my desk and headed immediately down to my car, cursing as I fumbled getting my keys into the ignition.

Thankfully, Carmen's apartment was only about ten blocks away. It took only minutes for me to get there. I wanted to rush right in but decided it would be wiser to check the area first, so I circled around a couple of times. I didn't see any bad guys.

I parked on the street in front of the building. It was an old, two-story duplex that had been further sliced into four apartments. Carmen had said that her apartment was on the bottom floor, but she hadn't given me the apartment number. I realized then that she had also neglected to give me her last name. I checked the mailboxes and found that the ground level apartments were inhabited by a Ferguson and a Reilly. With her dark skin, brown eyes, and long, straight tresses, Carmen didn't look to me like either a Ferguson or a Reilly.

I knocked first on the Ferguson apartment. No answer. So, I tried the one across the hall. The door had one of those glass, fisheye peepholes and I heard some shuffling behind the door before the dot of light in the peephole went dark. It was dark a long time. Finally, the light in the peephole returned and the lock slid back.

"Ms. Reilly?" I asked as Carmen opened the door.

She gave me a timid smile, ushered me inside, pushed the door closed, and slapped the lock into place with authority. "Did anybody follow you?" Her voice quavered, but I didn't see any real fear in her eyes.

"I don't think anybody will be following me for at least the rest of the day," I said.

"What do you mean by that?"

"Nothing," I assured her. "Don't worry about it."

She smiled again. She wore the same pair of acid-washed jeans she'd worn in Farnum's apartment but had replaced the silky purple top with a simple, maroon blouse. Maroon was also a color that she wore well.

I must have been staring again. She looked up at me with clear eyes and set her mouth in a tight little grin. I smiled and turned to look around the room.

It was not the apartment that I would have expected of someone used to the luxury of Farnum's lifestyle. The wallpaper was an old floral print with a background that was probably once cream-colored but had yellowed like the parchment of an ancient Psalter. It had bubbled away from the wall in several places and, in one spot, directly over a full-sized bed, a section had been torn away completely. The tear was shaped like the silhouette of a bird—not soft and round like a dove, but with sharp-edged wings outstretched in flight, like a hawk or a vulture.

At the other end of the room, through an open arch, sat a sofa covered with a multicolored bedspread, an armchair, and an old stereo with a turntable, beside which was stacked a prodigious collection of 45s. In one corner there was a huge, old Zenith television set with a cathode ray tube like your grandparents might still have. The apartment did not come off as timeless. Just old.

In another corner stood an artificial Christmas tree. The tree was about four and a half feet tall with perfectly straight branches that sprouted not pine needles, but rather filmy, silver strips that looked like tin-foil hair. It had a roughly tree-like shape, but more closely resembled an alien homing beacon from a "B" sci-fi movie. It was strung with faded, colored lights, and a weathered Christmas angel perched on top. A white bed sheet was draped beneath to serve as a tree skirt. There were no presents under the tree.

I walked through the room, popped my head into the small kitchen at the back of the apartment, looked out the kitchen window into the alley, and finally peeked into the bathroom. We were alone.

Carmen followed, staying a few steps behind me. When I'd finished searching the place, I turned to her and smiled again. "You really don't look like a Reilly."

When she smiled back, little fingers of glee drummed inside of me. "Do I look like a Popkin?" she asked. "That was my father's name."

"No. You're infinitely more exotic."

"You must think I'm a fool," she said, her smile melting away. "It's just that I've been so frightened today. When I got home the place just looked…I don't know. It just looked different. I thought maybe…maybe someone had been in here while I was gone. When I left this morning, I swear I put a coffee cup on that TV over there. When I got back, it was in the kitchen. I don't know, maybe I'm imagining things." She paused. "I overreacted. I shouldn't have bothered you. I'm sorry."

"I'm just glad you're all right."

She lowered her eyes and shook her head. When she looked back up, her eyes gleamed with tears. "Oh, Lyle," she said. "I feel…I just feel so all…so all alone."

Emotion swallowed her words. She rushed to the sofa, threw herself down, and curled up into a ball, her head turned against the cushions. Her small frame was wracked with sobs.

I hesitated, looking at her, noting particularly the way her long, dark hair was sticking slightly to her wet cheek. An emptiness opened within me.

I went to her. I sat on the sofa next to her, lifted her, and turned her head to rest against my shoulder. She came willingly, burying her face into my chest and placing her delicate, little girl hands—palms open—against me. I stroked her hair as she sobbed.

When her tears began to subside, I raised her face up to look at me. "Tell me what's wrong."

Tears still welled in her dark, harlequin eyes. She bit down gently on her lower lip. She looked at her hands, still placed against my chest. "I need to trust you, Lyle," she said. "I need so much to trust you."

She pushed herself from me tentatively, like a newly hatched chick, its feathers still sticky, moving for the first time from the safety of its mother. She got to her feet and stood in the middle of the room with her head turned away.

"I don't know what you must think of me, Lyle," she said, turning back, her voice regaining strength. "Here I've invited you to my home and I haven't even offered you anything. I'm afraid I've forgotten my manners. I don't have much. I think there's some lemonade in the refrigerator. Would you like some?"

"No, thank you."

She stared for a moment before taking a seat in an armchair opposite me. "It's Alexander," she said at last.

I nodded. "Why are you so afraid of him?"

Carmen sighed, her eyes flickering about the room. "The first thing I want you to know, Lyle, is that it hasn't always been like this between Alexander and me. In the beginning he was more like a...Oh, I don't know, I guess he was more like a father to me. Things have never really been easy for me. I don't mean to complain, but...Well, when I met Alexander, I was broke and alone and I'd been looking for a job for months. I'd just wanted some kind of clerical job, working in an office somewhere, but I couldn't find anything. I couldn't even get an interview. Then I saw this ad. It said they wanted dancers. I didn't want to go, but...I really needed to make some money. Anyway, I got a job as a dancer at a club downtown. The Elite. Maybe you've heard of it?"

I said that I had.

"I'm not proud of that," she continued. "But I refuse to be ashamed either. I needed to support myself and I wasn't willing to cheat or steal to do it. So, I worked at the Elite. Anyway, one night after I finished on stage, the manager came back and told me that the owner wanted me to join him at his table. I was scared, but I didn't see that I had any choice. So, I went to his table. Alexander owns the club. You can't imagine how surprised I was when I met him. He was so gracious. He was there with a couple of colleagues and when I got to the table, he stood and introduced himself. He took my hand and introduced me to the other men at the table. The way he looked at me, it was as if, for that moment, I was the most important person there. At least that's how he made me feel. We talked about his family and about this basset hound that he'd bought for hunting that turned out to be afraid of the woods."

Carmen chuckled lightly. "You could tell he loved that dog," she said. "He asked about my family, but I-I let him know that I'd prefer not talking about them. Instead of being irritated, he just smiled. It was such a kind, knowing smile. We spent the whole night talking about...about nothing really. You know, our favorite TV shows. Songs on the radio. Stuff like that. I was happy talking to him. He made me feel like somebody.

"When the club closed for the night, he walked me to the door and offered to escort me to my car. When I told him that I took the bus to work, he immediately asked Mr. Angelino to give me a ride home. I remember he told Michael to 'take this enchanting young woman anywhere she likes.' Pretty hokey, huh? But it made me feel special. A couple of nights later, he came back to the club and asked the manager if I could join him at his table, even before I went on stage. That night he told me that he would like to make it possible for me to quit working in the club. He said that he didn't want to offend me, but that there was something about me that made him feel that I didn't belong there. He said that he was afraid that the work made me sad. That he didn't want me to be sad. Not ever. He offered me some money—a lot of money. He didn't ask for anything in return. He told me that he considered the money an investment. He said that I should go to school. He said that after a few courses, he might be able to give me a job in one of his businesses. He said that it didn't really matter what I decided to do with the money. Above all, he said, he just wanted to know that he had helped make me happy."

Carmen paused. Her expression took on a large measure of defiance. "And he did make me happy. No one, not even my own father had ever made me feel like that. He made me feel that if I were happy, it would be something he could share. As if it would be as important to him as it would be to me. I slept with him that night. He didn't ask me. I asked him. I wanted to be with him. I've been with him ever since. Until recently I thought I would always be with him. But…things have changed."

"How have things changed?"

Carmen picked up a magazine that was sitting on a table by the armchair. She didn't look at it; she merely opened it on her lap and turned back one of the pages.

"It started a few months ago. I think he was having some financial problems. Alexander never talked to me about the business, but I could tell when things weren't going well. He'd ask me to come to the apartment and when I'd get there he'd always put on a brave front, like there was nothing wrong. But something was wrong. Ted Rovig started coming by quite often. Before, Alexander would hold most of his business meetings at his company's offices downtown. But he started having more and more business meetings at the apartment. He even apologized for it once. He told me that he was sorry to have all these people coming to our special place all the time. I told him that I didn't mind, but actually, I began to worry. I wondered what it was that they had to discuss that could not be talked about at the office. But I never listened to the meetings. I stayed in the back and watched television. Sometimes I would read."

"Why do you think that Farnum had you there at all? You had this place then, didn't you?"

"I've had this apartment since before I met him."

"Well?"

"I don't know for sure," Carmen said. "I don't mean to flatter myself, but I think that he just wanted me near.

I think that Alexander's world may be starting to fall apart. I think with so much slipping away, I'm something that he can hold on to. The trouble is…" She paused. "The trouble is that he's started holding on too tight."

"Tell me about that."

"He's been asking me to spend all my time at the apartment, whether he's there or not. He's been looking for signs of betrayal in everything that I do. He's told me again and again that if he ever lost me, he wouldn't know what to do. He's been pressuring me to give up this apartment and to live in our 'special place' full time. I've explained to him that I need a place to call my own, but he doesn't want to listen. One time, he blew up at me. He grabbed ahold of me and demanded to know who I was seeing behind his back. He scared me. The next day he gave me flowers and apologized. He assured me that nothing like that would ever happen again. He begged me to stay with him. I stayed. But it's happened over and over. Once he even hit me. I've been hit before, Lyle. I've been hit a number of times before and I promised myself that I would never let it happen again.

"I walked out on him that night, Lyle. He came to me on his knees. He begged me to come back to him. He told me how much I meant to him, and he promised never to strike me again. I did go back to him. And he's not raised a hand to me again."

Carmen got out of her chair and went over to the tree. I hadn't noticed it when I first came in, but a round contraption was sitting on there on the floor. It was basically a spotlight designed to shine through four rotating plastic cells—red, green, blue, and gold. Carmen reached over and plugged it into the wall bathing the tin-foil tree changing colored light. Then she went to the stereo and began leafing through the stack of 45s until she had selected about a half a dozen. I watched her in silence.

"I hope you like the old songs, Lyle," she said placing the records on the stereo. The record changer clicked, and the first record dropped onto the spinning turntable. The tone arm jerked over to drop its needle on the record. It was Bing Crosby's "White Christmas."

She snapped off a nearby floor lamp and the room glowed with soft, multicolored shadows. She returned to her chair and appeared to be listening intently to the music, her eyes avoiding mine. Finally, she looked up at me. "He never hit me again," she repeated. "But he has made things hard for me. Outwardly, he treats me like I'm the most important thing in his life. But he has me followed. His men tail me everywhere. He keeps telling me that he can't live without me. He says that if I ever leave him, something horrible would happen. He never says what that would be, just that it would be horrible. His men read my mail. They come into this apartment when I'm gone. He's suffocating me. He fights with any man who even looks at me. Remember? He wanted to fight with you when we met yesterday. I don't think he'll ever let me go. I think that he'd kill me before he'd let me leave him. I think...I think maybe he killed Ted Rovig over me."

The hairs at the back of my neck sprang up like snipers from a hidden bunker. "What makes you think that?" I asked her.

Carmen's eyes welled up again. As I waited for her answer, the tone arm on the stereo clicked again and dropped the needle on the opening notes of Andy Williams' rendition of "Sleigh Ride."

"They had an argument," Carmen said. "Alexander and Ted. Ted was always nice to me. He was nice to everyone. A few days before he was murdered, he was over at the apartment. He and Alexander were going over the books or something. I was back in the bedroom watching television. I heard voices. Loud voices. Alexander was accusing Ted of being my lover. He used such coarse language. Finally, I heard Alexander swear that he was going to kill Ted. That he'd kill him in the most painful way possible. He told him that even his family wasn't going to be able to recognize him. He said that when he was through, even Ted's sainted mother would turn away in disgust."

Chapter Nine

The idea that Farnum killed Rovig had, of course, occurred to me before. If the scene that Carmen described between Farnum and the dead man had occurred, then her fear of Farnum was quite justified. She'd make a helluva witness for the prosecution.

"What exactly was your relationship with Rovig?"

She looked at me with a pained expression.

"I need to know, Carmen."

"I liked Ted," she said. "He was nice to me. He wasn't like so many of Alexander's other associates. He wasn't a tough guy. He was a sweet, little man who had lost his wife and who needed somebody to listen to him talk about his troubles. We talked a couple of times. I told him that I didn't understand why his wife had left him. He seemed to find some comfort in that. I guess I'd say that our talks made us close. I'd say that he began to look on me as...I don't know, a little sister or a daughter, or something."

She laughed. "I know what that sounds like, believe me. Over the years I've had more than one man tell me that I reminded him of his daughter. Most of them just wanted to get me into bed. Maybe it makes it more exciting for them, I don't know. But Ted was different. Or at least I think he was different. Maybe he just ended up dead before he could make his move."

"Did you ever visit Rovig at his home?"

She arched her back in her chair and her breasts pressed firmly against the fabric of her blouse. She exhaled deeply and a space opened between two of the buttons.

"No," she replied. "I'd never been to Ted's house."

I nodded. "You're in trouble," I told her.

"I know. That's why I need you so much now, Lyle. I've no one else to turn to. Nowhere to go."

I nodded again.

"We'll have to set you up someplace. You can't stay here. If Farnum's the killer, you'll need to be where he can't get to you. Do you know anybody that Farnum doesn't know about who you might stay with for a few days?"

"I have a brother. Alexander's never met him. I've told him about him, but I've never told him where he lives."

"No good. Farnum's certain to have had you checked out pretty thoroughly. He'd have the address or at least be able to get it. No, I think a motel's probably our best bet. Maybe someplace out of town. If we're not followed, and I know how to avoid that, you'd be safe."

She smiled. "That would be better than staying with Terry, my brother. His wife just had a baby and…Well, let's just say that my brother and I haven't got along since we were much younger."

She fell silent, lowering her gaze and pretending to examine a few threads that had strayed from the seam of her jeans. "What's wrong with men, Lyle?" she asked suddenly.

"Pardon me?"

"Why is it that when men see a pretty girl the first thing they think of is getting her into bed?"

I started to protest, but she cut me off.

"I don't know why I'm telling you this, Lyle. But, you see, my mother died a few years ago and my relationship with my dad and brother is not good. You see…You see, I moved away from home when I was quite young because my father used to…He used to…you know, he used to touch me. It went on for a long time. Since I was just a little girl. I think my mother knew about it. I used to wonder why she didn't stop him. Anyway, I moved out of his house when I was sixteen. I came across the country, here, to Minnesota, to stay with my brother. Terry had moved here to go to college. I thought I would be safe so far away from my father. He's still in New York. But…"

She sniffled and got up from her chair to rearrange some framed photographs that were on a nightstand by her bed. One was a picture of a short, barrel-chested, white man of about fifty standing proudly beside a blue, Lincoln Continental. Behind the car, stood a woman of about the same age with dark, East Indian features, her head lowered as though embarrassed to be in the photograph. Next to this was what I took for Terry's high school portrait—a handsome, dark-skinned man sitting with his head turned slightly from the camera, one hand raised across his chest, his thumb and forefinger held just apart as if he were about to pinch something floating unseen in the air before him. The last photograph on the nightstand particularly caught my interest. There, Carmen stood next to a young man with lots of blond hair and a hook-shaped nose. They were both beaming at the camera. Between the man and Carmen stood a little girl, maybe two or three years old, happily embracing Carmen's leg.

Carmen turned back to me with weary, vacant eyes, as if some memory was draining her. She rubbed at her nose with a balled hand. "I had been staying with Terry for a few months," she said. "It was a small apartment. Only one bedroom. Terry had the bedroom because it was his apartment and because he needed somewhere private to study. I slept on the hide-a-bed in the living room. One night, Terry had been out with some friends, and I guess they'd been drinking. It was late and I was sleeping when they came in. Terry had brought three friends with him. They were laughing and they woke me up. I remember sitting up and pulling the covers around me so they wouldn't see me in my night things. Somehow, they thought that was funny. Terry was laughing when he came over to me. He patted me on the head, and he laughed. He laughed when he pulled the covers away. Then he stopped laughing. Suddenly his hands were on me. I pleaded with him to stop. He told me to shut up. I tried to scream, but he put his hand over my mouth. I tried to squirm away, but he slapped me hard. Then he raped me. The others watched and shouted things as he did it. When Terry crawled off me, the others took turns. When it was over and the others were about to leave, one of them came over to where I was lying. He tried to kiss me good-bye. Can you imagine? Did he think that would make it all right? It's funny, but that kiss stands out in my mind as the worst thing that happened that night."

I stared at her for some time, blinking, a fist-sized lump in my throat blocking my words. Shaking, I got up and walked into the kitchen. I found a glass in one of the cupboards and poured myself some lemonade. I stood in the light of the open refrigerator door as I gulped it down.

When I got back to the room, she was standing by the nightstand, staring at the photographs. Bing Crosby and the Andrews Sisters were merrily swinging on "Jingle Bells." Carmen and I didn't look at each other.

"It's good for me to talk, Lyle. It was a long time ago, and yet, sometimes it's like it was just yesterday. Or like it's still happening. I feel like a little girl on a merry-go-round, speeding ahead. But it's only the illusion of moving forward. Really, I'm just going in circles."

I sat back on the sofa and lit a cigarette. She turned toward me and smiled. But there was nothing like joy in her eyes. Instead, they shivered, as if she was fighting back her tears with her smile.

"Did you know that I was married once?" she asked. "After that night at Terry's, I moved in with a girl I knew. She and her parents lived in a nice home down in Lakeville. Her parents never asked why I had to move in with them, but they must have known because they were always very careful when they talked to me. They spoke in these really gentle voices as if they thought that if they raised their voices around me, I might shatter right there in their living room. They were very sweet people, but after a few months of being treated like a china doll, I just had to leave. I got a job working nights after school at a restaurant on the highway just north of town. There was a cook there. His name was Billy Reilly, he was twenty-two, he was tall, lanky, had long hair, and I thought he was the answer to all my problems. When he asked me to marry him, I jumped at the chance. We lived in a little trailer park, and we had a few good months. I got pregnant almost right away and you should have seen Billy's face when I told him. He was so proud I thought he would bust. He went right out and bought a box of cigars and started handing them out to everybody at the restaurant where we worked. He even handed them out to customers. They must have thought he was crazy."

Carmen chuckled lightly at the memory. I smiled too. I pulled at my cigarette and looked around for an ashtray. I didn't find one.

"I enjoyed being pregnant," Carmen said, her grin breaking wide and bright across her face. I dropped a long ash into the palm of my hand and tried to act as if this was something I did all the time.

"Billy was so sweet," she said. "I was only a couple of months along when he insisted that I quit work. He said he didn't want anything to happen to me or the baby. He was so worried. He acted as if we were the first couple ever to have a baby and it was a miracle that had to be carefully tended. He worked double shifts to make up for my lost income and spent his time off fixing up a little nursery in one corner of our bedroom. I was happier than I've ever been in my life."

The smile slowly faded from Carmen's face. "But it didn't last. I guess working double shifts sort of got Billy used to being away from home. He spent more and more time away from me. Before long, he'd come home smelling like beer and other women. I tried to make myself more attractive to him. But I was eight months pregnant and as big as a house. One night I broke down and asked him why he was doing this to us. You know what he told me? He said it was because I was too fat to make love to. We stayed together until after the baby was born, but when he didn't give up the other women, I took Angela and moved into this apartment."

"Where's Angela now?" I asked.

It took Carmen awhile to answer. "I couldn't keep

her," she said, at last. "I just didn't have enough money. Angela was with me for a couple of years, but I couldn't seem to keep a job. I just couldn't seem to focus on work when all the time I was wondering what my daughter was doing and thinking how I should be with her. It just wasn't the life I wanted to give her. At one point it got so bad that my father even asked us to come live with him. He said that he wanted to make up for what he had done to me when I was little. But the thought of that man touching my Angela..." Carmen paused. "Finally, I sent Angela to live with her father. That was before I met Alexander. Billy had settled down with a woman named Linda. They live together in the trailer that we lived in. He told me that he missed Angela and that he would take good care of her. He said that he could take better care of her than I could. I hated that he was right, but I let her go. After I began my relationship with Alexander, I wanted Angela to come home and live with me, but...Well, I've told Alexander about Angela and he hasn't exactly insisted that she join us. I don't think he relishes the idea of being with me with another man's child sleeping in the next room."

Carmen picked up the photograph of herself with Billy and Angela. She looked at it silently for some time. When she turned toward me, a cruel smile had appeared on her face. "You see," she said, "I've screwed up every relationship I've ever had. You better get out of here, Lyle, before I screw things up for you."

"I'm well past screwing up, Carmen."

"Do you want to help me?"

"Yes."

I not only wanted to help her, I wanted to be her goddamned knight in shining armor. I wanted to rescue her from Farnum, beat the crap out of Reilly, reunite her with her daughter, and help them live happily ever after far away from every man that had ever wronged her or caused her to doubt herself.

Hell, that should be easy, I thought. But first I had to figure what to do with the cigarette that had burnt down to the filter between my fingers.

I solved the cigarette problem by going into the kitchen and running water over the smoldering butt, then tossing the thing into the wastebasket. I stood in the kitchen for a moment thinking about how the world had changed. Until that moment I'd been working for Farnum. Now, I wanted him out of the way. The best way to do that would be to prove he'd killed Rovig. That would get him out of the picture for a long time.

I shook my head, swallowed hard, and went back to the living room. Carmen had sat back down, and the Chipmunks' Christmas Song was filling the room. Maybe the world hadn't changed that much, I thought. Alvin still wanted that hula-hoop.

It had grown quite dark outside. Carmen switched on a tarnished brass floor lamp that was decorated with rusty maple leaves around a yellowed shade. The lamp gave off a soft yellow light that shone on one side of her face, leaving the other side in shadow. She smiled as I sat on the sofa across from her.

"I think you'd better start packing," I said.

"Where are we going?"

"The motel, remember. You're not safe here."

"Lyle, I really can't leave just now. I have some things that I need to do tomorrow."

"What kind of things?"

"Just some things. Anyway, you're here. I feel safe

with you here. Couldn't you take me to that motel tomorrow?"

"Tonight would be better."

"Tomorrow, please, Lyle. Couldn't you just stay with me tonight?"

It wasn't until then that I realized how hard my heart was pounding. I was also feeling a little light-headed, like too much blood was welling up in my skull.

"Sure, Carmen," I heard myself say. "We can stay here tonight. But we gotta get you safe tomorrow."

"Great," she said. "Are you hungry? I have some tuna. I could make us some sandwiches."

"That sounds wonderful."

She went in the kitchen to make our meal while I stayed out front checking the window every couple of seconds and wishing that my mother had produced a smarter child.

Carmen came back with the sandwiches and changed the stack of records on the stereo. We ate serenaded by a host of Christmas classics. Sinatra, Nat "King" Cole, Perry Como, and, of course, Spike Jones and His City Slickers' immortal, "All I Want for Christmas Is My Two Front Teeth." As I ate my sandwich, I couldn't help imagining Farnum and Angelino busting in the door. I could clearly envision the grin on Farnum's face as he tells Angelino to disembowel me on the spot. I was reacting with some horror to the idea that the last thing I might hear on this earth were the words "sister Susie sitting on a thistle," when Carmen glanced over at me and giggled.

"What's so funny?" I asked.

"We are," she said. "We're funny. This whole thing is funny. Here we are talking about the danger I might be in, but instead of being scared, I feel like a teen-ager who sneaked her boyfriend into her parents' house. It's silly, but…I don't know, it's also kinda daring. Do you know what I mean?"

Her face was filled with such delight, that I couldn't keep from chuckling. "Yeah, I know what you mean."

We finished eating and I helped take the dishes into kitchen. Carmen said that she was tired, then she took some things out of her closet and disappeared into the bathroom. I went back on patrol in the living room— walking the perimeter and listening at the door for any signs of the enemy.

After several minutes, Carmen called to me from the bathroom. As I walked toward her voice, the bathroom door swung open. She had turned out the bathroom light, so the only illumination in the apartment was the glow of the floor lamp and the soft, changing colors that swathed the tin foil tree. She wore a stark, white nightshirt that buttoned up the front, the top buttons undone, revealing her slender neck and her skin which seemed to glisten in the dusky light and shadow of the room.

Again, I was struck by her skin—skin stretched taut over her collar bone, then smoothing out across the flat plain of her upper chest, then rising gently and full over her breasts, and finally disappearing in a tantalizing invitation beneath the nightshirt. As I got closer, she backed farther into the darkened bathroom, and when I entered the tiny room, she sat down on the toilet. Just enough light entered the room from the open door for me to see the curve of her body under the nightshirt. I dropped to my knees in front of her, edged close, and raised my face to kiss her. Her mouth met mine, opened slightly, and I felt the brush of her tongue against mine.

"Lyle," she said softly. "I need you to hold me tonight."

I didn't say anything as I undid a couple more buttons and slid my hands beneath the nightshirt. She arched her back, her breasts rose, and I kissed them both gently. She softly stroked my face. Then she stood, took my hand, and led me toward her bed.

I kissed her again as we lay down together.

"Don't say anything," she said. "It's best if we don't say anything."

The turntable clicked and the room went quiet. We made love.

We lay awake in each other's arms for a long time. I listened as her breathing slowed to the regular rhythm of sleep. I closed my eyes and lay my head on her soft shoulder.

I had been asleep for about three hours when I became aware that Carmen had awakened. She was lying next to me, staring at the ceiling.

"What's wrong?" I asked.

"What day is tomorrow?"

"Friday. Why? What's wrong?"

She turned to look at me. Her eyes were gleaming with tears.

"Nothing, Lyle. Nothing's wrong. In fact, this seems so right. It seems right to be here with you."

I searched for something comforting to say.

"It's just…" she continued. "It's just that I know that I'm putting you in danger. You shouldn't be here, Lyle. If Alexander finds out about this, he might kill you. I'm sorry. I'm really sorry, but you'll have to leave."

"Fine," I said, "but you're coming with me."

"No, not yet. There's something I have to do first.

Then I can come with you. Then I can let you take care of all this for me."

"What do you need to stay here?"

"I can't tell you just now. I want to, but I can't."

"Why not?"

"I just can't."

"Tell me why."

"I can't," she repeated. "I just can't, not now."

It didn't make any sense. I couldn't think of a single reason why she would have to stay in her apartment. Anything she needed to do she could do while staying somewhere else. It didn't make any sense.

I started to say something, but she put both of her hands softly on my bare chest and said, "Don't push on this one, Lyle. I can't tell you any more right now. Soon. But not right now."

"Fine. If you're going to stay, I'm going to stay."

"Lyle," she said abruptly. "Where are you parked?"

"What difference does that make?"

"Are you parked out front?"

"Yes."

"You have to go. You can't be here in the morning. You have to go now. Maybe they won't know that you've been here. You have to go before they spot your car. It's too dangerous for you to stay."

"If it's dangerous for me, it's dangerous for you too," I said.

She was fighting back tears. "Your being here might make it even more dangerous for me."

"Then we leave together. Right now."

Carmen reached out and placed her fingers on my lips. "Please, Lyle. Please go now," she implored. "I'll be with you tomorrow."

I dressed in silence. I felt foolish, confused, vulnerable. As I went to the door and slipped on my coat, Carmen raised herself from the bed and stood before me, her nakedness half in shadow and half bathed by the soft light coming from the back of the room. Slowly, she picked up her nightshirt from where it lay beside the bed. She slipped into it, but instead of buttoning it, she drew it around her, as though hugging herself.

"Tomorrow," I said. "Call me."

"I will," she promised, her little hands holding the nightshirt tightly around her.

I closed the door behind me and waited until I heard the dead-bolt snap into place. It took some seconds for my eyes to adjust from the darkness of Carmen's apartment to the harsh brightness of the hallway. I climbed up the steps from the lower level to the front entryway.

Angelino was leaning beside the front door. "Cold night outside," he said.

"Good evening, Mr. Angelino."

"Nearly morning."

I looked past him through the glass door and into the street. I could see my car parked out there, right in front of the building, only a few feet from where we stood. It seemed very far away.

Angelino straightened and rubbed the back of his neck. Then he leveled his clear gaze on me. "I don't want to tell you your business, Dahms," he said. "But I don't think this is such a good idea. Your being here, I mean. This is the kind of thing that can get you dead."

"That thought had crossed my mind."

"Good. Then you're not completely stupid."

"Oh, I don't know about that."

Saying nothing, Angelino simply nodded.

"Did Farnum send you to warn me off?"

"Farnum never sends me to warn people," Angelino said. "He's got others to do that for him. If he sends me, it's because the situation has gone way past warning."

"That don't sound too good for my side."

"On the contrary," Angelino replied, "my visit is about the best thing that could happen to you. Farnum didn't send me. I came on my own. I came to help you. I knew you'd be here. Farnum doesn't. Farnum won't know about it unless I decide to tell him."

I lit a cigarette with a vague hope that it would make me look tough. I watched Angelino pretty closely. It didn't seem to give him the "willies." But then, he was watching pretty closely himself and I gotta think he saw my hands shaking. "So, you gonna tell him?" I asked.

Angelino shook his head. "That wouldn't be much help to you and, like I said, I came here to help you."

The smoke from the cigarette got into my eyes. I had to close one to soothe the burning. I must have looked like Popeye the Sailor Man. "Okay, I'll bite," I said. "Why have you appointed yourself my guardian angel?"

The expression on Angelino's face remained clear and impassive. "I've got my reasons, Dahms. You can relax. I watch over Farnum's business affairs, not his amorous ones. But I figure someone has to clue you in before this thing caves in on you. You're probably not going to believe me anymore than Farnum did when I told him. Or Rovig either, as far as that goes. But I'll tell you anyway. That girl is not what she seems. It's a mistake to get involved with her. You should just take what she gave you tonight and get away from here."

"You're right, Mr. Angelino," I replied, puffing

furiously on my cigarette. "I don't believe you. The way I got it figured, you know that she can tie your boss to Rovig's murder and that would put Farnum out of business. If that happens, you'd be out looking for a job."

Angelino shook his head. "I was wrong about you, Dahms. You *are* completely stupid. Even if Farnum were on his way out, it wouldn't affect me. The people in charge like me. Farnum's not the issue here. My future is secure without him."

"Is Farnum on the way out?"

"That's none of your affair."

"Is there something wrong with the books?" I pressed. "Something that the bosses might find troubling."

"I didn't come here to discuss the business with you," Angelino said. "I came here to tell you to go away. For your own good."

"I don't much like being told what to do, Mr. Angelino."

"You're not gonna like getting hurt much either, Dahms."

"I thought you were like my buddy now," I said, forcing a smile. "That don't sound real friendly to me. Sounds kinda like a threat."

Angelino shrugged. "It's just advice. You should listen. You should just stay out of this."

"Can't do it, Mr. Angelino," I said, managing to keep my voice from quavering. "It's not good for business. I can't just quit because some tough guy tells me to. I've got a job to do."

"What job is that?"

"Finding Rovig's killer."

Angelino closed his eyes slowly, then opened them

again. "Farnum will call you tomorrow," he said. "He'll tell you that you're not working for him anymore."

"You'll tell him to call me?"

Angelino shrugged again.

"But will you tell him I was here tonight?"

"I don't think so."

I rubbed my eyes. It was late, I was tired, and I was having real trouble wrapping my mind around what Angelino was telling me. I couldn't think of a single reason for him to protect me or to try to help me.

"Did Farnum kill Rovig?"

There wasn't a trace of deceit in Angelino's eyes. "No," he said.

"Is Farnum on the way out? Are his bosses gonna put somebody more obedient in his place?"

Angelino made no answer.

"Are they gonna whack him?"

Angelino blinked slowly again. "Nobody's gonna get whacked," he said patiently. "You've been watching too much TV, Dahms. Whacking people lacks...It lacks respectability."

I burst out laughing.

"Yeah," I said. "Guys who peddle magazines with names like *Young and Shaved* are real worried about respectability."

"Dahms," Angelino said, a sigh softening his voice. "I'm not going to try to convince you that this isn't a dirty business. You know better. You're not exactly a stranger to the allure of the genre yourself. Remember?"

"No one's accusing me of being respectable, Mr. Angelino."

Angelino stared blankly at me. "Anyway," he continued, "we've had a nice talk, but it's late. I'm afraid

I must be going. I trust I have made myself clear. Your services are no longer required. You are no longer looking into the Rovig matter."

"Could it be that you're afraid of me, Mr. Angelino? Afraid of what I might uncover?"

Not a ripple of emotion passed over his features. "No, Dahms," he said. "I don't find you in the least bit frightening. You are a mild irritant at worst. But certainly not frightening."

"I was hired to find out who killed Rovig," I said. "That's want I'm going to do."

Then, for the first time ever, I witnessed Angelino show some real emotion. He laughed.

"Dahms," he chuckled. "You couldn't find Ted Rovig's killer if he was hiding in your pants."

Flushing deeply, I strode past Angelino and out into the cold night air. Angelino was a couple of steps behind me and made no effort to stop me. I headed to my car without looking back, focusing instead on my Ford, as if by ignoring Angelino, I could pretend he'd never been there. I was trying so hard to ignore him that I didn't hear the approaching car until it was nearly in front of me. It was a dark blur, fishtailing past.

By then, I was beside my own car, reaching for the door handle. Suddenly, my windshield exploded. I ducked down amid a stinging rain of shattered safety glass. There were flashes of weapons fire and bullets danced across the pavement, sparking like fireflies, leaving chalky trails etched in the concrete. I remained crouched behind the car, my head tucked under my jacket like a turtle caught in a strafing run. Then I heard gunfire behind me.

Startled, I pivoted in time to see Angelino standing

in the open, calmly returning fire. The sound of brakes screeching followed by an ugly, metallic crunch brought me to my feet. I turned to look at Angelino. He ignored me. Gun in hand, he started at a slow trot up the street, heading for something indistinct about a half a block away. I pulled my own gun from its holster and followed him toward a dark mass just beyond the circle of light cast by the nearest streetlight.

I didn't recognize the car or the driver. It was a dark blue Pontiac, its front end crumpled where it had slammed into another car unfortunate enough to have been parked in its way. Angelino opened the door of the Pontiac and the gunman spilled out of the driver's seat. Angelino caught him before he hit the ground. I moved in to get a look at the man who had tried to kill me. I didn't recognize him.

I could tell right away that the man was past saving. He was bleeding profusely from his right temple where a bullet had torn away skin, bone, and hair. Another bullet had caught him in the neck, and as he tried to breathe, a bloody hole under his Adam's apple bubbled with gurgling death. Soon his labored breathing stopped altogether.

Angelino holstered his gun and turned the man's bloody head to face me. "It's a friend of yours, Dahms."

"I don't know this guy," I told him.

"Sure, you do," Angelino said as he reached into the inside pocket of the dead man's jacket. "You and Egon here had quite an encounter earlier today. At least that's what I heard."

"Egon?"

"Yeah. Egon Trench. Works for Farnum."

Angelino pulled something out of the dead man's

pocket. "I guess old Egon didn't much like the way you showed him up this afternoon. Looks like he came for some payback."

I looked at what Angelino had taken off the dead guy. He was holding a pair of wraparound sunglasses with neon orange frames. I shuddered a little as Angelino placed them over the wide, open eyes of the corpse. In the distance, came the shrill sound of approaching sirens.

Chapter Ten

Calvin Gosden was an optimistic son of a bitch. You had to give him that. Despite the fact that he and I were sharing a holding cell in the bowels of police headquarters, Calvin had a bright vision of his future. A bright vision and a small problem with the law involving twenty-five cartons of cigarettes that he insisted he found in a dumpster in back of a Speedy Market on Fourth Avenue.

Calvin didn't mind spending the night in the cell, he told me. It was warm and he knew there was no way he was going to do real time for no cigarettes. Besides, he was waiting on a major payday that would result from what he called his "pending litigation" against General Motors.

It seems that a few years back Calvin had been experiencing a downturn in his fortunes and had unwisely decided to make an unauthorized withdrawal of funds from the cash register of a local 7-11. Having convinced the teenager behind the counter that he was concealing an AK-47 under his coat, Calvin jumped into his Chevy Citation and amid the squeal of tires and a plume of exhaust, he proceeded to make his getaway.

Unfortunately, the plume of exhaust turned out to be the result of a rapid loss of engine oil and Calvin had only made it about four blocks from the 7-11 when the Chevy's engine caught fire. The billowing smoke from the car fire made it astonishingly easy for the police to home in on Calvin's position.

To top off his run of bad luck, Calvin had been convicted of similar robberies on two occasions in the past, and he ended up serving three years in Stillwater for his ill-fated third offense. But Calvin managed to find the silver lining hiding within this dark cloud of circumstance. Calvin figured that if he'd been driving a different car, say a Porsche or even a Toyota Celica for God's sake, the authorities wouldn't have apprehended him. And if the authorities hadn't have apprehended him, he wouldn't have lost three years to the penal system.

"Not just any three years either," he told me. "Peak earning years."

Calvin smiled broadly at the thought, flashing brilliantly white teeth anchored in raw, bleeding gums. I winced every time he smiled. "They took something away from me that I can never get back," he said. "And I think GM owes me a little com-pen-sa-shun, Jack." He smiled again.

Christ, I thought, the guy could be a poster boy for gingivitis.

"I found me a lawyer that was all set to take the case too," Calvin said. "He told me that we'd be looking at a six-figure settlement. At least. Man, it was gonna be sweet. Then the bastard lawyer gets himself nabbed trying to move some rock he got off some client didn't have no other way to pay him. The judge says 'cause he's an officer of the court, he's gotta make an example of him. The lawyer does six months and gets himself disbarred. Last I hear he's working as a towel boy at a fitness center in Baton Rouge. Anyway, I'm looking for another lawyer."

I was feeling pretty lonely after they led Calvin off to morning arraignment and left me in the cell by myself. But it wasn't long before a uniformed officer came to take me to see the detectives. He handcuffed my hands behind my back and led me down a corridor and up a flight of stairs to the main lobby of the building. We waited for an eternity in front of a bank of three elevators, finally taking one up to the fifth floor and walked down the same corridor and past the same gray metal desks that I had passed on my visit to Tarkof just three days before. I didn't think he was going to be real pleased to see me again.

The officer who had served as my escort led me right up to Tarkof's desk, took off the cuffs, and left without a word. Tarkof was sitting behind his desk, popping sunflower seeds into his mouth and spitting the shells in the general direction of a nearby wastebasket. Bits of pulpy sunflower seed clung to the edges of his mustache.

He stared at me coldly as I took a seat in the chair opposite the desk. "This can be easy, or it can be hard, Dahms. It's your choice."

"I'll take 'Potent Potables for two hundred dollars,' Augie," I replied.

"Cut the smart-ass routine. You're so deep in the shitter right now, I'm surprised you can't taste it."

"Now that you mention it, I would appreciate a glass of water."

Tarkof ignored me. "Just tell me everything you know about the guy who got killed last night."

"I gotta think you know as much about the guy as I do. You must know he worked for Farnum. You must know that Angelino, another of Farnum's employees, shot him. What more can I tell ya?"

"You could tell me what you were doing there. While you're at it, you could tell me what Angelino and this Trench were doing there as well."

"Well, I was there on a date. That's all I know for sure. Maybe Angelino and Trench figured they needed to act as chaperones. I don't know."

"You three guys know each other well?"

"We'd only just met."

"Yeah?"

Tarkof and I stared at each other for a half a minute before he leaned forward in his chair. "Maybe it would help you be a little more forthcoming if I told you a little more of what we know, Dahms. We know that you went to see Farnum the day after I told you not to be sticking your nose in the Rovig thing. We got a report of someone matching your description impersonating a county employee at a rib joint in South Minneapolis. We have reliable information that following this little escapade, you and the dead guy, Trench, had yourselves a tussle in front of this same rib joint. You made a lot of noise, Dahms. People notice that kind of thing. Besides, you guys left quite of pile of glass on the street over there. We got ordinances that prohibit littering, you know. I'd cite you, but you got bigger problems."

"I didn't shoot Trench. You can't touch me for that. Angelino did that. And in self-defense."

"The way I figure it, Angelino wasn't defending himself. He was defending you. Trench was coming after you. Now I got to ask myself, what made you and Angelino such good buddies? I gotta wonder, what are you doing with Farnum? I gotta scratch my head and think, gee, why didn't old Dahms think I was serious when I told him not to go fucking around in this thing?"

"Augie, I—"

"I'll tell what it looks like," Tarkof interrupted. "It looks like you're working for Farnum. It looks like it was no coincidence that you were in Rovig's apartment the other day. It looks like Farnum sent you there. I don't know, maybe he forgot something there the day he iced Rovig. Maybe he hired you to retrieve it. Maybe you killed Rovig for him. That ain't real likely, I mean, a milquetoast like you, but it's a possibility."

"Augie, you know that I—"

"And even if we find out you didn't actually kill Rovig, we still have to work out a couple of problems. Did you know that we generally frown on citizens who interfere with police investigations? At the very least we're looking at having your P.I. license yanked. Depending on what we find out about your involvement with Farnum, you might be looking at spending the holidays in a cell with a bunch of guys with bad attitudes and even worse breath passing your fat ass between them like Aunt Edna's Christmas fruit cake."

The fruit cake remark got to me a little, but I held my tongue. Then I remembered something. "Why are you looking at Farnum for the Rovig murder all of a sudden? I thought you had the murderer all locked up. What happened to the Ehlers kid being the killer? Come to think of it, how can you accuse me of interfering with your investigation? Your investigation is over. I thought Ehlers did it. Case closed."

Tarkof eased back in his chair a bit. "Turns out there may be some reason to doubt that Ehlers did the murder. I'm not saying he's off the hook, but we're still looking into other possibilities."

"What's going on?"

Tarkof sighed and fingered the opening of the bag of sunflower seeds. Then he turned the bag around and pushed it gently toward me. I took a couple of seeds out and popped them into my mouth. I leaned forward to spit the shells into the wastebasket, but just didn't get enough behind the effort. The shells landed on my lap. Tarkof grunted but didn't laugh out loud.

"Ehlers was questioned on an unrelated matter the night of the Rovig murder," Tarkof said. "Seems he and some of his pals were in Loring Park that night picking on some poor pantywaist. Dispatch gets a call from some residents reporting that these assholes are stomping the shit out of some queer. We send a squad, but by the time the uniforms show up, the whole thing is over. They find the guy sitting on a park bench with a fat lip and a cut over his eye. Just up the street, they find Ehlers and three other punks sitting on the front steps of an apartment building. The victim doesn't identify Ehlers and his boys as the assailants, so the uniforms can't bring 'em in. They just warn 'em and take the victim to the E.R. According to their report, all this happened between about 9:30 and 10:30 p.m. The M.E. puts the time of the Rovig murder between nine and eleven. Of course, the exact time is impossible to determine. Ehlers could have had time to do the murder and then head over to the park. Or he could have done it after. But the incident does make for some doubt. The D.A. tells us he'll need a stronger case before he can indict."

"You still holding Ehlers?"

"No." Tarkof said. . "I was hoping we could hold him on yet another assault beef. The one we originally picked him up on. He beat on another faggot the night after the Rovig murder, but that victim also decided not to press charges. We let Ehlers go this morning. If we can't tie him to the Rovig thing, he won't even do time. He'll maybe get probation for taking the TV. Probably not though. The judge'll probably just give him a stern talking to." Augie shook his head.

" '*Queer, pantywaist, faggot*,' " I quoted back at him. "That sure is an enlightened way for a public servant such as yourself to be referring to the citizenry."

"What's it to you, Dahms?"

I shrugged. "Love is love. Anyway, did Ehlers tell you anything about him and Rovig? I mean, did he say why he and Rovig got to be such buddies?"

Augie gave me his cold, cop stare. "I think we got us a more immediately pressing question. How did you and Farnum and Angelino get to be such buddies?"

"You know what happened, Augie?" I asked, grinning. "I got real popular all of sudden. It's just the damnedest thing. I was working that problem of Luther Decker's and the next thing I know everybody wants to have me over for tea. First you, then Farnum. You wanted to know what I was doing in Rovig's house. Farnum not only wanted to know what I was doing there, but he also wanted to know what you and I talked about. By the way, Farnum's digs are quite a bit more comfortable than yours. Just a suggestion, but you guys could maybe change the furniture in here. Maybe add a couple of chintz curtains, that sort of thing. It's the little touches that truly made a room, you know."

"So Farnum asked you over," Augie pressed. "Then what?"

"Then he wrote me a check. How come you never do that?"

"Then you are working for Farnum?"

"I was. But that was before you solved the case by arresting Ehlers." I slapped myself a little harder than I had meant to on the forehead. "Oh, sorry! I forgot. Looks like Ehlers didn't do it. Hey! Maybe Farnum's still paying me. What do you think?"

"So, I tell you not to screw around in the Rovig thing and you go ahead and do it anyway? Is that what you're telling me?"

"Exasperating, isn't it?"

Tarkof just stared at me. At first, I wondered if he was silently planning how best to eliminate me without arousing any suspicion, but before long he smiled.

"Yeah," he agreed. "Exasperating."

"Anyway," I said, "I didn't find out much. I talked to Francine Ehlers and Lorraine Rovig. Then that Egon fellow and I met up and now I'm here. I'd still like to know why Rovig and Ehlers were hooked up. Ehlers tell you anything?"

"Nah. He stuck to that crap about Rovig being nothing more than his tutor."

"If you ask me, the whole thing is odd. This Rovig is stacking up to be one strange guy. Why the hell did he spend so much time with that street kid? At least with Farnum he ran with a better class of crook."

"Could be any number of reasons," Tarkof said. "My bet is that it was sexual. Ehlers would rather rip off his nuts than admit it, but I'll bet Rovig made himself the kid's bitch. I'll bet he picked Ehlers 'cause he thought the kid was dangerous. That's probably what got his rocks off."

"That would explain why Ehlers and the boys like to beat up on gays," I said. "You know, trying to exorcise their demons and all that."

"Ooh, how psychological!" Tarkof cracked.

"I don't think anybody's gonna accuse those youngsters of being well adjusted," I said. "But even if it turns out that a relationship with the kid is what drew Rovig to Ehlers, what's in it for Ehlers?"

"You mean besides packing Rovig's fudge?"

I cringed.

"Christ, Dahms," Tarkof continued. "That one's easy. Even for you. Rovig worked for Farnum. To a kid like Ehlers, Farnum is like the NBA. Ehlers is strictly a neighborhood player. He thinks he's hot shit shooting hoops in his own little playground. Thinks he's ready for the big time. Thinks playing up to Rovig will get him a shot at the big money."

"But that's never gonna happen," I said.

"Shit no," Tarkof continued. "A two-bit turd like Ehlers is never gonna be in the same league as say, a guy like Angelino. All the remedial reading classes on earth ain't gonna put him in that class. It's a dream. But hey, we all got dreams. The way I figure it, Ehlers and Rovig are swimming in the same sewer. Two scumbags feeding off each other's dreams."

"Nice image, Augie." I smiled. "And folks say you're not the artistic type. Have you talked to the wife?"

"Lorraine Rovig? Sure, but there ain't nothing there."

"She's hiding something."

Tarkof arched an eyebrow. "What?"

"I don't know. But something."

"You don't seem to know much, Dahms. Farnum's really getting his money's worth from you, isn't he?"

"Long as he keeps paying me. I don't need to solve

this thing. You guys can do that. I just need the paycheck."

"He paying you to schtup his girlfriend?" Augie asked abruptly. "Is that also part of the service?"

I winced a little, but I don't think it showed. "That Carmen's a sweet kid," I said. "She's definitely in this over her head, but she didn't get there through any fault of her own. She hooked up with Farnum because she was broke and more than a little gullible. Now she wants out and she needs some help. So, she called me. She's got nothing to do with Farnum's business or the Rovig murder."

"Now who's being gullible, Dahms?" Tarkof asked. "If she's so innocent, why the hell did she run?"

"What do you mean?"

"She took off, pal. She was gone before the first squad pulled up. Our guys have been looking all over for her. She's the one with something to hide. If not, then why is she running from the cops?"

"Christ, Augie," I said. "She's not running from the cops. She's running from Farnum."

"Yeah?"

"I told you. She's trying to leave him. Farnum don't like that. She's got no choice but to run. If Angelino showed up at your door just before someone started shooting the place up, what would you do?"

"Don't matter what I'd do. What matters now is, where the hell is she? What is she doing? Is she shacked up with some guy you don't know about? And wouldn't you like to know?"

I felt myself flush. "Fuck you."

Tarkof smiled. "She's got her hooks in you, don't she, Dahms?"

"Look, I'm not saying that I don't find this girl attractive. But I'm smart enough not to let that draw me into something that could get me killed. It's a pretty sobering experience, getting shot at. Last night is enough for me. I don't want anything else to do with Farnum or Angelino or this Carmen. I just want out of this thing."

"Well, you might be showing some sense at last, Dahms. Another sensible thing would be for you to tell me anything that you know about the Rovig murder. Particularly anything this Carmen might have told you."

"She said she made a point of staying out of Farnum's business. Really, she doesn't know anything about the murder."

Tarkof nodded ambiguously. "So, is there anything you can tell me about the Rovig thing?"

"The truth is," I said, "I don't know shit."

He eyed me for some time. "That's probably the only thing we can agree on."

Chapter Eleven

Tarkof made me go over everything a couple more times before he let me go. He probably didn't really think I was hiding anything from him. He was probably just using me to kill time until lunch.

Our session together didn't strike me as real profitable for either of us, except that just as I was leaving, he made a point of telling me that Angelino had also been released. I didn't know if Augie was offering me a friendly warning or if he just wanted to see what my reaction would be. If it was the reaction he was after, I'm afraid I disappointed him. I hadn't slept in a day and a half, and I was just too tired to react at all.

It was nearly one in the afternoon when the bus dropped me off back in Dinkytown. Although I wanted nothing more than to go home and sleep, I had a few things that I had to take care of first. Most importantly, I needed to find out if Carmen had tried to contact me. But there was also the question of sustenance. It had been a long, long time since the tuna sandwiches at Carmen's apartment and my stomach was groaning in despair. I stopped by a fast food joint and arrived back at my office clutching to my bosom the life-sustaining bounty of a cheeseburger combo meal.

I forced myself to put the food aside long enough to check my answering machine for a message from Carmen. No luck. The message light was dark. I punched the playback button anyway, but she hadn't called. Tomorrow, she'd said. She'd be with me tomorrow.

It was tomorrow.

I spread the burger and fries out on the desk in front of me, and while I ate, I let my fingers do the walking through the phone book listings for automobile glass companies. My car was still parked out in front of Carmen's apartment and the last time I'd seen it the windshield was missing. I had to call a couple of places before I found one that was willing to do the job right away, but I thought my luck might be changing when they told me they offered a free box of steaks with every windshield replacement.

By the time I finished calling around, my fries were cold, and I'd run out of those little packages of ketchup, so I wrapped up what remained of the meal and lobbed it across the room into the wastebasket by the coffee machine. Two points.

Then I walked over to Carmen's. It wasn't far and only took me about twenty minutes, so I was surprised when I got there to find the glass company van already waiting for me. A guy named Alf handed me a form to fill out while he and a partner went right to work replacing the windshield. It didn't take them long, but I had nowhere warm to wait while he worked, so I was chilled to the bone and shivering like a yellow fever victim by the time he finished. Alf then nodded at me, went into the back of the van, and emerged with my box of steaks. As he pulled away, I couldn't help wondering how long the steaks had been sitting in the back of that van. I shook the box and from the sounds of clunking inside, they sounded frozen enough, so I figured they were okay.

After some initial resistance on the part of my Ford, I managed to get it started, and a couple of minutes later I was parked in front of the Bijou. Getting out of the car, I spotted the two cops that Tarkof had sent to keep an eye on me. They were sitting in a brown Plymouth about a half a block away. I was tempted to wave to them, but I thought better of it. Instead, I tucked the box of steaks under my arm and headed for the house—visions of my room and my warm bed swaying like slow moving dancers in my sleepy head. Although I was acutely aware that someone had tried to kill me the night before and knew that it was entirely possible that some colleague of Trench's would want revenge, I was simply too tired to be afraid. I glanced back at the reassuring presence of the cops. I'd be afraid after I got some sleep.

I had to pass Edgerton's room on the way to my own and when I walked by, I heard clinking sounds coming from inside. I made it all the way to my own door before I turned to walk back and knocked on Edgerton's door.

"Come in," he called. "It's open."

Pushing the door open, I disturbed a large pile of comic books, each wrapped in a clear plastic envelope, stacked just inside. Edgerton was sitting on the bed. He had what looked like a long, coiled spring in one hand and in the other he was holding a pair of wire cutters. He looked up, glanced at the pile of comic books that I'd knocked over and frowned. He kept on snipping small rings of wire off the spring but nodded approvingly when I bent over to straighten up the comic books.

"Whatcha doing?" I asked closing the door.

Barely looking up, he said, "Making a mail coat."

"A *mail* coat?"

"Yeah. You know, a chain mail coat. You've seen

them. It's a coat made up of interlocking metal rings. The kind of armor that enabled the Norman invaders to defeat the numerically superior English forces at the Battle of Hastings in 1066. Highly effective in its time. You see, the mounted forces of William of Normandy, protected by their chain mail, were able to decimate the English forces. The English were, in essence, defeated by their inferior technology. They were stuck trying to protect themselves with nothing but shields—technology they'd inherited from the Vikings. Chain mail was far more effective. And chain mail remained the premier protection until the invention of single-plate armor. Now, single-plate armor was developed by the Italians and the Germans, who—"

"What are you going to do with it?" I interrupted.

"I'm going to wear it," he replied. Pausing a moment, he added, "You look beat."

I shrugged. "I didn't get any sleep last night."

"What kept you up?"

I shrugged again. "Nothing much. Some guy shot at me. He ended up dead. I got thrown in jail. Nothing unusual."

Edgerton put down the spring and the wire cutters. "How's that?"

I told him the whole story of the previous twenty-four hours: the interviews with Lorraine Rovig and Francine Ehlers, the incident with Egon Trench, most of the particulars of my meeting with Carmen, and finally, the drive-by shooting that formed the climax of the evening. Edgerton listened without much interruption. When I finished, he sat silently for some moments, while I leafed through a magazine, I found on his dresser that appeared to be the digest of a California-based UFO cult.

"So," he said at last, "if you are thinking about pursuing a new line of work, maybe something safer, I hear they're hiring at Bill's Burger Bonanza. I know a guy. I could put a word in for you."

"Maybe later. Right now, I'm going to bed."

I shut the door softly, but firmly on my way out.

When I got to my room, I realized with some irritation that I still had a box of steaks tucked under my arm. Exhausted, I just didn't feel like taking them all the way upstairs to the refrigerator. Instead, I looked around my room trying to think of somewhere I could stash them for a few hours. Finally, I hit upon the idea of sticking them in the window, between the inside, double-hung window and the storm window outside. With the weather we'd been having, I figured it would be cold enough in there. Somehow, I convinced myself that this was a good, even inspired idea and I was actually feeling kind of proud of myself as I switched off the light.

I slept hard. It was nearly 10:00 p.m. when I awoke to the sounds of loud voices and music coming from the Bijou's living room. Evidently, a few of my fellow residents were having some kind of soiree. I pried a little dried crud from the corner of one eye and stumbled to the little sink in my room. I splashed water on my face, brushed my teeth and, now semiconscious, made my way to the telephone. I dialed up my office answering machine, but Carmen had not tried to reach me. I hung up the phone and tried to ignore the little twinge of worry that nibbled at me. She was a grown woman, I told myself. She could look out for herself. But shouldn't she have called by now?

I sat and listened to the sounds coming from outside my room and tried to reconcile the laughter and loud conversation with the quiet but gnawing anxiety that I was feeling about Carmen. But something else was gnawing at me as well. I was hungry again. Really hungry. I got up and looked through my cupboards, The only food I could find was half a bag of mini rice cakes that I'd bought several months earlier. I nibbled at one but quickly discovered that the rice cakes had managed a new and hitherto unimagined level of staleness. Tossing the bag in the wastebasket, I glanced over at the box of steaks that I'd stuck in my window. Just then a peal of laughter sounded in the hallway outside my room, followed by the sound of people brushing past my door.

I really didn't want to face anyone just then, so I switched on the TV and flipped channels until I lighted on a station running *The Incredible Shrinking Man*. Although the noise continued outside my room, inside it felt safe, even quiet and cozy.

I watched the movie, one of Edgerton's favorites, while lying on my bed. After a while, I realized that a trip to the bathroom was seriously in order. Even so, I couldn't miss the film's climax. I crossed my legs and squirmed as the main character, the shrinking man, finally finds peace. As our hero shrinks toward nothingness, he realizes that the notion that existence begins or ends springs from humankind's limited imagination. It is humankind's conception. Not nature's. He is simply passing into another realm. Alone and impossibly small, he will, nevertheless, continue to exist.

I turned off the TV. Although I could still hear music playing faintly and people talking elsewhere in the house, it sounded like most of my neighbors had gone to bed. But, not wanting to chance a line for the bathroom, I peed in my sink.

I called my office machine one last time, but even as I was dialing, I knew there would be no messages that night. At least I wasn't disappointed. I looked at the clock. It was only a little after midnight. I didn't think I'd be able to sleep, and I knew that I wouldn't be able to start looking for Carmen until morning. I certainly didn't feel like waiting for sunup alone in my room, so I decided to head to McCauley's for some breakfast.

I grabbed my jacket, locked up, and went out into the hall. It was now dark. No sign of the earlier partiers. I was nearly to the front door when Edgerton emerged from his room. "Where you going?"

"McCauley's. Gonna get some breakfast."

"I'll come with you."

"Suit yourself."

Edgerton got his coat and we stepped out onto the porch. "A few of us got together in the living room tonight," he told me. "Listened to some music. Jansrud brought some beer. You might have enjoyed it."

I shrugged. "*Incredible Shrinking Man* was on."

"Damn. Sorry I missed that."

It was still quite cold, and the sidewalk was partially iced over. I slipped a bit and Edgerton had to reach out to steady me. As we approached Dinkytown, I caught sight of someone standing under the streetlight at the corner. Someone really big. Whoever it was hesitated for a moment, then began walking toward us.

A little trickle of fear ran up the back of my neck. It could be nobody, I thought. Or maybe it was another of Farnum's goons. Maybe it was someone looking for payback. Instinctively, I reached under my coat, but I'd left my .38 back in my room. I rarely took it out to breakfast with me.

I remembered the cops that I'd spotted earlier in the day. I wondered if they were still staking me out. Wouldn't matter anyway, I decided. Even if they were out there somewhere, they were there to watch. They'd just watch me get killed. My only comfort was that the guy coming at us was on foot. If he did take me out and the cops were still there, they'd have a shot at catching him after he killed me. Small comfort indeed.

I moved to the very edge of the sidewalk, wanting to put a little room between Edgerton and myself, and pulled my hands out of my coat pocket. I doubt if Edgerton even noticed that someone was coming toward us. He was humming something. "Little Drummer Boy," I think.

"Hang here a moment," I told him.

He stopped humming. "Huh?"

"Just stay here until I tell you it's all right."

He stopped and I quickened my pace so that I would reach the big guy well ahead of my friend. My heart was pounding, and my ears were filled with a dull roar, as if I could hear the blood rushing distinctly through each of my capillaries.

When I was within a couple feet of the approaching figure, I stopped and yelled, "You got business on this street?"

This seemed to confuse the big man. "I'm looking for someone," he said uncertainly. "Is that a problem? I mean, I know it's late and all. I could come back in the morning."

Hit men don't usually come off so apologetic, I thought. Then I recognized the voice. "Milkman?"

"That you, Dahms?"

"You scared the shit out of me, man." I sighed.

"Coming at me like that. Shit."

"Oh, Jeez. I'm sorry, Dahms. I didn't mean to. I know it's late. But I got to thinking and I'd really like to talk to you about something."

I turned back toward Edgerton. "It's okay."

Edgerton came up alongside of me and squinted at the stranger.

"What the hell are you doing out so late anyway, Milkman?" I asked. "What's it, two o'clock in morning?"

Mulligan rubbed a hand through his hair and shuffled his feet sheepishly. "Well," he said, "after my shift at Gateway House, I got the Holiday Lights parade, then after that I volunteer at Lifeline, that's a suicide prevention hotline. You know the holidays are an awfully hard time for some folks."

"The Holiday Lights parade?" I asked.

Mulligan smiled. "Yeah, you know. The parade they have every night downtown during the holidays. It's all lighted up and everything. Kids love it."

"I'm familiar with the parade, Milkman, but uh…what's it got to do with you."

"Oh, I volunteer. Sometimes I crew. Sometimes they let me wear a costume."

"Uh, okay. What do you want to talk to me about?"

"Huh?"

"You said you wanted to talk to me."

"Oh, yeah. Uh…you think we could go somewhere?" Mulligan asked.

"Sure, Milkman," I said. "We were just going to grab a bite. Why don't you come along? We can talk while we eat."

Edgerton, who'd been studying the big man's face,

suddenly broke into a huge grin. "Jesus Christ!" he exclaimed. "Are you Milkman Mulligan? For God's sake, Lyle, you didn't tell me you knew Milkman Mulligan."

"Just met him yesterday."

"Well, hell, Mr. Mulligan," Edgerton said, stepping forward and extending his hand. "I'm a big fan. Dahms here was at the Civic Center the night that you partnered with Jesse 'the Body.' He told me all about it. You know, the night the 'Bod' got frustrated and left you alone in the ring to get pummeled by the Fabulous Ones? Hell of a night, man."

Mulligan shook Edgerton's hand, then turned to me. "Glad you enjoyed the show," he said, smiling.

Edgerton just kept shaking his head. "Milkman Mulligan."

"So," I said to Mulligan, "will you join us? For breakfast, I mean."

I got the impression that Mulligan wasn't one for quick changes in plans. He stared at me with a helplessly blank expression.

"I was wanting to talk to you about something," he said.

"Then come along. We'll eat. We'll talk."

Mulligan glanced at Edgerton, then back at me.

"It'll be okay," I assured him. "Edgerton here is the soul of discretion. What's bothering you anyway?"

Mulligan shuffled his feet in the darkness. "I want you to help me prove that Lorraine Rovig ain't no killer."

"You afraid maybe she is?"

"No way," he said loudly. "No way. It's just that…It's just that…" he stammered.

"Come on," I said. "We'll eat. We'll talk."

Chapter Twelve

McCauley's is really two operations working out of a single building—McCauley's Pub downstairs and McCauley's Restaurant upstairs. Since the pub had closed by the time we got there, we went into the restaurant and joined what restaurant workers call "the bar rush." A hostess came by to add our names to the waiting list and we pushed into the packed lobby to wait for a table.

We didn't do much talking. I was content to wait for the Milkman to explain what he wanted and Edgerton—who I knew was anxious to engage the Milkman in conversation about his days in the ring—kept shuffling and sneaking sidelong glances at the enormous, former wrestler as he waited for the proper opening. He wasn't the only one sneaking looks at Mulligan. Every guy in the lobby peered over at the big man, most backing off as they did, making sure that they weren't crowding him. I couldn't help noticing that no one felt it necessary to show the same deference to me.

After about ten minutes, we were shown to a booth and once seated, we each turned our attention to the menu. When our waitress came, I ordered breakfast—a mushroom and cheese omelet, crispy hash browns, wheat toast, and a side of pork sausage. Edgerton opted for a Mexican pizza with four sides of sour cream and the Milkman chose an e-coli special—a half-pound, blood-rare hamburger with fried onions and a side of fries. We all had coffee. We were still waiting for our food when Edgerton cleared his throat.

"So, Mr. Mulligan, do you keep in touch with any of the lights of the AWA? I mean do you ever have a guy like George 'Scrap Iron' Gadaski or former British champion Billy Robinson over for drinks? Did you get an invite to Jesse the Body's inaugural party?"

"I really don't keep in touch much," Mulligan said. "I mean, Gadaski's been dead quite a few years now. Robinson checked out a while back too. The governor's party wasn't for me, and as for drinks, I kinda got a little problem with that. It's not a really good idea for me to drink no more."

"Oh," Edgerton said, wincing. "I didn't mean to…you know, dredge up bad memories or anything. It's just that in the old days I used to spend every Saturday morning watching the AWA broadcast." Edgerton grinned. "Meeting you, thinking about those times…makes me feel young."

"I hear that," Mulligan said, smiling. "I like looking back on them days, too. I mean, some of it I don't like to think about. But hey, some of it was pretty good. Sometimes the crowd was behind me. Sometimes I didn't get hurt too bad. Then there was the stuff that weren't too good."

Mulligan's smile faded. His eyes went vacant, and his brow furrowed as if he were laboring to remember something. At last, a sloppy grin appeared on his face. "Where fault can be found, the good is ignored."

Edgerton blinked, then furrowed his own brow. I drained the last of my coffee and glanced around for the waitress. I spotted her a few tables away carrying a pot in each hand—one ringed in orange, the other in black. I tried to get her attention, but she didn't notice me.

"By *fault*, what do you mean?" Edgerton asked.

"Oh, you know," Mulligan said, "being on the road all the time, no chance for family, the drinking, guys using drugs, like steroids and stuff."

"You ever use steroids?"

Mulligan looked shocked. "Me? Ah, hell no, man. You see up close what happens to some of those guys taking them steroids, it'll scare you right quick. This one guy I used to work with? After a while, the stuff went after his legs. Above the waist, he was all rippling muscles. Below, the guy was withered like dried beef."

Our food arrived, and the waitress returned to fill our coffee cups. Between bites of my omelet, I asked, "So, Milkman, why did you want to see me?"

Mulligan nodded his head slowly a couple of times. "I'm worried about Mrs. Rovig."

"Yeah, you mentioned something about proving she isn't a murderer."

"Oh, um…" he began nervously. "I probably shouldn't a put it that way. I mean, I know that Mrs. Rovig didn't hurt anybody. No way. No way that coulda happened. But there's something…It's like, I don't know what. But it's there. There's something wrong. We gotta take care of it. We gotta protect her."

"Uh huh. What makes you think something's wrong?"

"Some of the things she told you in her office. Some of those things aren't right."

"You mean she lied?"

Anger flashed across Mulligan's face. "I wouldn't say that, exactly," he said.

"It's okay, Irv," I assured him. "I could tell when I was talking to her that she wasn't telling me the truth. If she's hiding something that might harm her, maybe you could tell me. Maybe we could do something about it."

"That's just what I was thinking," Mulligan said, his features smoothing and the vaguely vacant look returning to his eyes. "She's acting funny. Suspicious. If I'm picking up on it and you, well, you gotta figure the cops'll pick up on it too, and there's no telling what they'll think. I'm not saying she did anything wrong, mind you. It's just that, you know, the cops are poking around. You're poking around. I figure it's time for me to do something. I'm here to tell ya, I don't think I could let anyone cause any more problems for Mrs. Rovig."

There was nothing in his tone that suggested that he was threatening me. Even so, I caught myself rubbing my neck, remembering the way he'd handled me when we first met.

"I'm on your side, Milkman," I said. "You talk to me, maybe I can help."

He stared at me for a moment, his expression as blank as a bowling ball. "She didn't tell you the truth about the Ehlers kid."

"No?"

"Nor her ex-husband, neither."

"She left something out?"

"Yeah," Mulligan nodded. "A couple of things. She told you that she only talked to Rovig about work. That ain't true. They talked plenty. They argued plenty. They'd be in her office, and you could hear them out in the hall. You didn't even have to work at it. They'd argue about that Al Farnum guy."

"Yeah?"

"Yeah. I think Mrs. Rovig is involved in some kind of business deal with that Farnum. I think I heard Rovig tell her that the deal wasn't safe. He told her to get out of it. Mrs. Rovig didn't like him telling her what to do. She told him off but good."

"Did you hear what kind of business deal this was?"

"No. I didn't hear that. Just Rovig telling her not to trust him. That something was gonna blow up in their faces."

"And what about Ehlers?" I asked. "You said she might be hiding something about the Ehlers kid."

"Yeah."

"Well, what's she hiding?"

"I don't want to sit here and state totally fact that I know for certain, but I think she knew the kid pretty good."

"What makes you say that?"

"I saw them out the window one time. A couple weeks ago. They were in the parking lot. By Mrs. Rovig's car. She and Ehlers were talking. They were going at it pretty good. Then this Ehlers, he takes hold of Mrs. Rovig's arm. Looked like he was squeezing pretty tight. Looked like it maybe hurt Mrs. Rovig. I was gonna go down there and make him let go, but she pulled away and got in her car. I watched long enough to see that Ehlers didn't follow her, but he stomped around the parking lot afterward like he was pretty upset about something. He was like, smacking his fist into his hand. Stuff like that. Mrs. Rovig musta stood up to him. I figure he was trying to pull something on her, but she wouldn't have none of it. Still, she shouldn't have to put with stuff like that. Then later, when you were in the office and you guys were talking about how Ehlers and Rovig were buddies, I got to thinking, maybe Rovig was behind it. Maybe he sent Ehlers to scare off Mrs. Rovig. Maybe they and this Farnum were all trying to pull something. Maybe they put Mrs. Rovig in a bad situation and maybe she needs some help getting out of it."

"Maybe," I said. "And maybe she and her husband really did just argue about some business deal and maybe Ehlers was having trouble in the program and just lost his temper when he talked to Mrs. Rovig about it. There doesn't have to be anything sinister here at all."

"I need to be sure," Mulligan said. "I can't be thinking that Mrs. Rovig needs help and not do nothing to help her."

"Maybe she can take care of her own problems," I suggested. "Maybe she doesn't need or want your help."

"I gotta do something."

"You're not going to like hearing this, Milkman," I said, "but I'm going to say it anyway. Let's just say that Mrs. Rovig is involved in the murder—"

"I'm telling ya," Mulligan shouted, "there ain't no way she is!"

Several heads swiveled around to stare at us. Edgerton winced, then looked up at the ceiling as if pretending he wasn't really with us.

"We're just talking possibilities here, Irv," I assured him. "There's no need to holler at me."

The corner of Mulligan's mouth twitched a couple of times and his eyes softened with genuine regret. "Sorry," he said, "I didn't mean to yell."

"That's okay. But again, I just have to mention, if you stir things up and she is involved, you could be making things much worse for her. It could be better if you leave it alone."

Mulligan nodded and again appeared to be in deep thought. He then looked up. "I need to do this, but I appreciate what you've said. You know what they say, 'Warning wards off blame.' "

I frankly didn't know that they said that, but I didn't say so to the Milkman. I glanced over at Edgerton who was narrowly eyeing the remains of his meal. I took this to indicate that he was either really fascinated with spent sour cream packets or he was searching his memory to see if he'd ever known that they said that. There's a lot of stuff clunking around in Edgerton's head. I figured he might be at it awhile.

"Okay, Irv," I said, "so you got to do something to help Lorraine Rovig. Where do I come in? Do you want to hire me?"

"Uh, no. I figured you were already working the case. I mean, somebody's already paying you, right?"

"Uh, yeah."

"Well, I'll just be helping you then."

"You know, Milkman. I usually work alone."

"So, this time you'll have help."

I looked closely at the Milkman. Again, there was nothing about him that indicated that he'd snap me like a twig if I told him no. But there wasn't anything there that said he wouldn't.

"A thing like this can take a lot of time," I told him. "It could get really messy. Hell, it already is. A guy took some shots at me the other night. He's in the morgue. It could have been me. If you'd been with me, it could have been you. Bullets don't care who they hit, Milkman."

"I gotta do something," Mulligan repeated. "Don't matter what happens. I gotta know I tried to help."

"If you sign on," I pressed, "you sign on all the way.

We follow things where they lead us. I'm not going protect anyone. If Lorraine Rovig's got something to hide, we're probably going to find out what it is. Even if it's not pretty."

"I understand."

"Okay then, I'll bring you up to speed."

The waitress came by and refilled our coffee cups. She had to come by again before I was done telling the Milkman everything I knew about Rovig, Farnum, Angelino, and Ehlers. I was careful about what I told him about Carmen.

When I finished, the Milkman nodded a couple of times, then asked, "When do we get started?"

"In the morning. We got lots of work to do. Lots of steps to take. We can't wait around."

Mulligan stared at the table for a couple of seconds. " 'A tree does not fall at the first stroke,' " he said at last.

"I got it!" Edgerton exclaimed suddenly. "I think I do, anyway. It's from Icelandic saga, right? *Where fault can be found, the good is ignored. Warning wards off blame. A tree does not fall at the first stroke.* Gotta be Icelandic saga."

Mulligan beamed over at Edgerton. "*Njal's Saga*," he said with pride.

"You a saga aficionado, Milkman?" Edgerton asked, leaning forward excitedly. "Have you read any others? You know, Snorri Sturulson's *Heimskringla*, or maybe *Egil's Saga*, *Laxdaela Saga* or *Gisli's Saga*? Shit, there's hundreds of 'em."

Mulligan shook his head. "No. Just *Njal's*. Had me an idea in my wrestling days. I was gonna partner up with a guy and we figured if we was gonna hit big, we needed to come up with a couple of characters. You know, like personas? Anyway, I ask around and somebody says maybe we should be like Icelandic warriors, you know. Said we got all that Viking stuff going on up here anyway and maybe we could cash in. So, I go to a bookstore and pick up a copy of *Njal's Saga*. First time through was kinda tough going, but I went through it a couple more times and damned if I didn't start to liking it. Got a couple of names out of it. Me, I was gonna be Ulf the Unwashed. Other guy was gonna be Grim War-Tooth. He had kind of a dental thing going on. We were gonna wear bearskins and carry war axes. Stuff like that." He gave a deep sigh. "Anyway, the partnership didn't take. That was a while ago."

"You must have a pretty good memory to still be able to quote from it like that," Edgerton offered.

"Not really," Mulligan said, grinning crookedly. "Just that I don't have many books. The ones I do, I read more than once. I musta been through *Njal's Saga* a couple dozen times since I bought it. Keeps the words in my head. You know."

"Yeah, I know," Edgerton said, "I've read it a couple of times myself. There's just something about saga. The whole milieu." He paused. "It's not unlike professional wrestling, actually. You know, good guys and bad guys. Good men doing bad things. A world where vengeance is justice and bloody revenge is a perfectly acceptable and expected remedy for wrongs committed. Where things like raiding are appropriate career options. Too bad the partner thing didn't work out for you, Milkman. I'd have loved to have seen it."

Edgerton thought for a moment before a big smile spread across his face. "So, I guess Lyle is the first partner you've had since back in your wrestling days."

"I guess so," the big man said.

"But instead of Ulf the Unwashed and Grim War-Tooth, you'll to be like Watson to Lyle's Holmes."

Mulligan smiled. "I like that," he chuckled.

I nodded and grinned at both of them. But truthfully, I was more than a little wary of my new partner's motives. I had to wonder just how far Mulligan would go to protect Lorraine Rovig. I wondered if he were partnering with me to help get at the truth or to make certain that I'd be no threat to her. What if I found out something that could harm her? Would he play Watson to my Holmes, or would he elect to play Myron Floren with my neck again?

I finished the last morsel of hash browns and leaned back in the booth. I'd have to trust him, I decided. But trust, even the hard-won kind, is often a slippery thing. And this was slipperier than a bag of eels.

Chapter Thirteen

The Milkman told me that he had a commitment early the next morning but would be free by midday to help me with the investigation. I assured him that I could hardly wait. We left the big man at the bus stop and returned to the Bijou, Edgerton heading off to bed, while I sat up in my room waiting for dawn to streak the sky.

I dozed briefly but woke early to a bitterly cold, gray morning. I was tired; so tired that as I walked to my office I wondered if, as I'd napped, someone had stolen in and replaced my leg muscles with something gooey.

The cops that Augie had assigned to watch me had reappeared. They weren't real hard to spot. As I made my way to my office, the unmarked car tailed along about a half a block behind me, blocking traffic as it inched down the street like a snail on tranquilizers.

When I opened the office door, the first thing I saw was the blinking light of my answering machine. I stared at it a moment, competing torrents of relief and anxiety coursing through me. I approached it slowly, as a starving man would the jaws of a bear trap baited with a rump roast. When Farnum's voice echoed in the room instead of Carmen's, the relief drained away, leaving only a spiraling whirlpool of anxiety.

Farnum was hardly my first priority that morning, but from his tone it was pretty clear that he wasn't particularly pleased with me. In suggesting that I call him at my earliest convenience, he managed to use the f-word as every part of speech. A bit samey, but he got his message across. I was going to have to deal with him.

I set up the coffee maker and sat down behind my desk to watch the glass carafe fill up. Then I got out his card and made the call. Listening to the ring, I wondered if Farnum would fire me right away or if he would threaten me first.

"That you Dahms?" Farnum asked, a quaver of barely checked anger edging his voice.

"No, Al," I replied. "It's your podiatrist. Just calling to remind you that it's time to have your feet scraped."

"Dahms!" he exclaimed angrily, but then stopped himself, taking a moment to regain his composure. "Perhaps," he continued in a considerably more dulcet manner, "you could tell me if your investigation is bearing any fruit?"

"Hot damn, Al. Things have been going great. Let's see, where do I start? One of your boys tried to kill me, I spent a night in jail, the cops are following me, and…Oh, did you know that your girlfriend is missing? I don't suppose she let you know where she headed, did she?"

"No," he replied. "I haven't heard from Carmen."

"Don't that bother you some?"

Farnum sighed. "Unfortunately, I have been rather preoccupied with other matters. I had hoped that she was under your protection."

"Nope, but while we're at it, just what are these other matters you're preoccupied with?"

"I'm wondering if it is in my best interest to tell."

"You mean you don't trust me? I think I'll cry now."

"I'm a busy man, Lyle. Perhaps we could stick to the matter for which you were hired. Are you able to report any progress with regard to the apprehension of Ted's murderer?"

"No. I've been stirring things up the best I can but nothing's shook loose yet."

When Farnum finally spoke, it was slow like if he was assembling a puzzle he had to painstakingly piece together. "That is...ah...unfortunate. But I'm sure that you are doing your best. I'm certain you'll find a solution to the mystery soon. I want you to know that you still have my full confidence."

I'll admit I was momentarily speechless. I mean, you gotta figure that after sleeping with his mistress and being responsible for the death of one of his associates, he'd at least have some hard feelings. But Farnum apparently still wanted me on the payroll. Something was definitely going on.

"You know," I ventured, "You're being rather more understanding about the direction of my investigation than I had expected."

"I know little of the direction of your investigation. That is why I thought it imperative that you call me. I understand that you had an altercation with my Mr. Trench. I must tell you I feel myself partially to blame for that. As you began your inquiries, I'd asked him to keep an eye on you. But when he came to me with the message that you'd rather be left to your own devices, I told him to give you a wide berth. I'm afraid Mr. Trench disregarded my wishes."

"You could say that, yeah. If not for Angelino's timely aid, you might be looking for a new investigator. Which brings up an interesting question, Al. You got any idea why your boys are shooting at each other?"

"I wouldn't characterize the situation with such a

generalization, Lyle."

"Okay. How does Angelino characterize the situation?"

"Come again?"

"What did he say about the night Trench died?"

He paused again, clearing his throat a couple of times in false starts. Finally, he said, "Michael has not shared his impression of that evening's events with me."

"Did you ask him?"

"I haven't had an opportunity. In fact, I'm not entirely certain that Michael is still in my employ."

"You fired him?"

Farnum paused again. "Not exactly."

"He walked out on you?"

"Not exactly."

"Well, what exactly?"

"Michael simply has not appeared for work since the incident."

"He's disappeared?"

"Has not appeared for work."

"Shit."

Farnum responded with a resigned sigh.

"So, you want me to stay on the Rovig thing?"

"Oh, heavens yes. As we discussed at the time of your hire, I believe that our solving the case is the best way to protect me from the unfounded suspicions of the police."

"Uh huh. So, you're still worried about the cops?"

"Not worried, Lyle. Instead, they are an element with which I'd rather not have to concern myself."

"What with other matters concerning you at present?"

"Yes."

"Like Angelino jumping ship?"

"Again, I'd rather characterize his departure differently."

"Any of your other lads decide to take a sudden vacation?"

Sharpness crept into Farnum's voice. "I have plenty of loyal employees, Lyle. What I need to know is, can I count *you* among them?"

"You keep paying me, I'll keep cashing the checks."

"What a confidence-inspiring way of putting it, Lyle. I'm deeply touched."

"You need me more than ever, don't you?" I pressed. "You need as many people on your side as possible. Don't you?"

"Your loyalty will be rewarded, Lyle."

"It had better be."

"Please try to keep me better informed as to developments in your investigation. You've been rather lax about that thus far."

"I'll do my best, Boss."

"Well, then, if you've nothing else that you care to tell me at this time, I'd best be attending to other matters."

"Take care, Al," I said. "Watch out for Angelino."

"You do the same, Lyle," he said as he hung up the phone.

The instant I placed the receiver back on the cradle, the phone rang again. Startled, I knocked the phone over and had to scramble to pick it up, finally mumbling a greeting into the mouthpiece.

"I'm gonna need you to pick me up," a voice informed me.

"Huh? Who's this?"

"It's me, Irv."

"Who?"

"The Milkman. It's the Milkman."

"Oh, hey, man. Yeah. Right. Why?"

"Ain't we gonna start investigating today?"

"Uh, yeah," I said, stretching the phone cord to its utmost as I reached for the coffeepot on the other side of the room. "I'm sitting here marking out our strategy right now."

"Good man," Mulligan said. "I figured we'd go after the kid first. That is, if you agree it's a good idea."

"The kid?"

"Yeah, Ehlers. I mean, we know he was involved with Mr. Rovig and that probably means he's trouble for Mrs. Rovig. Don't you think? Me, I think we should do him first."

"Well, yeah," I admitted, pouring the coffee, "that'd be one way to go, but I gotta tell you, I thought I'd go looking for Farnum's missing girlfriend first."

"You think she killed Rovig?"

"No, I just think she's in trouble. I'm worried about her."

Mulligan was quiet for a while. "You think she's in big trouble?"

"I don't know. Maybe."

"Is she in the kind of trouble that you got to do something about it today?"

"I really don't know. Maybe. Maybe not. What are you thinking?"

"It's just that, um...I got some time today, you know. I'm free after noon and I got all day tomorrow and I kinda...I kinda wanted to...you know, get on with something that'd help out Mrs. Rovig. I think that the

Ehlers kid is the way to go. But you're the boss."

I thought for a moment. The truth was that although looking for Carmen would make me feel better, it would probably be a waste of time. Finding her, unless she wanted to be found, would be nearly impossible. Where would I begin? I could start with the brother she'd told me about, but from what she'd said, it was unlikely she'd go to him. I could find the ex-husband, but...would she go to him?

"Okay, Milkman," I said at last. "We do it your way. Where are you? I'll come get you."

"Great. I'm at the Midway YMCA in St. Paul. On University Avenue. I'll be here 'til twelve o'clock. Them bad guys probably ain't out of bed much before noon anyway, huh?"

"Probably not. You working out?"

"Not right now. I worked out earlier. I'm working right now."

"You work at the 'Y' too?"

"Just Saturday mornings. If you put in a shift, they give you a break on your membership."

"What do you do? Demonstrate equipment? Give tips on using free weights?"

"Nah. I do the nine to noon shift in the nursery. Me and another gal. In fact, I really gotta be getting back there. We're making paper snowflakes. You really gotta watch them kids and scissors."

"Um, yeah. I suppose you do," I said. "So, I'll see you at noon?"

"I'll be ready."

"Great. Watch out for paper cuts."

After Mulligan hung up, I had some time to kill, so I sat in the office for another hour or so making notes with a blue pen on a yellow legal pad. It wasn't real useful, but the yellow and blue somehow made me think of spring.

As the gray morning turned toward a gray afternoon, I locked up the office and hoofed it back to the Bijou. The cops followed me, then followed me some more as I got in my car and drove over to the YMCA.

A large woman at the front desk asked me for my membership card and eyed me suspiciously when I told her that I didn't have one. I explained that I was there to pick up Irv Mulligan and she pointed to a flight of steps behind her and told me that the nursery was at the top of the stairs, on the right.

The door had a sign on it that read "Y Men's Club Room," but alongside that was a hand-lettered piece of paper that read "Babysitting." I opened the door and at first wondered if I was in the wrong place. Nothing about the room suggested that it was a nursery. The walls were plain white and in need of repainting. There were a couple of stacks of chairs pushed against one wall and a folding table pushed against another. There were no bright posters, no big plastic climbers, or teeter-totters, or any of the kid stuff that you'd expect to see. But then there was only one kid—a boy about a year old with a runny nose in blue overalls holding on to a round, plastic chicken that jingled when he shook it. Mulligan sat cross-legged on the floor next to him, grinning as the kid rattled the chicken.

"That's right, Adam," the big man said. "The chickee's making music."

"Can I help you?" a woman's voice sounded from a corner.

I turned and faced a pleasant-looking brunette

wearing gray slacks, a navy-blue turtleneck, and a colorful vest that I guessed was a Latin American design.

"I'm here to pick up the Milkman," I told her

She looked confused, but I pointed at Mulligan and the lines in her face smoothed.

Mulligan smiled up at me. "Hey, Lyle. Thanks for coming. We'll only be a couple more minutes."

The woman looked around the room, then smiled at Mulligan. "Ah come on, Irv," she said. "You might as well take off. It's almost time to close up. All the other kids are gone. The toys are picked up. Adam's momma'll be here any time now. You go on and get out of here. I'm sure I'll manage."

"You sure?" Mulligan asked without taking his eyes off the toddler

"I'm sure."

Mulligan smiled broadly at the child. "Adam, my man. I gotta be going. You be here next Saturday? I'll be here next Saturday. Maybe I'll see you next Saturday."

The kid gargled at him.

"Okay. Bye-bye," Mulligan responded. "Have fun with your chickee."

When he stood up, Mulligan towered over the child like a grizzly over a field mouse. The boy cooed at him and shook the chicken a couple more times. Mulligan grinned so widely most of his face disappeared.

"It really makes you feel good," Mulligan told me in the hall. "Being with the kids reminds you of what's really important."

"He sure liked that chicken," I said.

"Yeah. It's a simple toy. But he likes it. Sometimes they like the simple things best."

I held my tongue.

"Let's go get my gym bag," Mulligan said.

Mulligan led me down the locker rooms. When he had retrieved his gym bag he asked, "Where do we start?"

"Well, if we want to find out how Ehlers is involved," I told him, "we basically got two ways to go. We can get him to confess, which isn't too likely unless we get pretty forceful with him, or we can watch him, see what his movements are, who his friends are, that kind of stuff."

"Which way we gonna go?"

I sighed. "It's tempting to just pull the kid aside for a little talk. But my read is that he fancies himself a pretty tough hombre and the odds are that he'd clam up on us unless we beat his balls off. Even then, we don't know who he's tied in with and we don't want to risk retribution without anything to show for it. I figure we set up on the kid and see what develops."

"We do that from a car?"

"Yeah. Mostly."

"Cold day. Windows'll be closed up. You better drive me home to ditch this gym bag. You don't want to spend the day in a closed car sniffing this bad boy."

I smiled. "Fair enough," I told him.

We left the 'Y' and got into my Ford and we all—me, Mulligan, the gym bag, and the cops—drove back to Minneapolis and Mulligan's place just off La Salle near Stevens Square. Mulligan lived in a well-kept building with a small front courtyard. There, the skeletal limbs of a couple of grim-looking, leafless trees reached toward the gray sky, but hunched closer to the ground, evergreen shrubs added color to the cramped space. Three bird feeders hung on a wire that stretched from one corner of the courtyard to the other. The snow below them was heavily littered with spent birdseed. But the thing that impressed me the most was the quiet. It was a soundless, unpeopled tableau. I didn't hear a single tenant, a single television set, not so much as a sigh. Even the birds outside munched in silence.

Mulligan lived on the ground floor. He unlocked the front security door and we proceeded down the hallway, stepping carefully, quietly, to preserve the silence. There was something unsafe about all that quiet. I scanned the hallway, noting that the doors to each of the apartments were recessed, but not quite enough for a man to hide in effectively. If someone were waiting for us, I thought, I'd probably see him.

Mulligan unlocked his apartment and the door opened into a small, dark efficiency. It was quiet in there too, but unlike the hall, there are plenty of places in an apartment where someone might hide. I stepped in behind the Milkman, slowly surveying the room, when he tensed and brought his hands together suddenly, violently. The silence was shattered by a loud crack.

I was carrying a .38-caliber Smith and Wesson in a shoulder holster under my left arm. I gulped a breath, grabbed for the gun, and crouched low. Fear crackling inside my head, the lights in the apartment suddenly came on.

Mulligan was staring at me, wide-eyed, his mouth agape. Then he lowered his eyes, frowned sheepishly, and shuffled his feet. "I didn't mean to startle you."

"What the…" I began, still in a defensive crouch, still holding the revolver before me with both hands.

"I was just turning on the lights."

"The lights?"

"Yeah. You know," he said, "like the commercial."

"The commercial?"

Mulligan grinned. "Yeah, you know." He hummed briefly to find the right key, then began to sing: *Clap on. Clap off. Clap on. Clap off. The Clapper.*

"The Clapper?" I asked incredulously, finally standing up and letting my gun sink back into the holster.

Mulligan nodded.

I shook my head. "The Clapper," I repeated, taking a couple of deep breaths, before managing a weak chuckle.

While I waited for my heart to stop pounding, I took a long look around the apartment. It was furnished simply and with modest means. The sofa bed and armchair were the sort you'd pick up at the Salvation Army or from along the side of the road somewhere. The walls were mostly bare except for a couple of old wrestling posters hanging on the wall above the TV. I peeked into the small kitchen, then into the closet. When I was sure there were no bad guys in there, I turned and smiled. "Tell me, Milkman," I asked, "you got any Chia pets in this place?"

He looked a little dumbfounded. "I used to," he replied. "But the fur all died. How'd you know?"

"Just a hunch."

He shrugged and dropped the gym bag next to the sofa bed. "Okay, let's hit it. Unless you want I quick make us up some sandwiches?" He pointed to the kitchen. "I think I got some braunschweiger. And sardines. I got sardines."

"Um...That's okay," I told him. "We can grab something out."

We left Mulligan's quiet neighborhood and drove

over to the apartment that Thomas Ehlers shared with his mom. The Ehlers' neighborhood wasn't so quiet. Despite the cold, the street was pretty crowded. A group of kids were playing king of the hill on top of a large mound of snow that had been pushed into the yard when the parking lot next door was cleared.

A kid wearing a black and orange down coat and a Chicago Bears stocking cap was standing on top of the snow pile, his arms held defiantly above his head. Another kid in a brown overcoat salted with snow was sitting at the base of the hill. His little frame was racked with sobs. Several other kids stood around him, laughing and pointing.

A group of young men standing nearby were laughing too, but not at the kids and their game. There were four of them, huddled together on the front steps of the Ehlers apartment. Each wore an oversized starter jacket, each emblazoned with the insignia of a different sports team. Tommy Ehlers favored the Florida Marlins.

I parked the car on a side street about a half a block away that had a partially obstructed view of the men on the front steps. The cops parked about a half a block behind me. We sat there a long time. I only ran the engine for a few minutes a couple of times each hour to keep us from getting frostbite.

Tired as I was, I didn't feel much like talking. Mulligan followed my lead and we waited in silence. I kept yawning and Mulligan seemed content to watch the boys at play and to fiddle with the Velcro wristband on his down jacket.

After about the first hour, he asked, "Just what exactly are were looking for?"

"We don't know," I told him.

A couple of times the cops drove away and came back a few minutes later, large Styrofoam cups in their hands. God, I thought, coffee would be good. But I didn't want to move the car and it was too cold to walk even to the nearest gas station for coffee.

The cold got to the boys on the steps too. It was like they'd set up a rotation where one or two would go inside for a few minutes, then return so a different one could go in and warm up. But they seemed determined to maintain a continual presence on the steps, as if keeping watch at some border outpost. Besides laughing and stamping their feet, they didn't seem to be doing anything.

By and by, shadows began to lengthen, and it was becoming difficult to see the young men in the recessed doorway of the apartment building. I was seriously considering heading home when one of the guys stepped out into the light and pulled a cell phone from his pocket.

Following a brief conversation, he turned and said something to the others. They slapped each other on the back and stamped their feet even more vigorously. One of them doubled over with laughter.

A few minutes later, a yellow Caddy with a serious rust problem pulled up in front of the apartment. Two men sat in the front seat, two women in the back.

It was a tight fit, but they all managed to pile into the Caddy. Three of the men sat in the front and three sat in the back. In order to make room for everyone, the women had to get out, then climb back in and sit on the laps of two of the guys in the back.

One of the women took a couple of quick steps away from the car before being yanked back in by one of the laughing men. I didn't like it. The men seemed awfully big, and the women seemed awfully small.

"Something don't feel right," I told Mulligan as the Caddy pulled away from the curb.

He nodded. "We gonna follow 'em?"

"Damn right we are."

Chapter Fourteen

They didn't go far.

We followed the big yellow barge for a few miles before arriving at a single-level bungalow located on busy Cedar Avenue South. I found a parking spot only a few houses down the street, pulled into it and watched as Ehlers and his companions crawled out of their car tugging the two women by their arms. We were too far away to hear anything, but the Milkman and I watched as one of the women managed to squirm from the grasp of the man pulling her toward the house, only to be blocked by two others who grabbed her, picked her up and carried her bodily inside.

I glanced all around to see if the cops who had been tailing us previously had followed, but I couldn't spot their unit. The group disappeared inside, and we waited a few minutes in silence as I thought about the best way to handle things.

Finally, the Milkman turned to me. "It's not good," he said. "I don't think them girls want anything to do with them guys."

"I don't think so either."

"So, what are we going to do about it?"

I shrugged. "Let's go ask them."

The Milkman and I climbed out of my car, and I pulled the .38 from under my jacket as we approached.

While a realtor might have described the house as a

"fixer upper," others might have called it a "tearer downer." Several of the roof's asphalt shingles had peeled back and the soffit under the roof line showed massive wood rot. The faded yellow exterior appeared speckled with mildew and the cement stairway that led up to the front porch had sunk and pulled away from the house leaving a wide gap. The windows were completely blacked out with what appeared to be cardboard.

When we reached the front porch, we paused. I heard muffled laughter coming from inside. I thought about it. We didn't have anything approaching probable cause to bust in there. Legally, the thing to do was to call the police, tell them what we saw, and ask them to investigate.

I was about to suggest this to the Milkman when a woman's scream sounded from inside the house. He put his sizeable bulk into ramming the door. It flew open with a crack like a tree giving way in a windstorm.

The house, though not furnished, was far from empty. Bags of garbage and Styrofoam take-out containers, some still filled with half-eaten meals, were strewn about what was once a living room. It was unclear if the house had electricity. With the windows covered, the only illumination inside was from a Coleman lantern the boys had set up in the middle of the room. There were no pictures on the walls and nowhere to sit. But there were a couple of sleeping bags along one of the walls.

One of the women lay curled up atop one, naked and sobbing. She was pretty, Asian, and didn't look older than sixteen. Her sobbing was convulsive, her body tightening like a fist with each breath.

Two men stood near her. Both turned when they heard the door crash open. Both had their pants around their ankles. Both held their manhood in their hands.

The other girl was also a child. One of the men, this one fully dressed, hovered over her while another was on top of her. It was Ehlers, still wearing that Florida Marlins jacket. This girl wasn't crying. Behind wisps of dark hair clinging to her face, I saw no fear, no hate in her almond eyes. Her face was stony, without expression, as if all feeling had been taken from her.

The men all stared at us. "What the hell?" one exclaimed.

I glanced at the Milkman, then back at what the men were doing to the girls. A warm sensation began to spread within me, as though a valve had suddenly been turned on. It went quickly from warm to intolerably hot. Flames licked at my insides. I looked down at the gun in my hand.

Ehlers rolled off his victim while the guy standing nearest him fumbled under his coat. He stopped when he saw my .38. He sneered. "What the fuck do you guys want?" He pointed at the girl at his feet. "A turn?"

Mulligan brushed past me and rushed toward him. He picked him up and heaved. The man went flying across the room. Yelping, he crashed into one of guys who had their pants down. Sprawling, they fell to the ground. The one left standing stooped down revealing a butt tattoo as he snatched something from the floor. It was a handgun. A 9mm. His mistake was that he tried to aim and pull his pants up at the same time. He got a couple of rounds off, but they went wide. I shot in him in the right thigh. I was aiming higher.

Tattoo Butt hit the floor screaming, the gun still in his hand. His buddy, pants still around his ankles, got to his feet and tried to grab the gun from Tattoo Butt, but he tripped over his pants and went down. He rolled, desperately trying to reach the gun, but I moved in and kicked him hard in the head. Then I stomped on Tattoo Butt's hand to get him to release the gun. I scooped up the 9mm. and kicked them both again. My foot against their heads made delightful "thunking" sounds.

I stepped back to both better cover the two men on the floor as well as to see what was going on with Mulligan. The Milkman had grabbed Tommy Ehlers and I watched as he rammed Ehlers' head into the living room wall. It made a dent in the sheetrock. Ehlers' eyes crossed and he crumpled into a heap.

Tattoo Butt and the other guy with the unfortunately downed trousers lay on the ground moaning, but the one that Mulligan had thrown was on his feet again and moving toward Mulligan. He produced a gravity knife. He flicked his wrist, the knife opened and, flashing the long, slender blade, he said, "Gonna cut you, man. Gonna cut off your gonads."

One of his friends mumbled, "Get 'em, Cheech."

Mulligan took a step forward, but I shouted for him to stop. Both men turned to look at me.

Cheech remained defiant. "First I cut him, then I eviscerate you, fat boy."

I managed a smile, shrugged and pointed at him with the guns that I held in each hand. "I don't think so, Cheech."

"You think I'm afraid of you, lard ass?" He laughed at his joke, smiled, and raised the knife. "I'll cut out your liver and feed it to that bitch over there."

"Milkman," I said. "Let me have this guy."

He nodded and backed away. "I'll watch the others."

I made a great show of lowering the handguns. I

opened my coat and slid the 9mm butt first into my belt at the small of my back. Then I tucked the .38 into my belt in front of me and smiled sweetly. Cheech nodded, closing his eyelids halfway as if he were dozing. Still nodding, he let his heavily lidded eyes survey the room leisurely. I let my eyes wander as well.

Cheech burst toward me like a sprinter leaving the blocks. His knife in the lantern light cut an arc between us. He'd almost reached me when I snatched the .38 from my belt and pulled the trigger. He stared at me before he hit the ground, then fell backward, still clutching the knife.

I moved in and stomped on his hand. He released the knife, but then rolled and tried to grab my foot with his other hand. I stumbled out of his grasp and kicked the knife into the darkness. Cheech flailed at me one last time before rolling over on his back. Then, exhaling deeply, he stopped moving. I peered down at him.

Cheech's eyes were beginning to cloud over, but it was clear he could still see me standing over him. He sneered again and tried to spit at me but didn't get enough behind it. His spittle landed in a long strand on his chest, mixing with the blood that was now soaking through his shirt. He started to cough—small coughs that were barely audible. His mouth tightened into a macabre grin. He wasn't coughing, I realized. He was laughing.

That valve inside me opened up again. Then I was on top of Cheech, the barrel of my gun in his mouth. I stared first at the top of his head, then the floor he was lying on. I desperately wanted his brains on that floor.

A loud voice sounded from behind me. "Police! Hands up! All of you!"

The cops had tailed us there after all.

Chapter Fifteen

Four units of uniformed officers soon arrived to back up the detectives who'd been watching us. The women were transported to the hospital via ambulance while Ehlers and his friends were placed, none too gently, into the back of the squad cars. Mulligan and I got a ride with the detectives in the back of their vehicle and soon we were all at police headquarters.

Central booking was a madhouse. We were muscled through the crowd to the front desk where the detectives had a couple of words with the desk sergeant.

"We gotta hold you," one of them told us. "But we damn sure ain't going to put you in a cell with any of those assholes you followed into that house. So, we got a nice bench for you. We'll have to leave the cuffs on you, but..." He lowered his tone conspiratorially. "I don't think you'll be here very long."

I nodded gratefully and they led us through the maze of people to a bench along a wall. They were kind enough to re-cuff us so our hands were in front, then told us to take a seat. Cops got their own sense of time. It probably wasn't very long as they reckon things, but we were on the bench for what seemed an eternity. What made it worse was that I really had to go to the bathroom. I ended up squirming uncomfortably the whole time, doing a sit-down version of the pee dance.

They came for Mulligan first. After about twenty

minutes, a uniformed officer came for me as well. He took pity on me and let me go to the bathroom before ushering me into the elevator and up to the fifth floor and a room marked "Interrogation One." It was pretty spacious, but there wasn't much in there for furniture, just a rectangular wooden table with a recording device, and three chairs. Mulligan sat in one of the chairs, staring across the room at Augie Tarkof.

Tarkof was leaning against the wall, an unlit cigarette tucked behind his left ear. My escort left without a word. "I don't like working this late on a Saturday, Dahms," Tarkof said.

I gave him my best broad smile. "Then why don't we knock off, Augie? It's luau night at Hilo Harry's. We could all just head over there."

"Nah," Tarkof said without expression, "I've got a problem with poi. Besides, I've been seeing a little too much of you lately. Didn't I tell you to stay away from the Rovig investigation?"

I shrugged and took a seat in the chair beside Mulligan. "Yeah, but you knew I wouldn't," I said, yawning. "Isn't that why the last time we talked, you told me so much about Rovig and Ehlers? You were hoping I'd come up with something to help you out."

Tarkof moved away from the wall. "If I was, you sure as shit disappointed me."

"There's little in this life as sure as shit."

Tarkof nodded noncommittally. "That guy you shot?" he said. "Lopez?"

"The guy I shot in the chest? The one they called Cheech?"

"Yeah."

"What about him?"

"He croaked."

"No kidding."

"No kidding." He paused, staring fixedly at me for a few disquieting seconds. I stared back, pretending to pry wax out of my ear with my pinky. I removed the finger and examined the tip minutely.

"I heard he died thinking about you," Tarkof continued. "I hear he told the nurse that he was going to come back from the grave and cut the balls off the fat guy who shot him."

"That supposed to bother me?"

"I'm just passing along information, Dahms. It bothers you, that's your problem."

"What bothers me is I didn't take out more of them."

"Maybe we can come up with a few other things to bother you, Dahms," Tarkof said, the corner of his mouth curling into a smirk.

"What are you going to do," I asked, "charge us with trespassing?"

"Trespassing, illegal entry, destruction of property." Tarkof ticked each charge off with his fingers. "Ruining my day."

"Destruction of property?" I asked.

Tarkof nodded. "Those guys you shot bled all over the hardwoods. Gonna need refinishing. It'll set the homeowner back a bundle."

"We'll take our chances." I turned to Mulligan. "Won't we?"

The Milkman nodded but there was real apprehension in his eyes.

"Instead of threatening us with bogus charges," I said, "you should be thanking us. We helped get those guys off the streets." I paused. "What kind of time do you think they will do?"

"That's up to the ADA in charge of the case," Tarkof said.

I chuckled. "Seems to me you got Ehlers and his buddies by the short and curlies. It's not like they can afford a decent defense. What's a public defender gonna do? Kidnapping? Rape? Mulligan and me as witnesses? Shit, they'll plead out the first chance they get."

"Turns out you're wrong, Dahms," Tarkof said. "About Ehlers anyway. The kid's got himself a high-powered lawyer. The guy's with Pendergast and Associates. Pretty high buck outfit. Lawyer marched in here about an hour ago."

"How 'bout the other boys? They lawyer up, too?"

"Nah. Just Ehlers. Funny thing. After this lawyer shows up and talks to Ehlers, the kid starts looking at his running buddies like they're something he stepped on."

A chill ran through me. "But you'll nail him for the rape? Right? Ehlers pays for what he did to those two kids. Right?"

Tarkof stared impassively at me.

"Jesus. Tell me you're gonna nail these guys for what they did to those two girls."

"That's hard to say."

"Bullshit."

Tarkof spread his hands wide in a gesture of helplessness. "It's complicated, Dahms. What can I tell ya? I've been talking with them and I gotta say, they're acting pretty cocky about the whole thing. Like they figure they're some kind of criminal masterminds or something. They've even been dropping hints, trying to rub our noses in it. You remember a couple of years ago over in St. Paul some Asian gang members set up an online forum? They used it to charm young girls into meeting with them and when the girls showed up for their dates they got raped?"

"I remember. What's that got to do with these guys?"

"Remember that the gangbangers chose Hmong girls because of the stigma rape carries in their society? They figured the girls would never testify."

"Some did though, right?"

"Yeah. But not all of them. That's why these guys chose those two girls. They read about how the slants worked it and figured they could pull it off without getting caught. They figured them Hmong girls would never testify against them. Them being so bad and all. They figured if the social implications weren't enough to keep them from pressing charges, they'd just make a few threats. They still figure that'll work."

"No way," I said. "We'll testify. And let them threaten us. Let them give me a reason to go after them."

Mulligan nodded.

"Anyway, I'm just telling ya," Tarkof said, "the rape charge isn't them boys' big concern right now. Ehlers is breaking ranks with them. That's got them wondering. They don't know what that means."

"What do you think it means?"

"Somebody's paying for that lawyer." He paused. "Farnum?"

I thought for a moment. "I don't think so. I can't see a connection between Farnum and Ehlers."

"Ehlers hung with Farnum's accountant."

"Yeah. Ehlers has a connection with Rovig, but none I know about with Farnum."

"But then, as we have observed in the past, you

don't know very much."

"Sweet of you to point that out."

"I'm a sweet guy."

"So, you can't say if you're going to get those guys for the rapes?"

"I didn't say we weren't going to try." He checked his watch. "We'll hold them as long as we can. My guess is that his lawyer will get Ehlers sprung before the others. In the meantime, if we need you, we'll let you know."

I stared at Tarkof until the silence got real awkward. "You need us for anything else right now?" I asked.

"Nothing springs to mind."

"I could use some sleep."

"Don't let the door hit you on the way out," Tarkof said, removing the unlit cigarette from behind his ear, then taking a couple of draws on it.

Mulligan had kept his eyes lowered through much of our exchange but looked up expectantly when he heard we could go. We stood and Mulligan crossed quickly to the door.

"See you, Augie," I said, following Mulligan.

I was nearly out of the room when Tarkof called me back. "Just idle curiosity," he said, "but have you heard anything from that chippy you're sweet on? That Carmen?"

I didn't turn around. I didn't say a word. And it's embarrassing to admit, but you know, the door actually did hit me on the way out.

I checked with the desk sergeant and found out that my car was still parked in front of the house where we'd confronted Ehlers and his cronies. Once outside headquarters, I called for an Uber and before long we arrived at my car. During the ride, Mulligan and I neither talked nor even looked at each other.

After we got in my ride and I coaxed the engine to life, which was more than I could do with the car's heater. I cursed when frigid air blasted through the vents.

Mulligan grunted. I turned to him and watched as lines of thought creased his forehead. "You upset about killing that guy?" he asked.

I answered before I took the time to think about it. "Yeah. More than I'd like to admit. Yeah."

"You ever kill anyone before?"

"I've had my gun out. Even shot at a couple of people. None of 'em ever died before."

Mulligan's expression clouded over, and his brow furrowed. "More people become killers than I ever expected."

"Say what?"

"It's from *Njal's Saga*. Njal's wife is out for revenge, so she sends this guy Thord out to kill this other guy named Brynjolf."

"That's easy for you to say," I quipped, but I couldn't muster a smile.

"Anyway," Mulligan continued, "this guy Thord never killed no one before, so when the killing of Brynjolf was reported, Njal couldn't believe it. So, he says, 'More people become killers than I ever expected.' "

"I guess I always hoped it wouldn't happen to me."

"What?"

"That I'd become a killer."

"Ah! You ain't no killer."

"Cheech might not agree with you there, Milkman."

Mulligan stroked his chin with his thick fingers. "Killing somebody don't make you a killer."

"I'm afraid you're wrong there, buddy."

"That didn't come out right. What I mean is, you know, you call somebody a killer and it's like that's all there is. You know. Like they ain't nothing else. Like their whole thing is just being a killer."

"That's the trouble with labels, Milkman. But in this case, the label fits. I wanted him dead. I wanted them all dead. I saw what they were doing to those girls and I wanted them all dead. The cops got there before I could kill them all. I had to settle for Cheech. But now…It just looks different now. This thing's gonna be with me awhile. You know."

Mulligan was silent for a moment. "You're a good guy, Dahms," he said at last. "There's a lot of good stuff in you."

"Yeah, but like you said the other night, 'where fault is found, the good is ignored.' "

Mulligan grinned. "Ah, forget that," he said, waving a big mitt at me. "What the hell do I know?"

Chapter Sixteen

Before he got out of my car to go into his apartment, Mulligan leaned forward and asked me what our plans were for the next day. I told him I planned to sleep in. He nodded, a disappointed heaviness settling about his features. He reminded me that he had the day off and told me that he would call. I told him to call late.

I drove back to my office and when I opened the door the message light was blinking merrily away. Oddly, I actually hoped it hadn't been her. I hoped I hadn't missed her call.

Hope sucks.

According to the answering machine, Carmen called at 2:27 p.m. She didn't say much. Just that she was frightened, that she was sorry that she'd missed me, and that she'd try to call again. There was only the one message.

Carmen had been smart not to leave more information, I told myself. If she had left her location on the machine and somebody was looking for her, it's possible they could have broken into the office and listened to it. I checked the door again. Nobody'd broken in, but they could have. She'd done the right thing not letting me know where she was. I cursed her for it.

Since Carmen only had my office number, I elected to spend the night there. My desk chair wasn't particularly comfortable, but I was really tired and before

I knew it, I was waking up to sunlight streaming in through the windows. I cursed the sunlight. Before it woke me, I'd been in a dark place, holding Carmen. Her face had been wet with grateful tears, her tiny frame shivering, clinging to me for warmth and protection.

I looked at the clock. It was after eight in the morning. I waited around the office until nearly ten o'clock; then I couldn't make myself wait any longer. I looked up the addresses of both Terry Popkin and William Reilly. I didn't really think she be hiding with either her brother or her ex-husband, but there was a chance that she'd contacted them. They might be able to tell me where she was.

Her brother's place was the closest. He was living in an apartment on Elliot Avenue, just at the edge of downtown Minneapolis. Terry's neighborhood was undergoing something of a renaissance. The façade of his building had been recently sandblasted, a new sidewalk had been laid, and a few of the surrounding houses were being rehabbed. But it was a place still weighted with its share of hopelessness. Some of the housing stock was distinguished by peeling paint and listing porches and ne'er-do-wells continued to march past Terry's building in a daily parade between Elliot Liquors at one end of his street and the Albert Alonzo Ames Memorial Park at the other. The neon of the liquor store glowed like a boozy beacon. The park was a patch of concrete and broken glass, the swing set and jungle gym cordoned off by a phalanx of drug dealers.

Next to the security doors that barred entry into Terry's building was a framed list of residents done up in calligraphy. Using the adjacent phone, I dialed up Terry's number and listened to it ring three times before a woman's voice answered. "Hello." She spoke so softly I had to guess at what she actually said.

"Hey. Is Terry there? This is Lyle. I'm down here in the lobby and I gotta talk to him."

There was a long pause. Finally, the woman said that she would check. There were some muffled noises before a man's voice came on the line. "Who is it that you want?" In the background, I heard what sounded like the cooing of an infant.

"Is that you, Terry?" I asked. "This is Lyle. Man, we gotta talk. I know we haven't actually met, but I'm sure Carmen's told you all about me. I wouldn't bother you if it wasn't important. Let me in, huh?"

He let me listen to the baby in the background for a while. "You got the wrong place, mister," he said at last. "I never heard of you."

"Terry," I said, sounding less cheerful, "I know you gotta be careful. You got a family. You can't just let anybody into your home. But I'm a friend of Carmen's. She's in trouble and needs your help. Really, man. It's important."

"Tell me on the phone," Terry insisted. "You don't need to come in."

"This isn't the kind of thing I can discuss with you standing out here in the lobby. This isn't the kind of that you'll be wanting to share with your neighbors."

"What kind of…" he began, but he didn't finish the sentence. Instead, he buzzed me in.

The man who opened the door was shorter than I'd imagined. He was in his early thirties and wore a pair of khaki pants, brown loafers, and a white cotton pullover. He wasn't the friendly type. He glared at me with what I'm assuming was all the menace he could muster, but he was a good foot shorter than me, and I probably outweighed him by something like seventy-five pounds. He looked like he was trying to catch up though. His cheeks were far pudgier than the ones in the photograph I'd seen back at Carmen's apartment and a spare tire had settled comfortably around his middle. My Aunt Agnes would say that married life agreed with him.

"What kind of trouble is Carmen in?" he asked, blocking the doorway.

"You sure you want to talk about this in the hall?"

He didn't answer, but he did move out of the way and pushed the door open wide enough for me to enter. As the door clicked shut behind me, I surveyed the room, nodding at a woman sitting silently on the sofa. She didn't return my greeting. Instead, she bent down to adjust a blanket that covered a baby in one of those carrier deals at her feet. The baby made a little google noise. Babies like me.

I turned to Terry and smiled. "Did you hear about the shooting?"

His glare melted away. "Maybe we should talk in the dining room."

We left his wife and baby in the living room, Terry leading me around a small Christmas tree to a table in the dining area next to the kitchen. The tree blocked the view from the living room, but I was certain that, if she wanted to, his wife would be able to hear our every word.

"So, did you hear about the shooting?" I repeated.

Alarm crackled behind the suspicion in Terry's eyes.

"Don't worry," I assured him, "she wasn't hurt."

"What's this all about?"

"It's complicated. Carmen's on the run. She's

scared. She's got reason to be scar
involved with a guy named Farnum who
related trouble and may be mixed up in a
be looking for Carmen. We don't want h

"How are you involved in all of us?"

"That's complicated, too. I just want to make sure that she's okay."

"How do I know you're not in with this guy Farnum. How do I know you don't want to hurt her?"

"Good question. You don't."

Terry stiffened. "I think you should leave now."

"I don't think so, Terry."

The alarm came back into his eyes, stronger this time. "Are you saying that you're not going to leave?"

"That's what I'm saying."

"I'll call the police."

"Fair enough," I said. "But make it easy on yourself. Just stick your head out the window and holler. They'll probably hear you. The cops have been tailing me all week."

He tried to control it, but he was quivering like a Jell-O mold at a Luther League picnic. "What's going on here and what does it have to do with me?" A little boy whine edged his voice.

"Look, Terry. Carmen's in trouble. I can help her, but only if I can find her. You're her brother. I'm going to need your help."

Terry sighed and slumped lower in his chair. His mouth pursed slightly, not quite a pout, but awfully close. "I haven't talked to her in months," he told me. "I sure as hell don't know where she is now. If she got herself into trouble, that's her problem. I have a family to think about. I shouldn't have to deal with this. I ᴊuldn't have to deal with you."

"Your concern for your sister is really touching."

"Look, I don't have to explain myself to you. I don't know you. You could be anybody. You're probably not trying to help Carmen at all. You're probably..." He threw up his hands. "Oh, why is this my problem anyway?"

"You're right," I said. "You don't know me, and I could be anybody. So, let's just say that I am a bad guy. Let's say I'm looking to do some harm here. Here I am, sitting in your home. Your wife and baby are right over there. Does that help you understand why this is your problem?"

"See. Now you're trying to scare me."

"Damn right, Terry. And you should be scared. Now, the fact is that I'm one of the good guys. But bad guys might be looking for your sister. One bad guy shot another bad guy in front of your sister's apartment the other day. Your sister ran. If more bad guys are looking for her, they're going to eventually look here. You want that? You want them in here?"

"I, ah...I..."

"Let me help you, Terry. You don't want that. That would be a bad thing. If you help me find Carmen, maybe I can help keep these bad things from happening. You want to protect your family? Do the right thing here. Maybe everything will turn out okay."

"But I don't know where she is," he cried. "I told you. I haven't heard from her in months. She's never even come by to see the baby. Her own niece. She's got nothing to do with us."

"You must have some idea where she would go," I pressed.

"I got no idea. No idea at all."

"Think. Would she go to friends? What about other family members?"

Terry lowered his eyes, his head lolling atop his shoulders. "We're all the family she has in town," he said quietly. "She doesn't want anything to do with us. And her friends? I don't know anything about her friends. You just told me that one of her friends might be trying to hurt her. You said she's running from her friends."

Terry looked up and chuckled anxiously. "She's always running from something."

"What do you mean?"

"I mean it's like…I don't know. Like she can't stay close to anyone. You reach out to her, she runs away. She's not close to us. She's not close to her ex-husband. Nobody."

"Maybe she's been betrayed by those close to her," I said. "Maybe she doesn't figure she's got reason to trust you people."

"What do you mean by that?"

"She lived with you for a time, didn't she? Back when you were in college?"

"Yeah, so?"

"She left. Why?"

"Carmen is always leaving. I just told you that."

"You had nothing to do with her leaving?"

Terry stared at me for several seconds before answering, genuine sadness seeping into his eyes. "Maybe I rode her too hard," he said, at last. "It's just that I always figured that you had to work hard in this life to get ahead. I always told Carmen that nobody was going to hand her everything she wanted. She would have to work for it. I tried to get her to stay in school. To be serious. Maybe I pushed too hard. I don't know. But it was like she just didn't see it. It was like she figured that the world owed her. Like if she could just make the right connection, everything would be handed to her. Maybe I did have something to do with her leaving. But I don't know what else I could have done. It's just not my fault."

"Carmen tells it differently," I said.

"She would, wouldn't she?"

I stood, turned my back to him, and looked out the window. In the street below an old man in a shabby overcoat shuffled slowly across the intersection, holding up the progress of a car trying to make a left turn. Two young men on the sidewalk laughed at the old man as he waved a tired arm at the impatient driver.

I turned back to him. "You sure you can't help me?"

He glanced back toward the living room. "Maybe I can't help anybody."

I peered that way too, at the Christmas tree that stood between us and where his wife and child were sitting. There was a ribbon woven among the tree branches, gold letters on red silk that read, "The Season of Hope."

I turned back to Terry Popkin. I wondered why I'd come. I hadn't really thought he'd be able to help me find her. I could have just called. But maybe I just wanted to see what kind of man would rape his sister. Maybe I hadn't even done that.

I left Terry standing in his dining room. I went down to the street and got in my car to begin the forty-minute drive south to Lakeville, where Carmen's ex-husband still lived.

It was a nice drive. The farther you drive away from

the city, the more things spread out. The houses are built larger and farther apart, and the apartment houses and strip malls have these hugely expansive parking lots. Each thing seems to take up a whole lot more room. Towering above the freeway overpasses, impossibly tall poles hoist enormous signs and huge American flags to the sky, marking the location of gas stations, convenience stores, and family restaurants. It's as if by making things take up more space, they can claim to be living on a grander scale. As though it proves they've latched hold of that great big American dream.

Billy Reilly's great big American dream was located in a trailer park nuzzled up against the freeway. The trailer park was a relic, a reminder of a time before suburban sprawl had reached that far south of the Cities. It butted up against a tract of newly constructed "executive-style" houses, and you just knew looking at it that it wouldn't be long before the land was bought, the trailers moved out, and even larger houses built in their stead. But in the meantime, it was essentially a couple acres of mobile homes laid out on a barren piece of dirt called "Shady Vistas."

There was a sign on a trailer just inside the park that read "Manager," and I stopped to ask an old man in a plaid jacket for directions to Reilly's mobile home. I drove along a serpentine dirt road until I found number 28. It was pretty large, as mobile homes go, white with black trim, and in pretty good shape, although along the bottom edge some of the black didn't seem to be welded on as well as it should have been. I pulled my car off the road and into a spot in the small yard that had been shoveled clear to accommodate what looked to be a brand-new Dodge pickup truck. There was just enough room left over for me.

It was cold and overcast and walking up to the trailer the lights inside glowed brightly. Reilly must be cooking something, I thought. I could distinctly smell garlic as I knocked on the door.

The young woman who opened the door shivered as she looked out at me. She had reason to shiver. It had to be ten degrees below zero outside and she was wearing a baby T-shirt clipped just above her navel. As the cold outside air rolled past her into the warm trailer, the muscles of her abdomen contracted noticeably. She wrapped her arms around herself and leaned forward to get a better look at me. When she did, her long black hair cascaded down across her face, and she swept it back with an elegant wave of her arm. I noticed a soft shadow on her left cheek, barely perceptible beneath her makeup. An old bruise, I thought.

Her dark eyes glittered in the light from the porch, but they were cold eyes, reflecting outside light rather than glowing from within. Her jaw was set, and her mouth was a thin, grim line. She was perhaps eighteen years old, bony, and hard as granite.

"Who's there?" a man's voice called from inside the trailer.

"What do you want?" the young woman asked me.

"I need to talk to Billy," I said, pushing past her and into the trailer.

"Hey!" she shouted, but I was already in their living room.

Reilly was just coming out of the kitchen carrying two plates of spaghetti. In front of the sofa, a pair of place settings had been laid out on a coffee table. The TV was on, and I spotted Rudolph the Red Nosed Reindeer capering across the screen. Unfortunately, it wasn't the original production, but rather the lackluster sequel, *Rudolph's Shiny New Year*. I didn't think I'd stay to watch it with them. Reilly came to a stop when he saw me, each hand helplessly holding a plate of pasta.

"Who the hell are you?" he shouted, looking around for a place to set down the food.

"Relax, pal," I told him. "I'm an old friend of the family, just come to wish you compliments of the season."

"Get the hell out of my house. I don't know you. Get out or I'll…I'll…"

I unzipped my coat and pulled it back far enough so he could see the gun in my shoulder holster. "You'll have to wait on dinner, Billy."

I glanced back at the door. Billy's girlfriend was still holding it open, a puzzled look on her face. "Why don't the two of you have a seat on the sofa. I've got a couple of questions."

Billy studied me briefly, his eyes darting a couple of times to the gun under my arm. "Why don't you close the door and come have a seat, Cheryl," he said cautiously.

I stepped back eyeing them both. Cheryl was not happy. Neither was I. I distinctly remembered that Carmen had told me that Reilly was living with a woman named Linda. Something wasn't right.

"Who the fuck is this dufus?" Cheryl asked Reilly. "What the fuck kind of trouble are you in now? Why the hell don't you do something besides stand there?"

Reilly winced at Cheryl and then glared at me. But there wasn't much he could do but look pathetic. "I told you to sit down," he snapped.

Cheryl closed the front door and sauntered over to the sofa, shaking her head and smirking. As she took a seat, her hair again fell across her face. When she pushed it away, I was reminded of the bruise.

"You two been together long?" I asked her.

She stared at me.

"Does Billy here hit you a lot?"

"That's none of your business, fat boy," she hissed in reply.

I turned to Billy. "Sit down," I told him. "And for God's sake put down those dinners. You look like a goddamned bird feeder."

Reilly set the pasta down on the coffee table and took a seat next to Cheryl. I pulled a metal folding chair from the nearby dinette set and sat myself across from them. "This is only going to take a minute or two. I'm sorry for all the dramatics, but I just don't have the time to be friendly." I scowled at Reilly. "Or the inclination. I got a couple of questions, then I'm outta here."

"We don't have to tell you anything, ass wipe," Cheryl said. "Billy, why don't you just pound this guy into a pile of slop? He's just a fat guy, for christsakes."

"Shut up, Cheryl!" Reilly said.

"Don't you tell me to shut up, you mother-grabbing little pansy. I'll take this guy myself if you ain't man enough."

I smiled at her. "Shut up, Cheryl."

Cheryl shut up and I stared at Billy for a while. His eyes shifted aimlessly, refusing to meet mine. When I figured I'd been at it long enough, I abruptly asked, "Where's Carmen?"

This was too much for Cheryl. "Who's Carmen?" she shrieked. "If you've been running around behind my back, I'm gonna superglue your nuts to the—"

"Shut up, Cheryl," I interrupted and turned back to Reilly. "Where's Carmen?"

"I ain't seen her," he insisted. "I ain't even heard from her in years. Really. You gotta believe me. I don't know nothing about Carmen."

"No, Billy," I told him. "I don't have to believe you. Now, where's Carmen?"

"Jesus, man. I can't tell you what I don't know. I ain't laid eyes on the bitch in a long time."

I took the gun out from under my arm and held it in my lap. The sight of the gun got a tiny gasp out of Cheryl. Reilly looked like he might mess himself. "Then tell me what you do know," I said.

"I'm telling you, I don't know anything, man."

"She called you. She needed help. She told you where she was going."

Reilly was sweating. He tried to respond but could only manage a frightened squelch. He took a couple of deep breaths. "I ain't heard from her," he said at last. "I don't know what you want from me."

"She's on the run," I said. "She was married to you. If she didn't go to you, then who would she go to?"

"How should I know. I—"

"You were married!" Cheryl squealed. "You bastard. You never told me you were married. I'd like to know what else you haven't told me, you two-faced, dickless, little—"

"Shut up, Cheryl," I told her.

She glared at me but stopped talking.

"Where would she go?" I asked Reilly.

"Look, man," Reilly pleaded, "you gotta believe me. I just don't know. Carmen left me a long time ago. I never hear from her. I don't even know if she's still in the state. I'd tell you if I knew. Honest. I just want you to go. I just want you to believe me and go. I just don't want…I just don't want you to hurt us."

Tears welled in his eyes.

"That's touching, Billy. That really is. And I'd go. I really would. Except, I don't believe you. I don't believe that Carmen would cut off all contact with you. You see, I know about Angela."

Cheryl was beside herself. "Who the hell is Angela?" she screamed. "Who the hell are all of these women? You bastard! You told me I was the only one for you. You remember that? Do you remember telling me that you piece of shit? You weaselly little—"

"Baby, there is no Angela," Billy sobbed loudly. "I don't know nobody named Angela. This guy's got it all wrong. Why can't I make you believe that? You got it all wrong."

There was a tightness in my chest. I sucked in a little extra air and hoped that whatever it was would quit pressing down on me. "Billy," I said, straining to keep my voice calm, "did you and Carmen have any children?"

"No. No, sir. We didn't have no kids. We was only together for a few months."

Cheryl was staring at me with crazy eyes. Reilly, his head bowed, continued to sob softly. He wasn't lying, I realized. He hadn't heard from Carmen. There was no reason for me to be there.

I looked down shamefully at the gun in my lap. At first, I struggled to think of a way to make a graceful exit, but then I began to wonder what would happen after I'd gone. I'd hurt Billy. I'd made him cry in front of his lady.

When he stopped crying, he was going to want to make her forget that she saw him weak. I thought of the bruise.

Once I'd gone, Cheryl would pay a price for my having been there.

I stood up suddenly, violently overturning the coffee table, dumping the pasta at the feet of the still seated couple. I grabbed Reilly by the collar and lurched him to his feet. I put the barrel of my gun to his head, wheeled around, and screamed at Cheryl.

"Get the hell out of here! Go get the cops! Run!"

Cheryl hesitated for a moment. A flash of fear joined the anger in her eyes. She turned and ran from the trailer out into the cold. I noticed that her feet were bare.

"Please don't kill me," Reilly entreated.

I let my grip slacken and he dropped to his knees, curled up, and buried his head beneath his arms. "Please don't kill me."

I wondered if the cops had followed me all the way to Lakeville. If they had, they'd be joining us at any moment. I had to go. "Be a good boy, Billy," I said. "Be a good boy, and I'll just be a memory. You don't want to see me again."

"Just don't hurt me," he sobbed.

"Nobody gets hurt. Remember that. Nobody gets hurt, or you'll get hurt. You gonna remember that, Reilly?"

He looked up at me. There was nothing but fear in his eyes. "I'll remember," he said.

I got out of there as fast as I could. I was the dumbest person I knew.

Chapter Seventeen

I checked the rear-view mirror several times on the way back to the office, but if the cops were still tailing me, I sure didn't spot them. Maybe Augie's given up on me, I thought.

I parked the car, entered through the back door, and feeling lazy, took the elevator up to my office. The door swung open, and I stared at the blinking message light on the answering machine. This time there was no message from Carmen, but there were two messages from Mulligan.

In the first, he'd eagerly asked me to get right back to him with our plans for the day. In the second, much later message, a mournful sounding Milkman hemmed and hawed through about two minutes of tape, apologizing for bothering me and making up excuses for the fact that I hadn't called him.

I was seriously unhappy with myself. I knew I'd really disappointed the big man, and for what? For all my efforts to track down Carmen, I'd accomplished exactly nothing. I sat looking out the window for about another hour or so, then locked up, and left for home. It was still bitterly cold, but there wasn't much wind so I decided to walk, hoping the stroll would help me unwind. And there was something soothing about the darkness and the contrast between the cold outside and the warm lights burning in the houses along the street.

When I reached the Bijou, I found a note taped to my door that read: "See me. Edgerton."

I unlocked my room and tossed my coat on the bed. I glanced up at my window and noted with pleasure the box of steaks still wedged between the windowpanes. I was hungry. I'd defrost a steak, I thought—two, if Edgerton hadn't eaten yet. We could nuke a couple of spuds and maybe open a can of asparagus.

I went next door and found Edgerton still snipping off metal rings for that chain mail coat of his. "You wanted to see me?" I asked.

"Huh?" he said looking up at me.

"Your note. It said you wanted to see me."

Edgerton nodded a couple of times and then returned his attention to his work. "You got mail," he said at last.

"It's Sunday. Last I heard they don't deliver mail on Sunday."

"Don't they deliver 'priority mail' on Sundays?"

"Was this 'priority mail?' "

"No."

"Then it's a little strange."

"It struck me as a bit strange as well," Edgerton said, finally putting aside his metal coil and searching his debris-covered bed for my mail. He handed me a five by nine padded mailer with neither postage nor a return address. In fact, the only writing on the thing was my name, hand-printed in block letters.

"It's not ticking," Edgerton said, handing it to me. "But I figured I'd let you open it just in case."

I smiled. "What are you doing with it, anyway? This some new duty you're taking on around here? You now the Bijou mailroom supervisor?"

"Nah. I found the thing just inside the door when I got home from work. Figured I'd better scoop it up before someone walked off with it." He paused. "Shit goes missing around here you know."

I shrugged and took the package from him. "Thanks," I muttered. "Have you eaten?"

"Yeah. Me, Don, and Jason from the armory hit the brunch buffet at La Cucaracha Sonriente. I ate till it hurt." He rubbed his belly. "Still does."

"I gotta get some food in me," I told him, turning to the door.

"Happy eating."

I got back to my room and tossed the mailer on my bed. Then I glanced over at the box of steaks in the window again. Too much trouble, I decided. A quick check of my cupboards confirmed my suspicion that there was nothing else edible in the place. I'd have to go to McCauley's. I was picking my coat up off the bed when I remembered the mailer.

Someone had sent me two DVDs. There was no identifying information on either one of them. No label, no title, no nothing. I put my coat back down on the bed and slid one of the discs into my DVD player.

The quality wasn't anything to brag about. It was grainy and in black and white. It was shot in a bedroom and the fixed camera was focused on a massive bed all puffy with pillows and a thick down comforter. There was a date stamp in the bottom left corner of the screen. The scene was shot nearly a month earlier.

Before long somebody entered the bedroom. It took me a couple of seconds to realize that it was Carmen. She was wearing a thick, white bathrobe. Her feet were bare. She sat on the corner of the bed staring at something out of the range of the camera. The something was Farnum. He walked into the shot buck-naked. He must be working out, I thought. Carmen stood as he approached her. Her robe fell open, then dropped to the floor. They moved onto the bed and made love. They made a lot of love—a lot of athletic, inventive love. It went on a long time. I had to fast forward through parts of it. And I had to hand it to Farnum. The guy had stamina.

When they finally finished, Farnum kissed her modestly on the cheek and left the room. Carmen pulled the comforter around her. Her features relaxed and she seemed to be thinking about something far away, something other than what she had just been doing with Farnum. It seemed that way to me, anyway. But I could've been wrong. Maybe she was just worn out.

I thought about the night we were together. I didn't think I'd left her worn out.

The other DVD was shot in the same room. The date in the corner was earlier, but only by a couple of months. Farnum was the same. And the lovemaking was roughly the same. A couple of the positions were different. But the woman wasn't Carmen. The woman was Lorraine Rovig.

Watching the DVDs started to get to me. I felt as though something were crawling on me—a lot of somethings, tickling me unpleasantly as they marched with tiny feet. This wasn't any of my business, I thought. I didn't want it to be my business.

I jumped at a sudden knock on the door. Edgerton stepped in. His face was all screwed up like something was bothering him. He drew a breath to make comment, but stopped himself, instead turning to stare silently at the TV screen. After a few seconds he declared, "If you're gonna waste time watching crap like this, at least pick something with better production values."

"This was in that package you picked up for me. It has something to do with the case I'm working. The old guy on the bed is Farnum."

Edgerton examined the TV screen minutely. "Bully for the old guy," he said. "Who sent you this? Farnum? He want to show you that he's still got it?"

"I don't think that the reason the disc was made was entirely voyeuristic," I said, switching off the DVD player. "Farnum's probably got security cameras all over his apartment. 'Course, he probably figures the recordings that come out of the bedroom are the ones most worth keeping. This thing is from a little while back and it's still kicking around. Usually, these things don't get saved unless the owner makes a point of doing so. But I don't think Farnum sent me this. He wouldn't have a reason. But whoever did send it would have to be someone close to Farnum. Someone with access to his collection. Angelino maybe?"

I hit the eject button and the DVD emerged from the machine. "I really don't know what message this is supposed to send me," I continued. "It's interesting enough. I didn't know that the murdered man's wife was getting it on with his employer. Gives her a motive. Him too, I guess."

"Doesn't Farnum already have a motive?" Edgerton asked.

"You can have more than one, Stephen."

Edgerton shuffled around the room and finally sat down on the metal folding chair at my small desk. "Looks like whoever it was sent you two discs," he said. "What was on the other one?"

"Same thing," I told him. "Different woman. It was Carmen on the other disc."

"Carmen that woman you're kinda sweet on?"

"Yeah."

"Ouch."

"Yeah."

"You think that's why this person sent you the disc? Maybe make you feel bad enough to drop the case?"

"Maybe. It's hard to say why anybody does anything."

"Ah!" Edgerton sighed. "The machinations of the criminal mind."

I went to my desk, picked up a marking pen and labeled the discs "Carmen Reilly" and "Lorraine Rovig" respectively. "By the way," I asked Edgerton, "you in here for any special reason?"

"Uh, yeah," he said. "I wanted to know if you wanted to go grab a beer."

Something in his tone didn't sound quite right. I figured he had some kind of agenda. "Beer would be good," I said. "Dinner would be better."

"You eat, I'll drink," he said.

We were almost out the door when my cell phone rang. I knew Carmen didn't have my cell phone number but that didn't stop me from sighing loudly when I realized that it was Mulligan and not her. Loud enough that Mulligan asked if I was all right.

"I'm fine, Milkman," I told him. "I thought it might be someone else."

"If you're expecting a call, I could call you back later. Or you could call me back. Either way. I don't want to keep you from nothing. I just—"

"It's fine, Irv. What did you want to tell me?"

"Uh. Oh. Nothing, I guess. I mean. You know. I didn't want to *tell* you anything. It's just that I didn't hear nothing from you today and I thought…well, I thought we'd be investigating and everything."

"Sorry, Milkman," I said. "I had to run down some leads regarding that girlfriend of Farnum's I told you I was looking for."

"The one in trouble?"

"Yeah."

"You find her?"

"No."

"Sorry."

"Thanks."

"Well," the big man went on, "I got to work at Gateway House tomorrow, then tomorrow night I got the Holiday Lights parade. By the way, they got an opening for Tuesday night. They might let me be a character. You know, in a costume and everything. You ever think about doing something like that? You should see the kids' faces when they see those nursery rhyme characters coming down the street all lit up and sparkling in the darkness. You should give it some thought."

"It would be a dream come true, Milkman," I deadpanned. "Sounds like you're all booked for tomorrow. I guess I'll just have to go solo."

"You sure I can't help out? I really worry about Mrs. Rovig."

"I know, Milkman, but there's not much we can do until something breaks loose. Just keep an eye on things down at the center and let me know if you notice anything you think is significant."

"I damn sure can do that much," Mulligan assured me. "I wish I could do more."

"You're doing plenty. Just keep your eyes peeled and we'll touch base tomorrow after the parade."

"Roger." Mulligan said.

"Wilco!" I countered as I hung up the phone.

Edgerton joined me for the frigid trek over to McCauley's Pub. When we got there, I asked Skip, the bartender, for a pitcher of dark beer and a menu. We staked out a booth along the wall and Edgerton poured us a couple of beers and sat quietly while I studied the menu. When Skip came by, I ordered a bacon cheeseburger and fries. Extra fried onions. After Skip had returned to the bar, Edgerton folded his hands on the table and leaned in toward me. "So, you gonna tell me what's going on with you?" he asked.

I sipped at my beer. "You know what's going on with me. What more do you want to know?"

"Let's try this another way," Edgerton said, his voice taking on a disagreeable edge. "I finally got around to taking a look at today's paper. You should check out the Metro section. Seems some local PI killed somebody yesterday. Now, if I can only remember the guy's name."

"So that made the paper?" I asked.

"Uh huh."

"Ever wonder why those guys only cover bad news?" I asked, "If they'd wanted, they coulda found something a lot more uplifting. A story about the return of a lost kitten maybe. You know, *Christmas just wouldn't have been the same without our dear little Scruffy*. But no, they gotta take the easy way." I took another sip of beer. "If it bleeds, it leads."

"You could have been killed."

"Yeah, but I wasn't."

Edgerton drummed his fingers on the table. "You

sure you don't want to talk about it?"

I picked up my beer and spent a moment watching the bubbles rise from the bottom of the glass and then bob and pop on the surface. "Nope," I said.

"Okay."

Neither of us said anything for a minute or so. I broke first.

"I mean…You know…This whole thing's really gotten away from me. I don't even know who I'm working for anymore. I killed some guy. Okay, he was trying to carve me up, but still…And then there's Carmen. You know how long it's been since I've been in a relationship. So hey, I go ahead and pick the girlfriend of some porn king to get all weak at the knees over. It's pathetic."

"It's not always possible to control who you care about," Edgerton said.

"Maybe that's it, man. All of a sudden, I have no control over anything. I can't shake the feeling that somebody's playing me here. But damned if I can decide who it is."

Edgerton leaned back in the booth. "You know the score, Lyle. We're all playing each other, or trying to, all the time. The ability to influence others is what gives us the illusion that we can control our own destinies."

"I really don't need a lot of philosophical bullshit right now, Stephen."

"Whatever. Remember, you're trying to uncover a murderer by pawing through other people's lives. You're gonna turn up a lot of stuff that stinks pretty bad. Stuff that those people are going to try to keep covered up."

"You'd think I'd learn to just let things be."

"Where's the fun in that?"

"Ask Cheech, man."

"Who's Cheech?"

"That guy I killed."

"The guy was evil. Screw him."

"That's a real caring attitude you got there, man."

I watched the bubbles in my beer glass some more.

"You're going to have let go of this thing, Lyle," Edgerton said quietly. "You're going to have to let this thing with Cheech just slip away."

"That's a pretty big job, Stephen."

"You're a big man."

Chapter Eighteen

Carmen called me the next morning. I was sitting in my office drinking coffee and looking out the window at Walking Phil as he made his way up Fourteenth Avenue toward the Dinkytown business district. Walking Phil got his moniker from his habit of walking silently all day through the streets of Dinkytown, barely pausing, just walking—walking and smiling this sweet, almost beatific smile. Walking and tipping his battered brown felt hat to people as he passed them. Walking and going nowhere. But, I figured, at least he knew where he was going.

When the phone rang and I heard her voice, I was overwhelmed. It was like I'd been suffocating and could suddenly breathe again. It was a voice I could follow.

I'd wanted to sound nonchalant, but all I could do was repeat her name into the phone.

"You sound glad to hear from me," she said.

"That would be one way to put it. Where have you been?"

"Safe. Like you said, I had to get safe. I've been too afraid to do anything. I've just been sitting here too scared to move. I can't live like this. I can't—"

"Where are you?" I interrupted.

She gave me the name of a motel only a couple of miles away, over by the University Hospital. I said that I'd be there right away.

On the way over I reminded myself that Carmen hadn't been entirely truthful with me, that there were some really bad people interested in her whereabouts, and that any contact with her could prove to be very dangerous. I knew I had a blind spot when it came to her and warned myself that I'd have to be careful. But mostly I thought about her smile.

There was a coffee urn in the lobby of the motel and a tall stack of Styrofoam cups next to it. I took a moment to fill two cups before working my way down the hallway to the room number she'd given me. When I knocked and finally saw her framed in the doorway, I noticed that my hands were shaking, rings rippling the surface of the coffee. I set the cups down on a wobbly table in one corner of the room and took a seat in the brown plaid armchair that sat next to it. I gestured to the cup nearest her. Carmen flashed me a smile of thanks but didn't pick up the cup.

"I'm so glad you weren't hurt, Lyle," she said.

"Hurt?"

"In the shooting outside my apartment. I read about it in the newspaper. They said you and Michael were not hurt. Only the other man. He worked for Alexander too. I knew him slightly. He frightened me."

"Yeah?"

"So much about that place frightens me. I can't tell you how glad I am that I'm leaving that place. Those people. I'm so grateful for your help. I can't tell you—"

"Well, you're not out yet," I interrupted. "Things have happened since we last talked. Lots of things."

"That doesn't sound good," she said, lowering her eyes.

"It's not."

She looked back up at me with soft eyes, deep and trusting.

"Maybe we can make it okay," I said.

"Money's going to be a problem," she told me.

"Yeah?" I asked.

"I'm afraid so. I mean, I got out of my apartment with my purse, and I've closed out both my checking and my savings accounts. I was hoping it would be enough, but…You know, staying in a motel. Meals. I guess I never realized how little I have in the world."

"If you need more money, I can probably give it to you."

"Oh, no, Lyle," she said, sounding flustered. "I didn't mean…You've done so much for me already. I can't take your money." She let out a clipped chuckle. "It's funny though. Here you are offering me money and we've only known each other a few days. There aren't many people who would do that. People I've known my whole life wouldn't help me out like you have. Like Terry. My own brother. When I asked him, he came up with every excuse in the book."

She smiled and tossed her head back. Her thick, black hair tumbled around her shoulders. I found myself wondering what attracted me to her more, the brightness of her smile or the touch of sadness that never seemed to be completely absent from her dark eyes.

"When did you talk to Terry?"

"The morning after the shooting. Why do you ask?"

"Oh, it's probably not important," I assured her. "It's also not true."

A cloud passed over her pretty face. "What do you mean, it's not true?"

I stood and turned away from her to look out the

window. There was a tall lilac bush planted in the yard of the motel. A few shriveled, brown leaves still clung to the tips of the otherwise bare branches. I sipped at my coffee and turned back to face her. "It turns out that's not the only thing you've told me that isn't true," I said. "It's not like I'm making a list or anything, but some of these things seem kind of important."

"Are you saying that you think I've been lying?"

"Yes."

I sat back down in the armchair and sipped at the coffee. "You didn't speak to Terry after the shooting."

"How could you know that?"

"Because I spoke to him."

A hardness that I hadn't seen before appeared in her eyes. "You what?"

"I went to his place to see if he could tell me where you were. If he'd spoken to you, he would have told me."

"You don't know that for certain."

"Yes, Carmen, I do."

She walked over to the table and picked up the cup of coffee that I'd brought her. She carried it over toward the bed, cupping her hand around it, and looked down at the floral print bedspread. Then she turned and stared at me. I smiled.

"I talked to Billy Reilly, too. Drove all the way down to Lakeville. Tell me, why did you make up that story about having a daughter?"

"You saw Billy?" she asked. There was a tremor in her voice. "Why would you do something like that? Why are you checking up on me? What is it you think I've done?"

"I wasn't checking up on you. I was worried. I was trying to find you. And I've no idea what you've done."

Tears began to well up in her eyes. She turned her head from me, and the ensuing silence was broken only once by a muffled sob. When she turned back to face me, her cheeks were streaked with tears. "Do you think I killed Ted?" she asked, lowering her gaze.

I couldn't help myself. I chuckled. "No," I said, uncomfortably aware of the sloppy grin on my face. "Hell, no. I think you're in a tough spot. You've been there for a long time. I think you're trying to play all the angles, and there's nothing wrong with that. I'd do that. I don't think you've told me all you know about Rovig's death, but why should I expect you to? You haven't known me long enough to trust me. You're right to be looking out for yourself. It's just that…It's just gonna be harder to help you if I don't know what to believe."

She raised her head. Her eyes shimmered, ringed by an arc of brilliant, reflected light that formed an outline, a boundary that struggled to contain both the welling tears and a swarm of dancing fireflies that gleamed there. Something deep inside me gave way. At that moment, I wanted her so much, I thought I would explode.

She was still crying, but so quietly that her sobs were the sounds of butterfly wings. She'd lied to me. She'd taken advantage of me. Angelino had warned me that she was not what she seemed. She needed me.

I put my arms around her and pressed her face to my chest. I held her closely as a shiver of belonging passed through me. She raised her head and kissed me hungrily. Wisps of her tear-moistened hair clung to my cheek as she stepped away. She stood before me and closed her eyes. Lightly, gently, I unbuttoned her blouse.

Her hands replaced mine and I watched as she removed the rest of her clothing. I got undressed, clumsily, her eyes watching me. Naked, I fell to my knees before her and kissed her belly. She folded her arms around me. I disappeared into her warmth. She raised me and led me over to the bed and then stretched herself before me. I'd never known anything so beautiful, so completely wondrous in my life. I lay down on her, pressing against her, wanting us to become but a single person. She wrapped her arms and legs around me in an embrace so complete that it was as if we were giving life to one another, as if she had been created in that moment, by that embrace.

We lay in bed for a long time afterward. She curled up in my arms, making contented, purring noises. I stared at the ceiling and wondered how I'd got there. It seemed like such a long time had passed since I'd been in Rovig's house, since I'd been pushed into that death chair. I closed my eyes and felt the warmth of her small body next to mine. I drifted into sleep, waking nearly an hour later to Carmen stroking my hair.

"You fell asleep," she murmured.

I rubbed my eyes. "Haven't been sleeping much lately. Must be tired. Sorry."

"Don't apologize," she said, smiling a soft, maternal smile as she continued to stroke my hair.

I liked it when she stroked my hair. I liked it a lot. I would have liked for it to have gone on a long, long time. But we had to go. We had to get her safe.

A lawyer whom I occasionally work for owned a cabin about an hour and a half north of the city. We'd never been especially friendly, in fact, once after I failed to obtain some information that he'd hired me to get for him, he referred to me as one of the most "coprocephalic" people he knew. I was plenty miffed when, later, Edgerton explained to me what he'd meant by that. But there was the time that his wife left him, and the poor son of a bitch found himself so hard up for friends that he had to turn to me when he was hurting.

When his wife hit the road, he called me up in the middle of the night, more than a little drunk, and muttering something about a road trip. He hung up before I could really figure out what it was that he wanted, but a short time later he was standing at my door. I figured he'd end up a drunk-driving statistic if I didn't intervene, so I got dressed, and drove him in his car up to his cabin.

By nine o'clock in the morning we were both more than a little drunk, bare-chested, and singing what we believed to be sea chanties on his porch overlooking the lake. By noon he was crying on my shoulder, telling me that I was the best friend he'd ever had and if I ever needed anything, like a spare kidney or something, I had but to ask.

Of course, early the next morning, after we'd slept it off, he abruptly announced that he needed to get back home, and we drove back to the city sharing nothing but a sullen silence. He even dropped me at a freeway exit better than a mile from my house, saying that taking me all the way to my door would be just too far out of the way for him. Well, I hadn't had any need of that kidney he offered me, but I did need an out-of-the-way place to hide Carmen. His cabin more than fit the bill.

She went to the desk to check out while I stowed what few belongings she had with her in the back of my car. Before long, we were heading north up Interstate 35, watching the housing developments of the northern suburbs give way to the stubble of harvested corn stalks peeking out from under snow covered fields. When we reached the sleepy town of North Branch, we stopped at a small grocery store just off the freeway exit. Since I wasn't sure how long Carmen would be holed up in the cabin, I piled the grocery cart high with everything from flour, eggs, and sugar to a half-pound of beef jerky and a family-sized bag of shortbread cookies.

Then we drove a few miles out of town, turned off the main road, and finally turned into rutted, gravel driveway that was posted: "Private Drive." I glanced at my watch. It was midday.

The cabin was locked, but it didn't take me long to figure out where the lawyer had hidden a spare key. The term "cabin" didn't really apply to the lawyer's lakeshore digs. The place was on the small side, I suppose, but only if your family name is Windsor. I could have fit my room at the Bijou into the cabin's foyer and had enough room left over to kennel an elephant with a glandular problem. I carried the groceries into the kitchen. It didn't look to me like the kitchen was big enough to fix dinner for more than a couple hundred people at one time, but I might have been wrong. When I switched on the lights in there, the glare from all the stainless steel made it hard to make out the actual dimensions. To one side of the kitchen was the dining room and an enormous oak table that looked sturdy enough to park that elephant on, and both the kitchen and dining room overlooked a spacious, sunken living room. The architect probably called it a "great room." And it was pretty great, especially the magnificent, stone fireplace that took up nearly an entire wall.

Carmen followed me into the kitchen and stared wide-eyed at the place for several seconds. "This is wonderful, Lyle."

"It gets better."

I pointed up at the loft above us, and then took her hand and led her to the back of the house where the bedrooms were and where the owner had installed North Branch's largest and best-appointed bathroom. The shower stall was huge and sported two shower heads, one on each side, and the bathtub was a whirlpool big enough to sink a battleship in.

"No outhouses for us," I told her. "This place has its own indoor privy. Mighty scarce in these parts."

She laughed. "You make a girl's head swim."

As we were coming in, I'd spotted some split wood piled next to a shed adjacent to the cabin. We decided Carmen would put the groceries away and make us some lunch while I brought in some wood for a fire.

When I returned, Carmen was in the kitchen smiling over a pair of grilled cheese sandwiches she had in a cast iron skillet on the massive stovetop. I dumped the wood next to the fireplace. It took some doing, but I got a fire going using the wood I'd brought in, most of that day's newspaper, some kindling I'd found next to the fireplace, and finally a couple of long squirts of lighter fluid.

When I arose from the fire, the room was filled with the smell of fresh coffee and Carmen came in from the kitchen carrying a plate with a sandwich in each hand. I walked right up to her between her outstretched hands and kissed her.

"Now stop that," she scolded, "you'll make me drop the plates." Then, laughing, she kissed me back.

We sat down on the rug and ate our sandwiches in front of the fire. Carmen cleared the plates while I lounged, finishing my coffee and watching the flames dance among the embers. When she returned, Carmen snuggled in next to me. "This is very special to me, Lyle," she said.

"Pretty special to me too," I said, tugging her even closer.

"The only thing missing is a Christmas tree."

"Should I go out in the woods and get you one?

Carmen nuzzled her head into my neck. "Maybe later."

After a couple of minutes of quiet cuddling, Carmen said, "You know, it wouldn't be all bad spending Christmas in a place like this. Places like this are made for Christmas. You know what I mean?"

"I do."

"Do you usually spend Christmas with family?"

"Yeah. My mom and dad live in the south suburbs. Burnsville. I have a brother, but he and his family live in New York. They don't often make it back here for the holidays. But Mom likes me to be with them on Christmas day."

"I don't want to keep you from your family on Christmas."

"Well, we got a few days. Let's see what happens. Heck, maybe you'll join us."

Carmen smiled but said nothing.

I put another piece of wood on the fire, and we snuggled some more. Finally, Carmen, in a very quiet voice, said, "I'd always wanted a daughter, you know."

"Yeah?"

"Yeah. The little girl in the photo. You know, the one back at my place. The one with Billy and me. She was a neighborhood girl I used to baby-sit sometimes. I used to dream that she was mine. Billy's and mine.

That's probably why I told you that…you know, about Billy and me having a daughter. I just wanted it so much. A family. Someone of my very own. Someone who wouldn't exist without me. Someone all helpless and looking to me for all the answers. Do you know? Do you ever want that?"

I held her as close as I could. "Yeah," I told her. "I do, sometimes."

She turned to study my face. She looked like she wanted to say something, but she just smiled and put her head down on my shoulder. We held each other until it was time for me to go. I had to get back. I had to see about making her safe. About getting answers to all those questions.

It was all I could do to leave her.

Chapter Nineteen

It was dark when I got back to my office. Mulligan had left me two messages. He sounded quite apologetic about bothering me, but he thought he had something that might interest me. I knew the big man was working the Holiday Lights parade at seven o'clock. I figured he'd be downtown already, but I called him at home just to make sure. I'd figured wrong.

"Mulligan," he answered.

"Milkman. Glad I caught you. I just got back. I was up north. Whatcha got for me?"

"Oh jeez, Dahms. I was just going out the door. I don't really have time…But then, again, Mrs. Rovig looked kinda scared when he showed up today."

"When who showed up, Irv?"

"Ehlers," he said. "Tommy Ehlers."

"What? For class or something?"

"Ah, heck no," Mulligan growled. "He showed up to talk to Mrs. Rovig."

"What did they talk about?"

"I don't know. They went into her office. They had the door closed. I wouldn't have wanted to spy on them or nothing."

"Of course not. But did you get some idea as to the gist of their conversation?"

"I did get some kind of gist. Yes. The gist was that they were mad at each other."

"Any idea what they were mad about?"

"No, sorry."

"That's okay," I assured him. "Sounds like you're busy. We can talk more tomorrow."

"Yeah, I do got to go. You don't think that this Ehlers will…you know, do anything, do ya?"

"No, Milkman. I don't think Mrs. Rovig's in any immediate danger. It looks like she and Tommy Ehlers had some kind of arrangement, and it sounds like things aren't working out just the way they wanted."

"What do you mean *arrangement*?" Mulligan asked defensively.

"I don't know Milkman. But we gotta find out."

"Can I help?"

"Yeah. You keep doing what you're doing. You keep your eyes open. We need to pay attention to anything out of the ordinary. We don't know exactly what we're looking for, so we gotta be ready to use whatever comes along."

Mulligan was silent for a couple of seconds. "There was another thing," he said at last.

"What was that?"

"Mrs. Rovig met with another guy today. He coulda been anybody. She has a lot of meetings. This guy was dressed real nice. Real expensive. Coulda been corporate. Mrs. Rovig does a lot of fundraising, you know, to keep the Center open. She's always schmoozing with them corporate types."

"Yeah."

"Yeah. But there was something about this guy. Something, I don't know…something hard."

"Was he a big guy? Dark complexion? Looks like he works out?"

"Yeah," Mulligan said. "He was really cut. And he had these eyes. Washed out blue eyes that didn't say nothing. You know, like...I don't know, like he was already dead inside. You know who he is?"

"I think so."

"Who?"

I thought for a moment. "Have a nice parade, Irv."

"Jeez, the time," the big man exclaimed. "I gotta go. But who's the guy?"

"I'll check it out to make sure, Irv. Tell you what. I'll meet you at the Center tomorrow. I think I'd better talk to Mrs. Rovig again. I think she can clear some things up for us."

"Who's the guy, Dahms?" Mulligan asked again.

"I'll talk to you in the morning, Milkman," I said as I hung up the phone.

Things were getting kind of thick, I thought. That was either good or bad, I didn't know which. I decided that of the two guys that had visited Lorraine Rovig that day, I'd have better luck getting something out of Tommy Ehlers.

I called Francine Ehlers. She answered in that fragile, little old lady voice of hers, but there was a distinct note of agitation in it this time. "You know Tommy got arrested again?" she asked. "I mean, he's out now, but—"

"Yeah, we know," I interrupted. "But down here at Rabinowitz and Rabinowitz, we believe that the police have charged Tommy unfairly. We think that they're carrying out a vendetta against him. We believe that our interest in your son's well-being frightens them and they're trying to discredit him in our eyes. They want to close the Rovig case and sending an innocent man to jail doesn't seem to bother them. We can't let that happen. We'd really like to talk with him and get his take on what's being done to him. Would you happen to know where he is?"

Francine sighed. "Was it you that got Tommy out of jail so quick? I know them other boys are still in the lockup."

"One of the partners was involved in Tommy's release earlier today. Yes. But we would like to continue our discussions with your son. Unfortunately, he has not made himself as available as we would like."

"He took off on me too." Francine giggled. "He said that he had some stuff to take care of and he was out the door. He took off so fast he nearly closed the door on poor Bosco. Like to have snapped him in two. I've heard of where they were able to save pets that were all crippled up like that, but I sure don't have the money to pay no vet to straighten Bosco's spine if he gets caught in the door. He's always trying to run out. I thought about that invisible fencing stuff. You know, that way he'd get a shock if he tried to run out the door. But I don't know. Them things could give off some dangerous kind of waves or something. A friend of mine. She lived near the power company and somebody on her block got leukemia. I could have him call you if he comes back."

"Who?"

"Tommy, of course."

"Oh yeah. Uh. Have you got his cell phone number?"

"I should have thought of that myself. It's like that when you get older, isn't it? Not that I'm ready to get out the rocking chair just yet, mind you."

"The number," I prompted.

She gave me the number and I promised to stay in touch.

I figured I had nothing to lose, so I sent Ehlers a text with just my office number for a message and waited for the kid to call back. After about a half-hour, I texted him again. Nothing. So much for my crack investigatory techniques.

Having failed to contact young Mr. Ehlers, I thought I'd turn my prodigious professional talents toward the investigation of some dinner. I decided to walk over to McCauley's.

Outside, a slightly musty smell to the air hinted a change in the weather was coming. But it was still brutally cold. The wind tearing down Fourteenth Avenue was a fountain of pain. By the time I reached the pub, my eyelids had nearly frozen together.

Food was not actually prepared in McCauley's downstairs pub. Instead, it was prepared in the restaurant upstairs and this thought comforted me more than a little as I entered and found Skip wiping up a spill with a bar rag that looked filthy enough to have been snipped from the Shroud of Turin. He nodded at me as I grabbed a menu from the stack on the corner of the bar and positioned myself in a booth along the wall. Skip brought me over a beer, and I ordered a patty melt.

Since it was a weekday and was getting late, the place was pretty empty. A few regulars were at the end of the bar, munching popcorn in front of the TV. A couple tables were occupied, but the place was essentially dead. Even the jukebox was silent. But the beer was cold and felt good going down. I knocked it back and was signaling to Skip for another when Ehlers came in. He wore that Marlins starter jacket and he unzipped it loudly as he stepped to the bar and spoke briefly with Skip who shrugged and pointed to my booth.

Ehlers loped up to me and towered over the booth, probably trying to look imposing. He stared hard at me for some time while I just smiled. He kept on staring—long enough so that even he realized he was overplaying it. Finally, he said, "I heard you've been bothering my moms."

"You gonna sit, Tommy?" I asked, batting my eyelashes at him. " 'Cause if you're not gonna sit, you're gonna have to leave. They don't allow loitering in here. They gotta discourage the wrong element."

Ehlers tried the imposing stare again. I batted at him some more. Finally, he sat down in booth opposite me as Skip brought me another beer and my patty melt. Skip didn't say anything to Ehlers. He just walked back behind the bar and watched us, occasionally wiping at something with the bar rag of Turin.

"How'd ya find me?" I asked, picking up the sandwich.

"You ain't hard to find, Fats. All a guy's gotta do is look for any place where they have food." He snickered at his little joke.

I took a bite of the patty melt. "That's pretty funny, Tommy. You're a pretty funny guy. That's what everybody says. Like that girl we pulled you off the other day. She couldn't stop laughing about you."

"You're gonna pay for that," Ehlers snapped. "You and that big guy. You're both gonna pay for what went down there. You're gonna pay for what happened to Cheech."

"You keep telling yourself that, junior."

"I could kill you right now. Right here."

214

"Whatever, Tommy. But before you do, just one thing. Why'd you come here? I mean, if you were going to kill me you wouldn't have sat down. You'd have just got right to blasting. Am I right?"

"I came to give you a warning."

"Oh goody. I haven't been warned in days. What was the warning going to be? You're not going to warn me about the dangers of gluten in my diet, are you? Because I'll put up with a little bloating in exchange for loaf of warm sourdough."

"You shoulda stayed away from the Rovig matter," Ehlers said. "You were told."

"That's right. I was warned." I looked at him. "Now if only I could remember who it was that warned me."

"You remember," Ehlers said. "No one forgets Michael Angelino."

"Oh yeah," I replied, nodding my head. "But how is it you know?"

Puzzlement began to crowd Ehlers' features. Behind the increasingly troubled expression, I could see his mind racing. It didn't seem to be going anywhere but it was clearly in something of a hurry. I carefully placed both of my hands, palms down, flat on the table in front of me. And I smiled. I smiled at him, then I slapped him. I slapped him hard.

The slap jolted the young man to his feet. With one hand he fumbled for the gun in his belt while the other hand flailed about like a porpoise that has lost its equilibrium. By the time he got the gun out of his belt, I had mine trained on him. He stared at it with exquisite bewilderment.

"You gonna shoot him or should I?" a voice boomed from behind the bar.

Slowly, Ehlers turned his head toward the voice to find Skip standing there with both hands wrapped around an enormous .44, his eyes squinting narrowly as he drew a bead on him.

"Ah, hell, Skip," I said. "I'd better do it. You're gonna make too much of a mess with that thing."

Ehlers's hand went limp, and his gun fell from his fingertips.

I picked up the gun and chuckled. "Don't worry, son. We're just funnin' you. You go ahead and take a seat now. If we decide to shoot you, we'll take you out back first. Easier to hose things down out there."

Ehlers was shaking as he sat down. Skip watched as I resumed my seat across from Ehlers, then he put his gun back in its little cubby under the bar, picked up his rag, and went down to reassure the folks at the end of the bar that order had been restored.

I smiled at Ehlers again. The muscles on one side of his face twitched. I smiled even more broadly. "Now where were we?" I asked. "Oh, yeah. You were going to tell me how you knew who'd warned me off. Was it the same guy who told you where to find me tonight?"

Ehlers didn't say anything.

"It's all right, Tommy," I assured him. "You don't have to tell me anything. And I wouldn't worry about it. I'll explain everything to Angelino. You know, I'll tell him how hard you tried, but how you just couldn't quite manage this little errand he sent you on. I'm sure he'll understand. I'm sure he'll give you another chance. I hear he's quite a forgiving man."

Tommy's lower lip began to tremble.

"You know, it's not unmanly to cry," I told him.

"You gonna let me go, now?" he asked.

"Hell yes, Tommy. You can go whenever you want. It's not like I won't be seeing you again. Hey, I know! Next time you and Angelino drop by to see Mrs. Rovig, why don't you give me a call? We could all have lunch. I know a great dim sum place. You three can discuss that little business arrangement you have, and I can load up on pot stickers. What do you say?"

"But Angelino, he don't know about..." Ehlers, began, but stopped before he let himself tell me more.

"Angelino don't know about you and Mr. and Mrs. Rovig?" I asked. "You don't think so? Come on, Tommy. Just how simple-minded are you? You think Angelino took you on 'cause you're such an asset to the organization. He's just keeping you around 'til he finds out all you've been up to. Then, when he knows all he needs to know, he can wax your ass. If I were you, I'd get me some life insurance. There's this guy on TV. He says if you're over sixty-five or a veteran you can't be turned down. You've done your time, right? 'Course maybe jail time doesn't count the same as a stint in the military. Still, I'd call anyway. You wouldn't want to leave Mom and Bosco unprovided for."

"You really think—" Ehlers began.

"I really do," I interrupted. "It's a pity that's something you never learned to do."

Ehlers looked at me with horror. He shuddered, got up slowly, then, as though flames were licking at his heels, he raced out of the pub.

Chapter Twenty

I'd been guessing about Ehlers and Angelino. I didn't know Angelino had sent the kid, but I knew Ehlers wasn't bright enough to track me down without help. The trouble was I wasn't bright enough to figure out why Angelino would have sent the kid to me at all. He'd warned me once, and that was out of character. I couldn't imagine that he'd bother to warn me again. Angelino just didn't do business that way. But then, maybe he'd changed, I thought. I figured I'd better find out a little more.

I got up the next morning and decided to go over to Gateway House first thing. During the night the temperature had climbed and when I emerged from the Bijou, it was downright balmy out there. It had to be at least a couple of degrees above freezing, warm enough for a light fog to be hanging in the air. The thin layer of snow that covered the sidewalk was just this side of slushy and a trickle of water ran along the curb where I'd parked my car. I was almost euphoric.

Mulligan was in the front hall when I came in. He was talking to a tall, well-dressed, black man who I took to be a teacher. Mulligan was holding a pail filled with greenish granules. The well-dressed man said something about the girls' bathroom. Something about how someone had been sick. When Mulligan spotted me, he looked a little desperate. He wanted to talk to me, but he knew his job. He nodded at the well-dressed man, turned, and walked quickly away toward the mess in that bathroom.

I circled around the hallway until I arrived at Lorraine Rovig's classroom. I pushed open the door without first checking through the window and made an unfortunate intrusion into a class that was in session. Most of the students turned to face me when I barged in, but Mrs. Rovig was busy. She had her back to the door, bending over a desk, helping one of her students—a young Native American woman with sunken cheeks and what looked like scar tissue around her eyes. After a couple of seconds of talk, the student smiled and nodded excitedly. Only then did Lorraine Rovig turn around to face me.

Her eyes were so impassive and cold they could have been fashioned from jade. "You're disturbing my class," she said evenly. "Please wait in the hall until we're finished."

Now everyone was staring at me. I didn't say anything. I just blushed and slunk back into the hall.

The class broke up about ten minutes later and as they filed out of the room, each of the students glanced over at me with knowing disdain, as if gloating. They could leave, but I had to stay after to account for my behavior. When the last of them had gone, I went back in to see Mrs. Rovig.

"I can't have anyone disturbing my classes."

"I'm sorry," I said. "I know you've had too many visitors lately. It must make it difficult for you to concentrate on your pupils."

"I'm afraid I don't know what you mean."

"I mean yesterday. You had both Tommy Ehlers and

Michael Angelino stop by. It must be hard to focus on your students with shit like that hanging over your head."

"Kindly watch your language."

"Sorry."

"Besides, I still don't know what you mean."

"Uh huh. Did you know that Farnum has a video camera in his bedroom?"

I thought I saw a ripple pass over her features. "You're blabbering, Mr. Dahms. Kindly leave my classroom."

"Tommy thinks he's working for Angelino now. He came to see me last night. He brought his gun. After I took it away from him, I explained to him that Angelino was just using him to find out about the plan. I don't know if he listened. It's just so hard to reach kids today, isn't it?"

"I believe I asked you to leave."

"Were you in on this thing with your husband from the beginning? I'm guessing not. I guessing it started off just Ehlers and Ted. Then you got involved somehow. That about right?"

"I have no idea what you are talking about. I have to prepare for another class. I am asking you for the last time to leave."

"Nope," I continued, "I figure if Angelino had been involved from the beginning you guys wouldn't have fucked up so badly. Oh, excuse me. My language again."

"You leave me no alternative but to call the police."

"Sounds good, Mrs. Rovig. You give them a call."

She didn't move. Her face was without a whisper of expression. I tried to imagine what was going through her mind. Her silence told me that my guess about her involvement was at least close to the truth. She didn't want the cops involved and certainly didn't want to tell me anything. Her ex-husband was dead and her partner, Ehlers, had betrayed her. She'd be looking for a way out.

"Who do you suppose would have sent me that DVD, Mrs. Rovig?" I pushed. "The one of you and Al Farnum in his bedroom. I'm guessing Angelino. But I can't for the life of me figure out why."

She continued to stare in silence.

"You could help me here," I told her. "I'm not one of the bad guys. If Angelino threatened you, maybe you could use some help."

Still nothing.

"Is it the money?" I asked.

Her mask slipped a bit, her eyes going cloudy for a moment. "What money?"

"This all started as a way to hurt Farnum, didn't it? You and Ted wanted to hurt him by skimming money from his operation, leaving him to explain it to his mob bosses. If the money was skimmed, you'll want to protect it, you being a widow and all. Is that why you won't go to the cops? Is that why you won't let me help you? Is it the money?"

She lowered her eyes. "I don't have the money."

"But can you get your hands on it?"

Her eyes snapped back to mine. "Will you please leave now?"

We stood staring at each other, my mind making lazy turns as I tried to think of a way to get her to open up to me, her mind firmly set on protecting her secrets. Then something flickered in her eyes. She glanced at the classroom door. I didn't turn around to see what it was. I wanted to watch her eyes.

"Irv," she said. "This man refuses to leave. Would

you please escort him out of the building?"

Then I turned to see the Milkman slowly moving through the doorway. "Lyle, maybe you'd better go."

I almost missed it. I almost didn't turn around in time, but a softness, a sadness appeared in Lorraine Rovig's eyes. He'd called me by my first name. It was almost chummy. Maybe he was in league with me. Maybe she was alone. The change in her eyes didn't last long. Almost immediately they iced over again. Isolation will do that to you, I thought.

"All right, Mrs. Rovig," I sighed. "I'll take off. But I got a bad feeling about this. I think something really bad is going to happen. I'm not just being melodramatic. The Milkman and I want to help you. You could let us do that."

"Good day, Mr. Dahms," she said.

Mulligan walked with me out to the parking lot. He didn't say anything until we were outside. "You really think Mrs. Rovig's in trouble?"

"I do, Irv. That big guy that came to see her yesterday? His name is Michael Angelino. He's a mob enforcer who used to work for Al Farnum. He's not someone you want to mess around with. Neither is Tommy Ehlers, for that matter. Although Angelino is the fucking Prince of Darkness and Ehlers is more like some malicious imp."

"I don't know this Angelino," Mulligan said, "but I know Ehlers. Ehlers is a chump."

"Agreed, but the bottom line is that Mrs. Rovig's been running with some pretty bad company. She'd been involved in an intimate relationship with Farnum. She either broke it off with him, or he dumped her for a new lady friend. I don't know which. In either case, I think she was very upset about the relationship. Her ex-husband was not happy with Farnum either. I have it on good authority that they'd been quarreling. And we know that Ted Rovig and Tommy Ehlers were involved in some kind of relationship. I think the three of them—Ted, Ehlers, and Lorraine Rovig—got together and cooked up a way to get to Farnum. Since Rovig was Farnum's accountant it probably had something to do with the books. Since Farnum is accountable to the mob for the money brought in by the porn operation, screwing with the books could get Farnum in very serious trouble with some very serious people.

"Trouble is that it's a dangerous game. The mob doesn't like to be messed with. You heard the experession, *'Don't mess with the messer'*? Ted Rovig sure got himself messed with, didn't he? If Lorraine Rovig was part of a scheme to hurt Farnum, she could be messed with too. Whatever started it, there's sure a whole bunch going on. So far, we got Ted Rovig dead, Farnum's cronies are deserting him en masse, and it looks like Angelino's using Ehlers and questioning Lorraine Rovig to root out details. Whatever happens next, my guess is it won't be good."

"You think she'll let us help her?" the big man asked.

"No, Irv. I don't think she will."

"We gonna help her anyway?"

"Oh, yeah."

"How do we do that?"

"I really don't know. I'm hoping we'll think of something."

Mulligan stared at me for some time, but I couldn't tell if he was thinking or just letting his mind drift. "We got the parade tonight," he said at last. "It's a commitment. Maybe we should cancel, but...I don't want to cancel if it won't do no good. It's a commitment."

"Go to your parade, Milkman. There isn't much else for you to do."

"We could follow her, wait outside her place. Like we did with them guys that raped them girls."

"We could. But I've done that many times and the truth is it doesn't usually lead to anything."

"Maybe if I talked to her. Maybe Mrs. Rovig would let me watch over her. Maybe I could sit up in her living room. Something."

"You could do that."

"You think she'll let me?"

"No."

Mulligan gave a helpless shrug. "What do you think we should do?"

"I'm heading over to talk to Farnum now," I told him. "Maybe he knows something. You stay here and keep an eye on things. Chances are that nothing's gonna happen today anyway. I'll hook up with you later and let you know anything I find out."

Mulligan thought that over. "Okay," he said, "we'll talk when you pick me up. Just make sure you're here around four-thirty. We gotta be downtown by five."

"Downtown for what?"

"For the parade."

"Milkman, I don't have time to watch the parade."

Mulligan shook his head. "I know that. You aren't gonna watch it, you're gonna be in it."

"You're losing me here."

Mulligan smiled like he was in on some joke. "Don't

you remember?" he asked. "We need someone for tonight. You were going to do it."

"This is the first I'm hearing of it, Irv."

"I had to have told you."

"Told me what?"

Mulligan's expression changed. He was still smiling, but now sheepishly. He shuffled his feet, looked at the ground, then back at me.

"Jeez, Lyle. I really thought I'd told you. I got this chance to be a character. You know, wear a costume. March in the parade. But they need another guy. I told them you'd do it."

"You what?"

"Come on, it's one evening and you won't believe how it makes you feel."

"Irv," I said, shaking my head in disbelief, "I'm investigating a murder. I don't have time to—"

"But you just said that nothing was probably gonna happen today anyway," Mulligan interrupted.

"Yes, but—"

"Look, Dahms," Mulligan broke in again, "I've been watching and the way you're working it is to just sorta wait for things to happen. You go places, shake things up, and then see what rattles loose. This parade thing, maybe it's one of them things that's supposed to happen."

There was something inordinately patient in his eyes, as though he was convinced that he need only wait for me to realize that he was right.

"Have you been like, discussing Zen with Edgerton or something?" I asked.

"Who's Zen?"

"Never mind."

"Pick me up at four-thirty. Okay?"

"I don't want to be in no parade."

"Nobody'll even know it's you. You'll be in a costume. All you gotta to do is walk. You put the costume on, and you walk. The whole thing only takes about forty-five minutes."

"No way," I said, shaking my head repeatedly. "This is nuts. Besides, if it only takes forty-five minutes, why am I picking you up at four-thirty?"

"We gotta show up early. Gotta get ready."

"Find somebody else."

"No time. Besides, they need a big guy."

"Why a big guy?"

"It's a big costume."

"What kind of costume is it?"

"Nursery rhyme character."

"Which nursery rhyme character?"

"Tweedledum."

"No way."

"I'm gonna be Tweedledee." Mulligan was now beaming with delight.

"I'm not doing it," I said, pulling a cigarette out of my pack and fumbling for a match.

"You'll do it," Mulligan said.

"Why the hell should I?" I asked, rather more loudly than I'd intended.

Across the parking lot two figures, unrecognizable beneath bulgy, down parkas turned to look at us, then hastened their steps toward a car parked a few rows away.

" 'Cause, it needs doing," Mulligan said. "We've got a commitment. It's for kids, Lyle."

"But it's not my commitment."

"Sure, it is. I told them you'd be there."

"But…" I started to protest, but as I did, the glee fell out of Mulligan's eyes.

"I went into that house with you, Lyle."

I kicked at a small clump of ice-encrusted, exhaust-darkened snow that lay at my feet. It broke into three smaller pieces that skittered across the parking lot, one taking a weird hop and pinging against the grill of an ancient pickup.

"Christ, Milkman," I whined. "I really don't feel like a parade right now, plus—"

"Good!" he exclaimed, breaking into grin so big and bright I had to squint to look at him. "For a minute there I didn't think you were gonna do it. You won't be sorry, man. You think it's dorky now, but just wait. You do that parade one time and you're gonna be hooked. Gives you a real rush. All them lights. Seeing them kids. It's like you get this joy just exploding in your chest. You ain't gonna believe it."

I managed a weak grin. "I don't believe it now."

Chapter Twenty-one

Mulligan went back to work, and I drove over to Farnum's apartment. The fog seemed even thicker down by the river and enough snow had melted that I got the tops of my tennis shoes wet while walking from the public parking lot to Al Farnum's very private apartment. I couldn't help but notice that things had got even more private since the last time I had been there. Farnum himself let me in. There didn't seem to be anyone else around to do it for him.

"Kinda lonely in here, Al," I noted, squishing across his white carpet in my slush-soaked shoes. "Is today the goon's day off?"

Farnum smiled his smile. "I'll admit that in the past I made a practice of surrounding myself with something of an entourage. I've recently come to view that as unnecessarily ostentatious. It's much better this way, don't you think?"

"So, they all quit on you, huh?"

Farnum chuckled. "Not all. Now, Lyle, I trust you have come to give me an update as to the status of your investigation. You know, I should be somewhat peeved about the infrequency with which you have kept me abreast of your activities. You are working for me you know."

"Haven't seen much in the way of wages lately."

"I believe it's customary to settle up the financial

end of things at the conclusion of your business," Farnum said, taking a seat in the center of the sofa.

"Customarily, yes," I agreed, sitting in the chair opposite him. "But there's a clause in my standard contract that allows me to demand early payment from those customers that I don't believe are going to live to the conclusion of my business."

"Come now, Lyle," Farnum said, tilting his head so that he could literally look down his nose at me. "Am I supposed to take that as a threat or just one of your little jokes?"

"Just a prediction, Al."

"Perhaps you could confine yourself to facts, Lyle. Now, have you made any progress? Are you any closer to helping us identify Ted's killer?"

"I've found out a few things."

"Would you like to share them with me?"

"My money, Al," I prompted.

"Excuse me."

"We were talking about my money, remember?"

He chuckled. "But you weren't serious."

"The hell I wasn't. I need to see some money."

"This is quite irregular, Lyle. I see no obligation on my part to pay you at this time. I—"

I abruptly stood and turned to the door. "See ya, Al."

"See here, Lyle. There's no need for this kind of melodrama."

I turned around and shrugged. "Dead men don't pay their bills, Al. I don't think you're going to be around very long, and I need to have the money in my hand before your family's trying to decide between the mahogany with the brass handles or a Hefty bag and a dumpster behind one of your strip joints."

He let me get all the way to the door. "I'll get my checkbook," he said quietly. He wasn't smiling anymore.

I turned around and grinned at him. "Did I ever tell you that I love having you for a client?"

Farnum was silent until after he'd written the check. He handed it to me and when we had resumed our seats, he allowed the smile to return to his face. "Have you made progress then?"

"Like I told you, I found out a few things. For example, someone with access to this place doesn't like you very much."

"Go on."

"Somebody dropped of a couple of DVDs at my place the other night. You were the star. Well, you had costars. One disc featured you and Lorraine Rovig. The other was you and Carmen. I must say you acquitted yourself very well. My hat's off to you."

Farnum's expression didn't change but he let his eyes wander in the direction of the bedroom. "I appreciate the complement, Lyle. It means a lot coming from someone like you. I know how you like to watch. Have you any idea who sent them to you? Or why?"

"I don't. I was hoping you could help me with that."

"I'm afraid that I'm at a loss."

"Oh, don't sweat it, I'm sure that whoever sent them will let us know somehow or another."

"I hope that's not all you have, Lyle. That's hardly my money's worth."

"I have another question, Al."

"I was hoping for answers, Lyle."

"Didn't you see it coming?"

"What do you mean?"

"The thing with the Rovigs. Didn't you see it coming?"

"The thing?"

"Yeah. You seduce the guy's wife, the same guy you entrust with your financial well-being. The guy who can do the most damage to you in terms of your relationship with your superiors at the…what should we call it, at the *corporate* level. The wife dumps him, then you dump the wife leaving the whole family angry and vindictive. But you, big-hearted guy that you are, you just leave the guy in charge. Didn't it occur to you that maybe that wasn't the smartest play in the world?"

Farnum didn't answer right away. Instead, he glanced around the room as if he were trying to remember where he'd set down his drink. "I thought I had the situation in hand," he said. "In retrospect, it appears that I may have mishandled it."

"I was thinking the same thing."

"The important thing," Farnum continued, "is that we learn from our mistakes. They can make us stronger."

"You and I both know that this mistake ain't gonna make you stronger. Look around, Al, it's all over. You put yourself in a vulnerable position and Rovig took advantage. Old Ted, his pal Ehlers, and his ex-wife came up with a scheme to make it look as if you'd been holding out on your bosses. They skimmed a bunch of money and left a paper trail with you the patsy at the end of it." I stared at him and lowered my voice dramatically. "And when you found out, you killed Rovig."

Farnum crooked his head. Then a corner of his mouth curled into a smirk. "Nice try, Lyle. Really, I've got to hand it to you. But there's a small problem with your scenario. I didn't kill Ted."

"I don't expect you to admit it, Al. It's enough that you know that I know."

The sound of Farnum's laughter could probably be heard in the next county. He doubled over, actually holding his sides. He raised his head to look at me but convulsed once more. He tried looking at me again, wiping tears from his eyes. It took some time, but he finally stopped laughing at me. "That right there, Lyle," he said, "that 'you know that I know' line, that's my money's worth right there."

"So, you're saying that you didn't kill Rovig?"

Farnum couldn't help himself. He collapsed into giggles again. When he was finally able to speak calmly, he said, "That's right, Lyle. I didn't kill Ted. I didn't even know that any money was missing until after Ted was dead, until after I hired you. So, you see, I had no motive to kill him. Not at the time of his death anyway."

I thought about that for a moment. "It doesn't make any difference," I said. "Even if you didn't kill Rovig, you're finished. You've been fired, Al. Your bosses don't trust you anymore. The only question is, are they gonna let you retire and hope you stay quiet or are they gonna quiet you themselves."

Farnum stood and walked around in back of the sofa. First, he went to the glass balcony doors and stopped to look out at the river and the tall buildings that lined the opposite bank. Then he turned and slowly surveyed the interior of the apartment, pausing to examine the gaudy Christmas tree that occupied so much of the room. He reached out and straightened a couple of strands of tinsel that were not hanging to his liking. Then he looked at me. His jaw was clenched. A vein was throbbing visibly in this neck.

"Where's Carmen?" he asked.

"Safe."

"You know this?"

"Yep. I stashed her away myself."

"She alone?"

"I don't think I'll tell you that, Al."

Farnum stared at me, nodding his head slightly. The vein in his neck stopped throbbing. "She's not safe," he said. "Nobody's safe."

"What's her part in all of this?" I asked.

"I love her," he said. "I've loved her from the instant I laid eyes on her. I thought she was with me. But now…Maybe not. Maybe I don't know what part she's playing."

"Well, you brought her into this. She was dancing for you at the Elite. You liked what you saw. You took what you wanted. It was easy. I'm sure you'd done it many times before. It was old hat. You telling me that she's different than the others?"

Farnum smiled, thin and knowing. "Did she tell you she worked at the Elite?"

"Yeah."

"I wonder why she told you that?"

I could feel my eyes crinkle into a puzzled squint, but Farnum didn't give me a chance to respond.

"She never worked for me, Dahms. Or in any of my businesses. We met at a party. She was there with some errand boy for the Zoning Commission. A young guy with great hair, plenty of ambition and not a fucking clue. I was there with my wife, but that didn't stop Carmen. Not the boyfriend, not my wife. Nothing much stops Carmen. She asked if we could meet sometime. I was agreeable. She said later that night. I was agreeable to that as well. Damn, that was a night! But that wasn't it. That's not it. Not all of it. I've put up with things from her that I'd never put up with before."

"You were jealous of her," I noted.

"Yes," Farnum chuckled. "I guess. I mean, I figured she had other guys. I figured that's why she insisted on keeping that apartment of hers. I'd never have allowed anything like that before. But with her...I just kept thinking I didn't want to lose her. You know? Mostly she was with me. That was good enough."

"But you had people watching her?"

"Did she tell you that?" Farnum asked with surprise. "That type of behavior is simply...It's not businesslike. As I said, I'm quite taken with her, but I would never let it go that far."

"She said you were jealous. She said you had her watched. That you were even jealous of her and Ted Rovig. She said she tried to leave you, but you wouldn't let her go."

Farnum sighed. "I was concerned that she might leave me. I've never been concerned that way before. I didn't like how it made me feel. I still don't. I'm aware of how boorish it sounds, but I'm not used to losing what I've come to think of as mine. And yet, I guess I've always known that she would never be mine. One of the things that most draws me to Carmen is that she is so much herself. So much her own person. She's strong. She's with me but not dependent on me. I'm not used to that. I like it."

"That's a load of crap, Al," I said. "The first time I came in here you got all macho when all I did was look at her. Or maybe you were afraid she was looking at me. You say you like her independence? Pull the other one."

Farnum smiled patiently. "All right," he admitted, confess, I don't like it all the time. Still, a man is drawn to a mystery. You like a mystery yourself, don't you, Dahms? And there's no mystery like a woman."

"Honesty's not bad either."

"Yes, but mystery is the spice. Honesty is better for you, but it's much too bland for a steady diet. You gotta mix in the spice, even if you risk a little…a little heartburn." He nodded to himself. "Still, you have to wonder. That's the trouble with mysteries. You have to separate what's true from what's false. And the stories we tell. The stories that Carmen's told. She told you she was a dancer?" He chuckled. "And she is. But, perhaps, mostly a choreographer. Maybe we're the ones dancing for her."

I got up and walked over to the Christmas tree to join Farnum. For a couple of minutes, we watched the twinkling lights reflect off the glass bulbs. I glanced down at the presents piled under the tree. Many had her name on them.

"But you think she's safe, yes?" Farnum asked.

"Safer than you are," I said, surprising myself with the concern in my voice.

Farnum nodded.

"You think you're gonna be okay?" I asked.

Farnum turned and smiled at me. There was that look in his eyes. I hated him for making me care. "I've been dealing with these guys for years, Lyle," he replied. "I can take care of myself. Just look after Carmen. That's what I'm paying you for."

I nodded, swallowed hard, and left him standing by the tree.

Chapter Twenty-two

After I left Farnum's I had some time to kill and since I was only a few blocks away and didn't know what else to do, I decided to drive into Nordeast and have lunch at Stan's Polka Lounge. I got there just as the place was opening and within minutes it was already starting to fill up.

Stan's is named for its founder, a former bad-guy pro-wrestler who became far more famous for his signature open-face garlic roast beef sandwich than he ever was for his ring exploits. And it is truly one of the finest sandwiches in Christendom—a full pound of thin-sliced roast beef, onions and pickled peppers dipped in a gritty, black sauce made from pan drippings and lots and lots of garlic. It is huge, fragrant, and imposing, much like Stan was himself. Big old Stan may be gone, but his big old sandwich remains, still served his way. We should all hope for such a legacy.

Fortified, and still without a clear idea as to what I should be doing, I drove back to the Bijou.

I went inside, plopped on my bed, and listened to an episode of the *Fibber McGee and Molly* show from Christmas 1947. It featured Marian Jordan's little kid character, Teeny, along with the Billy Mills Orchestra and the King's Men in a musical version of "The Night Before Christmas." It was relaxing and familiar and so wholesomely corny that for a half hour I almost forgot about murdered accountants, porn king Lotharios, and small-framed, dark-skinned girls with innocent eyes that begged for my protection. Almost.

When the episode ended, I got off the bed and spotted that box of steaks that I'd forgotten I'd stuck in the window. Unfortunately, all was not well; a small, red stain had appeared in one corner of the box. I opened the window and pulled it out to survey the damage. The change in the weather had not been kind. One side of each steak, the side that had faced the outside, was still partially frozen, but the other side, the side that had been facing the room, was completely thawed. Thawed and leaking beef blood. This was not good, I thought, poking at the steaks with a finger. I knew I couldn't eat them. Still, I couldn't just throw them away. This was a whole box of steaks, for God's sake. I just couldn't. Not right away, anyway. So, I took them up to the kitchen and set them on a plate in the bottom of the refrigerator. I'd throw them out later, I decided. It would give me time to grieve.

I passed the remainder of the afternoon leafing through my copy of William K. Everson's *Films of Laurel and Hardy*, napping, and only occasionally thinking about the Rovig murder. At about a quarter to four I grabbed my jacket and left to pick up the Milkman. I'd have bet my life that I'd never have had occasion to say it, but I had a parade to march in.

I really didn't feel like running into Lorraine Rovig, so I sat in my car in the parking lot with the engine running for about ten minutes waiting for Mulligan. When he came out of the building and spotted me, he smiled broadly and even broke into a little trot of excited delight.

"Damn, I'm psyched!" he exclaimed, climbing into the passenger's seat.

"Damn, I must be psychotic," I replied. "I gotta be losing touch with reality. You sure I have to be part of this thing?"

Mulligan clapped a meaty hand on my shoulder. "As they say in saga, 'Be of good heart, Lyle. And may your hands prosper!' "

"Maybe we'll get into an accident on the way over there," I said.

Mulligan chuckled.

The Holiday Lights parade on the Nicollet Mall in downtown Minneapolis was one of those truly inspired ideas. For decades, the downtown stores had lost business to the suburban shopping malls and the future looked pretty bleak. The problem was simple to diagnose, but awfully difficult to treat. Parking downtown is expensive and once you get out of your car, you have to choose between walking down freezing sidewalks or attempting to find your way through the maze of heated skyways that, like a spider web, link most, although not all, of the buildings together.

And then there are all those icky street people to consider. The downtown council tried to deal with the parking problem by offering discounts in the evenings and on weekends, but since parking in the suburbs is free all the time, the malls are spacious and heated, and street people aren't exactly a problem in tony Edina, it just didn't do the trick. Downtown needed something that the suburbs didn't have. It needed a draw. Then along came the Holiday Lights parade.

Somebody had the literally bright idea of having a holiday parade every night during the Christmas season.

Sponsors were lined up, volunteers were recruited, floats were built, and costumes were stitched together. And since the parade was to be held at night, the whole enterprise was splashed with light. The parade was a giant, brightly lit Christmas present to downtown retailers, a gaudy slot machine all primed and ready to pay off. And pay off it did. Hordes of shoppers descended on Minneapolis to line the eight-block parade route, then duck into the adjacent stores after it passed. The whole thing was a certified success.

The Milkman gave me directions and I managed to drive downtown without incident. We found a parking spot near the corner of Fourteenth Street and First Avenue, so we only had to walk about four blocks over to the start of the parade route. Excited, the Milkman started off at a pretty good pace, but I was in no hurry and my sauntering forced him to slow down considerably. Finally, he just strolled along side of me, his fists jammed into his pockets, a dreamy little smile on his face—the smile of someone who knows he is doing good.

I wasn't smiling.

At last, we reached a barricade at the Nicollet Mall, and Mulligan showed a pass to a couple of uniformed cops who were trying to keep the crowd out of the main parade staging area. I can't say if they were being successful. Despite their vigilance, there seemed to be one helluva lot of people milling around in front of the floats.

Mulligan led me through the crowd and finally pointed out a short, chubby fellow who he said was in charge. The guy was in his fifties and was wearing a grime-streaked, yellow, down coat and a woolen, Madbomber hat. He did not appear a leader that would inspire much confidence. Mulligan said his name was Frank and that he would give us instructions.

While we waited, I watched Frank, casually at first, then with increasing interest. As I watched, it became clear to me that despite appearances, he really was in charge. I learned later that Frank wasn't the director of the parade. That honor went to some corporate type on loan from some other locally based corporation that could use its involvement to illustrate its deep commitment to the community.

No, Frank was the foreman; he was the guy who got things done. Dumpy little Frank was in perpetual motion—a squat, pear-shaped ballet dancer, twirling and shouting instructions to ten people at once, fixing little bits of costume as characters came within reach, giving pats on the back to some and exaggerated stern looks to others, laughing and snarling and checking everything off a clipboard he held in a gloved hand. Slowly, methodically, yet with an easy, good-natured flair, he marshaled order from chaos.

Finally, he turned his attention to Mulligan and me. "Patty over there has your costumes ready for you boys. Irv, you're Tweedledee. This other guy is Tweedledum."

Frank glanced over at me and, after a moment, recognition blinked in his eyes. "You the guy that helped Irv here rescue them girls the other day?"

"I was there."

Frank beamed. "Well, all right. You got a name?"

"Dahms."

"All right, Dahms. Like I said, you're Dum, he's Dee."

"I ain't gonna do it if I have to be Dum," I said,

making an overblown pouty face.

Frank chuckled, but said, "Sorry, lad, but Dum it is. Somebody from the media called me earlier today and asked about you two. Specifically, they wanted to know which characters you were going to march as. I told 'em. That's that. Get on over to Patty so she can fix you up."

Frank turned around and was instantly immersed in tending to a few thousand parade details. There was nothing to do but head on over to Patty so she could *fix us up.*

She was a gray-haired woman in her early sixties with a soft, smooth voice so cloyingly sweet it seemed to seep out of her like molasses. First, she handed us each a bag and directed us into a tent where we began by putting on a pair of powder blue polar fleece sweat suits, complete with matching gloves. We returned to Patty and, cooing with delight, she led us over to our costumes. I'm pretty sure I gasped when I got my first look at them.

Both Mulligan and I are big guys, but the costumes we were supposed to be wearing dwarfed us. They each stood some eight feet tall and maybe four feet around. You didn't put these things on, you climbed into them. Each costume was basically two ovals, like eggs, one on top of the other, made of plasticized fabric stretched over a metal skeleton. The smaller egg on top was the head, complete with wide, unblinking eyes, a great dark blotch of a nose, and an eerily painted smile. The head was perched on top of the larger egg, which was painted with a bow tie, a short, schoolboy coat, and matching breeches. There were holes in the eggs where you put your arms and legs, and there were lights. Hundreds of colored lights sewn onto the fabric, outlining each piece of clothing, each painted eyelash. The costumes were huge, garish, and frightening.

"This one's yours," Patty told me, pointing to the one with the word "Dum" blinking in yellow lights across its backside.

"Thanks," I muttered, "I feel so special."

"It is a wonderful opportunity, isn't it," Patty oozed.

It took some doing and some assistance, but I managed to get into the thing. Inside the metal framework was a tangle of wires that led from the battery packs to all those light bulbs. There were holes that I could see through, but they were covered with gauze, turning world outside into a dreamy landscape filled with indistinct shapes and thousands of blinking, haloed, multicolored, pinpricks of light. I heard Patty say something about getting into line and I felt a thump on the back of the costume. I turned and saw the Tweedledee costume lumbering toward me making muffled noises as it approached.

"I'm gonna get you for this, Milkman," I shouted.

I don't think he heard me.

There was another thump on the back of my costume, and I took my first couple of steps forward. The costume was so top-heavy that I nearly went end-over-end with my first step, but somebody out there steadied me, and I tried again. The rigid framework of the costume extended nearly to my knees, so each step I took was a tiny, hobbled, wind-up toy robot scuffle. With every movement, my forehead banged painfully against a metal strut, a wire kept draping itself over my left ear like a hoop earring, and my breath inside the costume was heavy with the perfume of the garlic roast beef I'd had for lunch

I inched warily into line with several other

characters behind the large Mother Goose float which featured the host of a locally produced, afternoon talk show dressed in a padded, blue gingham dress, the hair of her gray wig pulled into a tight bun capped with a matching blue gingham bonnet. She smiled and waved while straddling a large plastic goose complete with moving wings and a steady and oh so annoying honk. Smiling, cherubic children surrounded Mother Goose, each dressed as a little gosling, clutching a basket filled with goodies to toss to the crowd thronging the parade route. And there were lights. Blinking lights, swirling lights, and steady lights. Search lights, pulsating lights, and lantern lights.

Music began to play somewhere ahead of us and the figures around me scooted into their respective places, awaiting the signal to move out. Suddenly a great fuzzy blare sounded quite close to me, reverberating inside the hollow of my costume like the furious yowl of some terrible techno-beast. It seemed to be coming from the Mother Goose float. I spotted Frank in his yellow coat, rushing aboard the float. Before long the din mellowed to become a sing-song little ditty about the good Mother and her timeless, yet mostly incomprehensible rhymes.

Then we got to march. By my second step I knew I was in big trouble. My shins banged against the bottom of the costume, while the top swayed back and forth like a buoy in a rough sea. Although I managed to hang on, I pictured myself falling—falling and then rolling down the street like a massive Tweedle steamroller, leaving flattened nursery rhyme characters in my path.

My breath became increasingly labored, and I could feel sweat beading on my brow. I tried to concentrate on each step that I took. I found that by taking only the tiniest of steps and holding my back ramrod straight, I could keep my balance. I dared not even look around me for fear that the slightest movement would send me over. Then I began to worry that I was moving too slowly. I decided to risk sneaking a glance to my left, hoping to see if I was keeping up with Mulligan. As I turned, I bobbled, but managed to stay on my feet. I didn't see Mulligan though. All I could see was the crowd lining the far side of the street, a great empty space separating me from the spectators. I felt quite alone.

By then I was really starting to heat up. Outside, although the mist lingered, it was becoming increasingly chilly. But inside the costume it was warm, moist and garlic scented. The beads of sweat became rivulets that trickled into my eyes. Soon the trickle became a torrent of perspiration that burned intensely, making it ever more difficult for me to see. My hands outside the costume flapped uselessly, unable to swipe at the sweat pouring from my brow. Unheard inside the costume, I roared with frustration.

I turned, again hoping to catch sight of my gigantic colleague. When I finally spotted him and watched him work the crowd, my frustration evaporated. Instead, I began to feel ashamed of myself. Mulligan was marching close to the edge of the street, near the crowd, saluting and waving and extending his hand to the people, mostly children, who lined the street. Little kids—some stepping gingerly toward him, others rushing past anxious looking parents—came forward to grasp the big man's hand. And the smiles on their faces were as bright as the lights burning on Tweedledee's backside.

There's something about a kid's smile, I thought. The kids on my side of the street weren't smiling. I was too busy being pissed off. It wasn't enough just to stay on my feet and move down the street. I had to make these people happy. Dammit, I had to be a better Tweedledum.

Vainly trying to blink away the sting in my eyes, I scuffled as quickly as I could over to the crowd on my side of the street. When I reached the first person—a boy about six years old wearing a fire engine red, one-piece, zip-up snowsuit—I zealously stuck out my hand. A little too zealously it turned out. I nearly toppled over onto the kid. His dad scooped him up and out of harm's way as I righted myself by flailing about with my arms and doing a dandy little Hitler jig.

As soon as I had steadied myself, I distinctly heard a small, squeaky voice yell, "Dumb Ass!"

I glanced back over at Mulligan and watched him working the crowd with considerably more grace. I took a step forward, waved weakly a couple of times, and tried the handshake again. A brave little girl all in pink ran toward me. I was wary but held my hand out for her to take. She bypassed the hand altogether and instead spread her little arms as wide as the whole world and hugged me so hard I was afraid she would crush the costume. It crinkled a bit but held together.

As she moved away, I reached out with a gloved hand and tousled her hair. She smiled up at me. She was missing a couple of teeth in front, but it was one of the most beautiful smiles I'd ever seen. I stuck my hand out again and a little boy took it. I didn't fall over. I tried again. Another beaming moppet grabbed ahold, and I was still on my feet. I blinked away at the sweat running into my eyes. I wanted to see them. I reveled in their smiles.

Infused with new confidence, I started to get fancy.

I would shake some hands and then open my arms wide and tip back and forth comically as if I was about to topple. I would then right myself and shake hands with a couple more kids. I even got to clap some adults on the back. Soon everyone was grinning at me.

I happily began to sneak glances at the costumes and techniques of my fellow marchers as we made our way down the mall under the canopy of shimmering Christmas lights that outlined the trees and skyways above the parade route. The Old Woman in the Shoe was behind me, as was Little Jack Horner eating his Christmas pie, and his cousin, the other Jack, the one condemned to jump that candlestick for all eternity. Before long, yet another Jack, this one holding hands with his paramour, Jill, came skipping by looking to fetch that pail of water. I found myself wondering where that Sprat fellow was, the one who could eat no fat. I also took to wondering why so many male nursery rhyme characters were named Jack.

But mostly I did my act, and when I could, I watched the Milkman do his. He was quite a bit lighter on his feet, but I was shaking just as many hands as he was, and besides, who would want to be stuck as Tweedledee when you could be Tweedledum. Dum's the good Tweedle, you know.

I looked down the street in front of me and watched the line of parade watchers ripple as I drew nearer, and kids prepared to dash up to shake my hand. It was a powerful, joyous feeling to have that kind of effect. I glanced at Mulligan's side of the street. Things were rippling over there too. But something odd caught my eye. There was a figure, too tall to be a kid, standing in the street a few feet away from Mulligan. His hands were in the pockets of his red, hooded starter jacket, and he stood stock still as if waiting for the Milkman to reach him. When Mulligan was some five feet away from him, the man pulled his right hand from his pocket and extended it toward Mulligan. The people standing close to the tall man began to fall back, the little ones tugged aside by their parents. Something glinted in the tall man's hand.

"Gun!" I shouted. My warning thundered futilely inside my costume. There was no way Mulligan could hear me.

The tall man was only a few feet away from Mulligan when I saw the muzzle flash and watched a larger stir go through the crowd. I tried to dart across the street but the strides I took were too big and I banged my shins hard against the metal framework of the costume.

The weight of the costume shifted abruptly, and I couldn't hold on. As I toppled over, I caught a glimpse of Mulligan, still on his feet, turning to face the gunman. The other characters in the parade began to break formation as they reacted to the gunfire, and someone knocked into me as I was going down. I landed on my side and someone else kicked me, rolling me over. The metal framework bent where it rammed into my forehead.

I lay on the cold asphalt wobbling desperately like a June bug that's been flipped onto its back. In time, I was able to roll onto my belly, and I pushed myself up to my knees. I tried to stand, but the weight of the costume overcame me, and I went down again. I tried again, this time managing to get to one knee. I pulled my right arm through the hole and into the costume to reach the little .22 that I had strapped to my leg in an ankle holster hidden under the sweatpants. My arm got tangled, and I ripped at the wires to free it. The right side of my costume went dark. I freed my arm and got my gloved hand on the gun. I carefully maneuvered the gun through the armhole and looked up to see if I had a shot at the gunman. No such luck. I was too far away and there were too many people racing past. Struggling to maintain my balance, I got to my feet and began to scuffle toward the spot where last I seen the Milkman. There was no sign of either he or the gunman.

Taking quick, teeny steps, I hobbled across the street. I got banged into again and was nearly knocked down. I recovered, then someone else ran into me. I scanned the crowd, then the street, then the gutter. I couldn't see much, nor very far from inside my costume. I was nonetheless encouraged to find no sign of the downed Milkman. Just the panicked crowd running blindly past.

I spotted the Tweedledee lights on the backside of Mulligan's costume from nearly a block away. He had left the parade route and was heading up Sixth Street toward Target Center. It took me a moment to realize what was happening. He hadn't been hurt. He was okay, and incredibly, he was chasing the bad guy. Chasing him in his giant, light-up, Tweedledee outfit.

I tried to run after him, cursing my slow progress. Then I cursed myself. I don't know why it hadn't occurred to me right away, but it finally dawned on me that I should get the hell out of that costume. I dropped to my knees and pulled both of my arms through the armholes. I jammed the gun into the waistband of my sweatpants and wriggled out of the bottom of the costume. Freed, I headed toward Sixth Street at a full run, hoping to catch up with Mulligan. It worried me that I could no longer see the lights of the Milkman's costume. When I reached the corner, I glanced quickly to my rear. The Tweedledum suit lay on the pavement where I'd left it, half the suit still merrily blinking away, the other half dark and lifeless—a Toy Land stroke victim.

I ran as fast as I could, grateful that I was able to wipe the sweat from my brow but alarmed that my breath was now coming in gasps. A pack of agitated pedestrians was moving down the street toward me—tight-faced and wide-eyed with fear. The crowd was running away, I realized. That meant that Mulligan and the gunman were ahead of me. I tried to pick up the pace but couldn't get my legs to pump any faster.

Another shot rang out. Less than a block ahead, I thought. My footfalls on the pavement thudded heavily and my entire body quaked with each stride. Ahead, where an alley spilled into the street, a man had plastered himself against an adjacent red brick wall and when he saw me, he started mouthing something and pointing up the dark alley. I barely glanced at him as I turned and plunged into the darkness. My shoes crunched on broken glass, then hit something slippery.

I tumbled forward, hit the ground, and slid a couple of feet across the rough pavement on my belly. My forward momentum ended abruptly when my skull crashed into a garbage dumpster. Stunned, I looked up and a fuzzy swarm of fireflies appeared at the far end of the alley. I closed my eyes. The fireflies were now inside my head. I opened my eyes and the blurry swirl of lights sharpened suddenly. It was Mulligan's costume. It cast a halo of light around him as he approached me.

"I lost him," Mulligan said.

I rolled over on my back and stared up at the smiling painted face of Tweedledee. There was a tear along the cheek of the costume that looked like a dueling scar. A bullet hole, I decided.

"Help me out of this thing, will ya?" Mulligan asked.

I sat up and sighed. A swirling red light appeared at the entrance to the alley, then the whole place lit up all bright and yellow. I was trying to get to my feet when an amplified voice blared, "Freeze! Nobody move!"

Chapter Twenty-three

It was pretty crowded in the holding cell, but even though there was plenty of room on the bench we'd staked out, none of the other guys would sit next to us. I think it was the powder blue sweat suits that got to them. A half dozen guys had grouped themselves on the other side of the cell, and they kept looking over at us, whispering to one another, and trying not to giggle.

Not that I minded being ostracized. I wanted to be left alone. Alone and wallowing in a pool of self-recrimination. I'd let myself get lost. Looking back, it all seemed so stupid. I decide that the only thing that matters is Carmen's welfare, so what do I do? I stash her in a cabin in the middle of the fucking boonies and go off playing dress-up with Irving "Captain Good Deeds" Mulligan. A goddamned, strategic masterstroke.

There was another fellow in the cell who, like us, was an outcast. He too had a bench to himself. He was a young guy, maybe twenty, with cool blue eyes and a lot of forehead. He wasn't balding; there was just this incredible space between his eyes and the shock of dark hair that perched atop his cranium. And since nature abhors a vacuum, his eyebrows had joined together in one bushy growth that appeared poised to make an ascent toward his hairline.

He glanced back and forth between the congenial group on one side of the cell and Mulligan and me on the other, flashing an anxious smile as if almost desperate to make new friends. It took him some time, but finally the kid got up the courage to speak. Unfortunately, he decided to speak to me.

He pointed at me with his chin a couple of times trying to get my attention. When I ignored him, he finally asked, "Whatcha get picked up for?"

I looked at Mulligan to see if he wanted to handle it. He didn't. He just sat there on the bench with faraway eyes and a languid little smile on his face.

I didn't answer, so the kid raised his voice a little. "Hey, you in the blue! Whatcha get picked up for?"

"Shooting up the Holiday Lights parade," I said, being sure not to make eye contact.

"Cool," the kid replied, nodding repeatedly. "What are those, like uniforms or something?"

I sighed heavily. "They're polar fleece, They hold in the warmth but allow moisture to escape. They're chic, yet very practical."

"Uh huh." He kept nodding. "Me? I'm in here for love."

I didn't say anything.

"Yep," he continued, "I'm in here for love, man. That's what they got on me. I ain't no criminal, I'm a lover. Maybe like…you could say…like…like a criminal lover."

The kid chortled. The other guys in the cell cracked up too, a couple literally shaking with laughter. The kid's face lit up with a great donkey smile. He didn't know they were laughing at him.

"Some guy didn't like me banging his daughter is all," he went on. "Like I was the only one or something." He laughed again and searched every face for approval.

"Man, I tell ya, though, she was sweet. Young and juicy and prime."

Something tickled at the base of my skull. Against my better judgement I asked, "How old?"

"How old am I?"

"No, the daughter."

The kid brayed some more. "I don't know. I don't ask 'em for ID or nothing."

"How old do you figure?"

"I don't know, maybe fourteen. Something like that."

Mulligan stirred a bit but didn't say anything.

"Tell you another thing, that bitch's old man better not be fucking me over with this bullshit very long. I got me a lot of ladies waiting on my ass."

"Probably that silver tongue of yours," I speculated.

"Yes sir," he continued. "While we going at it, she was calling my name so loud I was afraid the neighbors were gonna complain. When I got off her, she was begging me to stay. She couldn't get enough of me."

"That when daddy walked in?" asked one of our other cellmates, a tall guy about forty wearing a Kansas City Royals sweatshirt.

The kid smiled sheepishly and stepped to the middle of the cell. "Hell no, man. He'd been there all the time. He was downstairs having a few brewskies and watching a goddamned hockey game. Didn't bother him I was banging his little girl."

"Then what are you doing in here?"

The kid's expression suddenly changed. He was standing in this no man's land in the middle of the cell, Mulligan and me on his right and the other guys on his left. Once again, he was glancing back and forth, but this time his face was taut, his eyes filled with apprehension.

"The guy found out about a little problem I have is all," he said.

"What problem is that?" the Royals fan asked. "You try to make him, too?"

I almost didn't hear the kid over the laughter. "No," he said, "I got the HIV."

Nobody said anything for a moment or two. We all stared at the kid as he tried to mask his apprehension with a soft smile. Then Mulligan, whom I couldn't have sworn had even been listening, broke the silence. "I don't suppose you were wearing a condom?" he asked.

The kid took a deep breath, puffed up his chest, and raised his head arrogantly. "Shit, man," he drawled. "It ain't like I was gonna marry her."

There's this old blues song. I can't remember who wrote it, but it's called "Blood in My Eyes." That's what I had. All I could see was red. I don't even remember getting off the bench. I do remember slamming the kid into the cell wall. And I remember driving my fist hard into his belly and listening to his breath rush from him. Before I could hit him again, I was suddenly off balance. I had to step back to avoid falling.

Mulligan had his hand on my shoulder. He had a helluva grip. "Dahms, let me have this guy."

I turned to look into Mulligan's face. It took a moment before I could focus and even longer before I was capable of speech. I nodded at the big man and wordlessly returned to the bench.

Mulligan reached down and helped the kid to his feet. He wrapped an arm around him, and half led, half carried him over to the other empty bench. Mulligan sat down close to the kid, sheltering him like a great, gentle bear protecting a cub.

There was virtually no expression on Mulligan's face as he talked softly to him, and although I couldn't make out what Mulligan was saying, I had a clear view of the kid's expression. The kid said almost nothing. He gave a brief answer to something once, then sat in silence. It looked to me as if the kid was tuning Mulligan out. I thought I heard the words "Gateway House."

The kid was nodding mechanically, looking at his shoes. Then he looked up at Mulligan and his eyes grew wide. Mulligan's expression didn't change, and he didn't raise his voice, but whatever he was saying began to affect the kid. At one point Mulligan held up one of his massive hands then slowly clenched it into a fist. The fist shuddered slightly.

As he stared at Mulligan's fist, the kid's jaw quivered, and he brought his legs tightly together. He was still nodding, but now very slowly and deliberately. Mulligan stood and squeezed the kid's shoulder. I heard the kid say, "Yes, sir."

Before Mulligan was able to rejoin me, a uniformed officer appeared at the cell door. "Dahms! Mulligan!" he shouted. "They're ready for you."

The cop opened the cell door and led us out into the hall. Before we were out of sight, Mulligan turned back to the cell and said, "Bye, kid. Don't forget."

"I won't, sir."

The cop led us to the elevator and up to the fifth floor. He took us to the same interview room we'd been in two days before, but evidently they weren't quite ready for us because we had to wait outside the closed door for several minutes. I was only too happy to wait. I was still all balled up inside from my exchange with the kid in the cell and needed a chance to regain my equilibrium.

"What did you say to the kid?" I asked Mulligan.

The Milkman ran one of his big mitts through his hair and smiled almost shyly. "I told him he had to have more respect for himself, is all. I told him that if he had more respect for himself, he'd have more respect for others."

"He buy that?"

"Didn't seem to."

"What then?"

"Then I told him that you were a private investigator and had all kinds of friends on the force. I told him that you would ask one of those friends to keep an eye out and if he was picked up for something like that again, your friend would tell you, and then you would tell me."

"Yeah?"

"Yeah. And I would be deeply concerned."

"That's very touching."

"Touching's right," Mulligan said, grinning. "I told him that if I heard he'd endangered anyone else, I crush his nuts like a couple of grapes."

The door to the interview room finally swung open and we were ushered inside. Augie was in there, leaning against the wall and rolling that unlit cigarette between his fingers.

"Well, Dahms," Tarkof said, "what do you have to say for yourself this time?"

Launching into my best Lou Costello impression, I said, "I've been a baaad boy."

Tarkof ignored me, grunted, and pushed away from the wall. "Let's get this over with as quickly as possible. Dahms," he said. "Who was shooting out there?"

"I didn't get a good look at his face," I said, "but judging from what he was wearing, I'd say he was one of the crew from that rape house the other day."

"Was it Ehlers?"

"I wish I could tell you, Augie."

Tarkof eyed me strangely. "There were two of them, you know."

"Two?"

Tarkof smirked. "Yeah. According to witnesses there was a guy a couple of feet in front of you at the same time the other guy opened up on Mulligan. You saying you didn't even see him?"

I shook my head. "No, I didn't. I was busy taking off after the one shooting at the Milkman. Did my guy get any shots off?"

"No. According to people we talked to, the guy pulled out a piece, but ran scared when the other guy started shooting. You got lucky, Dahms. You both did."

I didn't respond.

"Mulligan," Tarkof asked, "did you get a look at either of these guys?"

"Yes, I did, Detective. Not the one over by Lyle, but the guy near me. Yeah."

"Was it Ehlers?"

"No."

"Did you recognize him?"

"No."

"But you could identify him if you saw him again?"

"I think so."

"Good. You stay. We'll set you up with some pictures."

Tarkof led us out of the interrogation room and down the hall toward his desk. On the way, he asked one of the nightshift cops to have Mulligan look at the mug shots. Then he announced that he was going home. The cop led Mulligan away and not knowing what else to do, I pulled up a chair next to Tarkof's desk.

Tarkof took his time leaving. He stood up, then picked up his phone, hesitated, then hung the phone back up. He opened a desk drawer, then closed it without so much as peeking inside. He straightened some papers that lay on the desk, then disturbed the pile as he reached for the unlit cigarette that he'd placed next to them.

Finally, he turned to gaze at me. "What the hell are you doing, Dahms?"

I tried to think of something clever to say, but nothing came to mind. "Just trying to work my way out of this, Augie."

Tarkof stared at me long and hard. "You're way out of your league here, Dahms. You need to go away. You don't, you're the one who's going to end up with a hole in the head."

"I appreciate the concern, but I think I'm okay here."

"What are you, just stupid? You think you got something going on that I don't know about? I'm telling you, you're fucking clueless here. You don't have the least fucking idea what you're dealing with."

"Thanks for the vote of confidence. Can I quote you in my brochure?"

"What is it, Dahms?" Tarkof asked, looking truly bewildered. "Is it the girl?"

"The girl?" I asked.

Tarkof's eyes brightened. "It's the fucking girl."

I smirked and shook my head. "I'd have to be a complete idiot to get messed up in this thing over a girl, Augie."

"It's the girl," he said. "And it's too late for you to worry about being an idiot. It's time for you to worry about being a corpse. They're going to kill you, Dahms. They're going to splatter your brains against some wall somewhere just like they did with Rovig."

"They. We're not talking tonight's shooter, are we? We're not talking about Ehlers and his bunch."

Tarkof raised his unlit cigarette to his nose and sniffed loudly. "Let's just say, you seem to be very popular lately."

"There are a lot of bad guys in this thing, aren't there? You know that Farnum's superiors have cut him loose?"

"Yeah."

"You figure he'll get to retire to the country? Live out his last days keeping bees or something?"

"I wouldn't sell him any life insurance if that's what you mean?" He paused. "You gonna tell me where she is?" he asked. "The girl, I mean."

I sighed.

"I didn't think so," Tarkof said.

"You know who I haven't seen lately," I said. "Angelino. Where is he? Do you guys know?"

"Truthfully, we've got no idea. And you know, I've got a feeling you're going to find out before we do. Trouble is, that might come with a price."

Tarkof stared at his cigarette again briefly. Shaking his head slowly, he tossed the cigarette into a metal wastebasket by the desk. It made a little pinging noise. Tarkof didn't even turn around to look at me as he left.

About a half hour later, a cop appeared leading Mulligan down the hallway toward me.

"Did you pick the guy out?" I asked him

"I think so," he said. "What now?"

"We leave."

On our way out, the desk sergeant handed me my gun, my cell phone, and the keys to my car. It was then that I realized that we had left our street clothes back where we got the costumes, and we were stuck making our way back to the car wearing the damned sweat suits. Maybe we'd look like we'd been jogging.

Outside, orange fingers of daylight were stretching across the sky. Unfortunately, the mercury had once again plunged. Stepping out into the frozen air, every fiber in my body contracted violently. Neither of us had an overcoat.

It was way too early in the morning to expect anyone with access to our clothes to be hanging around the parade staging area, but I insisted that we pass by there anyway. We kept right on passing as the sun rose gingerly and the orange of daybreak was overtaken by the cold, yellow morning. The fog that had enshrouded us the night before had flash frozen, glazing everything with hoarfrost. Beneath the new morn sun, our footsteps crunched on the sidewalk, car windows glittered with diamond dust, and each branch on each tree, each twig on each branch, was painted a radiant, pure white as if traced with a fine brush by the hand of God.

Only there wasn't any God. Or if there was, he was nothing more than a celestial prankster, and I was his favorite stooge. I thought about Ehlers and those girls on the floor in that house. I flashed on Cheech, laughing and spitting as he died at my hand. I thought of Angelino, out there somewhere. Was he laughing too? I thought of Carmen, in that cabin, waiting for me, counting on me. And the worst thing was that I had no idea at all what the hell I was going to do next. I was certain of only one thing. God hated me.

We reached my car, and I opened the doors, but Mulligan hesitated before getting in. "That kid in the cell?" he said. "And them guys in the house? I mean you had every right, but..." He put his head down and shuffled his feet. Looking up he said, "You got some kind of a temper. Don't ya?"

I nodded. "I'm sorry, man. I do sometimes let it get the better of me."

Mulligan sighed. "I had me the same problem. With me it was both my temper and the booze. In the ring, I was a fierce son of a bitch. At the bar too. After a while, I'd lost everything. Everything except the anger and the whiskey. All's I can say is that with everything else gone, they didn't seem much like prizes. Now, I try not to let them have me. You know?"

I knew. I looked into his innocent, compassionate eyes and felt a worm of shame wriggling inside me. "I know, Milkman," I told him. "I'll work on it."

I may have actually meant it.

Mulligan smiled and we got in the car. "What's our next move," he asked before we pulled into the street. "You gonna have to talk to Mrs. Rovig again? You need to get her to come clean?"

I shook my head. "She's not going to open up to me, Irv. Not unless I press real hard. Even then..." I let my voice trail off.

Mulligan stiffened, but there was nary a ripple in his tranquil, blue eyes.

"You know," I said, "nothing she can tell me is going to help. I know she was involved with Ehlers and her ex in some scheme to hurt Farnum. I don't know exactly how Angelino figured in the thing, but I'm not sure if that matters now. You go to Mrs. Rovig, Milkman. You go watch out for her. I'll try to approach this from some other angle."

"You're a good man, Lyle," Mulligan said. "I appreciate everything you are trying to do for Mrs. Rovig. And for me. We'll be okay. It's like Njal told his family when they were surrounded, 'Be of good heart, and speak no words of fear, for this is just a passing storm and it will be long before another like it comes.' "

"How did things turn out for them?"

"Well," Mulligan said, lowering his gaze, "maybe that's not the greatest example after all."

"Why? What happened?"

"They were burned alive."

I coughed up a little chuckle. "No, Irv, maybe that's not the greatest example."

Chapter Twenty-four

I dropped Mulligan off at his apartment, grabbed a breakfast sandwich, and drove home to the Bijou. When I opened the door, the distinct smell of fried meat filled the air. I glanced in the kitchen and spotted a greasy black iron frying pan atop the stove. There was no one around. I was unlocking my door when Edgerton came out into the hall.

"I thought I heard you come in," he said. Noting the powder blue sweat suit, he added, "Nice outfit." He paused. "You were out all night," he continued. "Does that mean that you got lucky?"

"Oh, hell, yes, Stephen," I told him. "I'm the luckiest man in the world."

Edgerton eyed me for a few seconds. "Not as lucky as Pete Jansrud," he said, grinning. "Jansrud was really holding court in the kitchen this morning. He claimed he found a box of steaks. He ate maybe three of them himself and then offered to fry one up for anybody in the place who wanted one."

"Did you have one?"

"*Found* steak?" Edgerton asked, screwing up his face with exaggerated incredulity. "Oh yeah, I trust *found* steak. The other thing I love is diarrhea. I was just saying as I rolled out of bed this morning, I don't spend enough time in the bathroom."

Edgerton smiled broadly, but the smile quickly

thinned to a fretful sliver. "So, are you going to tell me about your night?"

"No."

"Want to hear about mine?"

"Not really."

"I was up late," he said, ignoring me. "Working on the chain mail coat. I finally put it down and fell asleep when somebody comes knocking at the door. Guess who? Ah, don't bother. It was Farnum. Fucking two o'clock in the morning and we got a porn king banging at the door. I recognized him from the video, but barely. The guy was a wreck. Really shaky. He kept looking around like he was expecting something to fall on him. I told him you weren't here and he left."

"He say what he wanted?"

"No."

"Thanks, Stephen."

Without further explanation, I pushed past Edgerton and unlocked my room. I pulled my cell phone out of the pocket of my sweatpants and checked the list of incoming calls. Farnum had tried to reach me repeatedly while I'd been in police custody, but he hadn't bothered to leave a message. I closed the door to my room, sat on the bed, and stared at the phone.

A knock on the door startled me and I jumped up to answer it. When the door opened, Edgerton stood there with two cups of coffee. He handed one of them to me and sat down on my desk chair. I returned to the bed and stared at the phone some more. Edgerton said nothing.

It only took a couple of minutes before I started talking. Then I couldn't seem to shut up. I told him about how Carmen had called and how I had stashed her safe in the north woods. I told him about how Ehlers had come after me, and how Skip and I had scared him off. I told him about how Lorraine Rovig refused to talk, and what I guessed about her, her ex-husband, Ehlers, and Angelino. I even told him about chasing after a gunman in a giant, light-up nursery rhyme costume. Not many people could have listened to that story without so much as a guffaw, but Stephen Edgerton was made of stern stuff. Of course, I knew he'd remind me of the debacle later and for the rest of my life, but for the time being he was silent.

When I'd finished telling him about the lock-up, the kid I'd beat up, and Tarkof's suggestion that I should quit pursuing the case, Edgerton nodded, stroked the whiskers at the point of his chin and said, "You should listen to this Tarkof. I don't see how you can help here. You'll probably just get yourself hurt."

"If I pull out, who looks after Carmen?"

"The cops."

"Nah, the cops get suspicious when they're lied to. Carmen's got kind of a habit of lying when she gets in a jam. I don't think Augie would be very understanding.

"This Carmen," Edgerton asked, "she been lying to you?"

"Yes. I mean, well…Yes, but it's not like it sounds. Some awful things happened to her in the past. More awful things are happening now. She doesn't know who to trust, so she mixes the truth with what she thinks people want to hear. It's instinct for her. It's a matter of survival."

"Seems to me you've more than demonstrated your trustworthiness, Lyle. I mean, you been arrested several times, shot at twice, and threatened the gods only know how many times. And you're still protecting her. If she can't be honest with you, she'll never be honest with anyone."

"Maybe it doesn't matter, Stephen. Maybe the only thing that matters is that she has someone looking out for her. So, I've decided to believe her. At least until she decides to tell me nothing but the truth.

A scowl passed over Edgerton's face. "That's bullshit, Lyle,"

"What do you mean?"

"I mean you're not pressing this thing just because you want to look out for this Carmen."

"What are you getting at?"

"Well, you've told me a little about your relationship with Farnum."

"What of it?"

"You've always been afraid of his having something to hold over you. Right?"

"That's part of it, I guess," I admitted.

"I could be wrong," Edgerton continued, "but I think that relationships are largely a matter of conquest rather than compromise. By that I mean that most people pursue a relationship not just because they want to build something with someone, but also because they want to possess that someone. And in this situation, Lyle, you have the possibility of double prizes. It's possible that you're all wobbly kneed over this Carmen primarily because she is Farnum's girlfriend. Maybe you figure that by having his woman, you'll finally get over on him. So, you end up with the girl and the upper hand over Farnum. Those are some pretty big incentives."

"You know, you are completely insufferable."

"So, it's possible, huh?"

"What's possible?"

"That I'm right."

"Where do you get that?"

"You're not denying what I said, you're just insulting me. That's a pretty good indication that I've struck a nerve."

"You're the most misanthropic asshole I've ever known."

"See what I mean," Edgerton said.

Before I could reply, my phone rang. Edgerton was right. Farnum *was* shaky.

"Dahms, I've got to see you right away," he said, his voice quavering.

"Let me check my appointment calendar, Al."

"Dahms, please," he pleaded, "I really need to see you. This thing's getting out of hand."

"They coming after you?" I asked.

"I don't know. I think so."

"Tell me again why I should risk becoming collateral damage in a mob hit for you, Al."

"I paid you dammit! You work for me."

"Bye, Al," I said, continuing to hold the phone to my ear.

"Please, Lyle! Help me just this once. I gotta have time to think. I gotta hole up somewhere and figure a way out of this. You stashed Carmen. You can help me too."

"There's a difference, Al. The sad truth is that I don't much care if you live or die. In fact, you dying might work out pretty well for the rest of us."

"You can't mean that, Lyle."

"Ah, but I do, Al. If you're dead, the mob ain't gonna care if your girlfriend can implicate you in a murder, the cops will close the Rovig case, and I can stop wondering when I'm next going to run into Angelino.

Sounds like the best of all possible worlds."

"But…but," Farnum stammered.

"Maybe you'll get it like Rovig," I said. "Maybe you'll take one in the head and it won't hurt too much."

"Lyle, please, quit joking around. If it's money you need, I'll get it for you. Whatever you want. I-I-I just need some time to think this through."

I couldn't think of a single reason why I should lift a finger to help him. The truth was that I really would be better off with Farnum dead. Carmen would be too.

"How soon can you get to my office?" I asked him.

"Ten minutes."

"Get moving."

I hung up the phone and stared into Edgerton's disbelieving eyes. He started to say something but stopped himself. Instead, he stood and silently took the empty coffee cup from my hand. When he reached the door, without turning around, he said, "Be careful, Lyle."

I went to my sink and splashed some water on my face. I changed my clothes, replacing the powder blue sweats with jeans and a flannel shirt. I chose a long, woolen overcoat from my closet, slipped it on, and patted the .38 in my shoulder holster through the heavy fabric. I rolled up a pant leg and strapped on my ankle holster. I checked the load of my toy-sized .22 and slipped that into the holster. I dropped some spare ammunition into a pocket of the overcoat and paused to check myself in the mirror. I stared at myself for some time, noting the look of grim determination on my face, the purpose in my eyes. I was a well-armed fat man with places to go and people to see.

Driving over to my office, I vainly searched for any signs that Tarkof had someone tailing me. A small terrier with a red plaid handkerchief tied around his neck lazily sidled down the street in back of me. Other than the dog, I was alone.

I parked the car and started up the back stairs to my office. The stairway rang loudly with the sounds of an up-tempo jazz number and the rat-a-tat of tap shoes issuing forth from the cavernous dance studio on the first floor.

On a step very near the upper landing I spotted something tiny and dark. I bent down to get a better look. It was a drop. Liquid. Nearly black. Barely noticeable. I touched it and rubbed it between my thumb and forefinger. It was tacky and not quite black. Blood, I decided.

The door to my office was ajar, light streaming from within. Silently I pulled the .38 out from under my coat. So silently that I had to check to make certain that the gun was really in my hand before I entered the office.

Farnum was standing with his back to the door. He stood perfectly straight and still. I closed the door behind me with a soft, but reassuring click. Farnum didn't move. He was staring at something behind my desk.

Tommy Ehlers was sitting in my chair. He had goofy expression on his face—the look of an imbecile about to drool all over himself. His eyes were open, but he wasn't looking at anything. The back of his head had been blown off.

I stepped past Farnum toward the body. There was a little blood on the back of the chair and some more had dripped to the desk and on to the floor. But there was too little blood. Ehlers was upright, his arms resting on the desk. He'd been placed there like a mannequin in a store window. He hadn't been killed in my office. Someone had put him there. A shrill shriek of fear coursed through me, pushing aside everything except the message that had been left for me. The corpse was a warning. My time was up.

I turned to look at Farnum. He hadn't moved since I'd entered the room. I walked into his line of sight until his wide eyes stared directly at me. There was no recognition there, only a vast emptiness. "I didn't do it."

"I know," I told him. "We gotta get out of here."

Farnum came back to life. First his body twitched, then his eyes snapped into focus. As he looked at me, a grin slowly forced its way across his face—a macabre grin like the smile of dead man that comes by inches as his lips rot and fall away. "You'll help me, won't you?"

Farnum's grin ate at something inside of me. The grin was the evil twin of that damned paternal smile that he'd long used to shame and control me. His face was trying to follow the established pattern, but his fear was getting in the way. His white teeth gleamed; his lips were thin, cold, and colorless.

I hit him as hard as I could. I got the full force of my weight behind the blow. I hit him once, in the mouth, hoping to knock those shining teeth clean out of his skull. I laughed as he dropped to the floor, spitting out strings of salvia and blood.

He stayed down a long time. I hovered over him, wanting him to get up so I could hit him again. I broke into renewed laughter when he finally looked up at me. One of his front teeth was missing. His smile would not be the same again soon.

"You'll help me, now?" he asked.

"Yes," I said, "I'll help you now."

Chapter Twenty-five

I led Farnum out of the office and pushed him into the back seat of my Ford. I told him to stay down and to stay quiet. Once during the hour and a half drive north he asked if he could sit up. I told him if he did, I would shoot him myself.

He grunted a couple of times as we pulled off the paved road and onto the rutted, gravel drive that led to the cabin. He sighed when I parked the car and opened the back door to let him out. He rose weakly, then stretched dramatically to ease the stiffness that had settled in his joints. As he looked around, he crinkled his features, but didn't ask me where we were. I started for the cabin door without a word. Farnum followed meek as a lamb.

Carmen had been busy. The path along the outside of the cabin had been shoveled clear of snow and wisps of smoke arose from the chimney promising a cheery fire within. The door was locked, but I knocked once, announced myself, and Carmen opened it. She gasped when she saw Farnum on the porch next to me, but she said nothing.

I kicked the snow from my tennis shoes and motioned Farnum inside. His eyes lit up when he saw Carmen, but then he glanced at me and hurried into the living room silently.

Carmen pulled me aside and in a frightened whisper

asked, "What is he doing here?"

"I figured we needed to talk," I said.

Carmen followed me into the living room. Farnum had taken a seat in an easy chair near the fire and Carmen sat on a sofa directly across from him. A single, porcelain coffee cup and saucer, a matching sugar bowl, and a slightly tarnished silver spoon sat on a large, oak coffee table that formed a gulf between Carmen and her one-time lover. I took a chair from the dining area and placed it at the end of the room nearest the door so I could see both of their faces. I placed my gun in my lap as a reminder to Farnum that he was no longer in charge.

"Tommy Ehlers is dead," I said, staring into her unresponsive eyes. "Must have been Angelino that killed him. I heard he was using Ehlers to gain information. He must have found out whatever it was he wanted to know."

I waited for one of them to say something, but I was the only one who felt like talking. I turned to Farnum. "Ehlers had been working with Ted and Lorraine Rovig to make you look like a cheat to your handlers in the mob. I figure Ted concocted the scheme and shared the plan with his pal, Ehlers. He probably came up with it back when you were porking his wife. When you dumped her to take up with Carmen, he probably let Lorraine in on it. He hoped it would redeem him in her eyes. It probably didn't, but she wanted in anyway. By then she just wanted to hurt you, Al."

Farnum shifted in his chair and sneaked a glance at Carmen, but still said nothing.

"And it did hurt, didn't?" I continued. "I mean, I'm guessing there was a sizeable amount of money involved. Much more than you could pay back, much more than your board of directors could afford to forgive."

Farnum turned to Carmen again. "It hurt, yes," he said. "The loss of the money, the loss of my position. But there are hurts worse than these."

"Don't tell me your feelings are hurt, Al?" I said. "When you buy people's loyalty, you're going to have to expect some betrayal when the money runs out. Your goons, Angelino, even Carmen here…you didn't think they were with you because of all the goodness in your heart. It was the money, honey. The money and the power. Without those, you're just a broken-down old pornographer with a missing tooth and a teeny little life expectancy."

"You're enjoying this, aren't you?" Farnum asked me. "You're reveling in my loss."

"Jeez, Al. Does it show that much?"

"Never mind," he said, sadness seeping into his voice. "It doesn't matter."

"A couple of things still have me puzzled though," I said.

"You mean you don't have all the answers?" he asked, the sadness stiffening into sarcasm.

"Let's start with the timing. The timing of Rovig's death is troublesome. You told me yesterday that you hadn't discovered that any money was missing at the time of the murder."

"That's right."

"Well, if you and your hired hoodlums didn't know about it, why was Rovig killed?"

"Perhaps his partners turned on him. Perhaps this Ehlers—"

"No," I interrupted. "It couldn't have been Ehlers.

The cops checked that out."

"Lorraine then."

I pondered that for a moment. "With a shotgun? I can't buy that. Besides, I don't think she has the money. She wouldn't kill him before she had the money."

"How do you know she doesn't have the money?"

"She told me."

"You might want to make room for the possibility that people don't always tell the truth," Farnum said.

I stared at both Farnum and Carmen. The silence in the room grew weighty.

"Then there were the warnings," I said. "Angelino kept warning me off the case. He warned me that night your gunman, Trench, bought it outside Carmen's apartment. He sent Ehlers to warn me. The corpse in my office was another warning. Hell, it was probably Angelino that sent me the DVDs. I mean, who the hell else could it have been? And those discs were also some kind of warning."

"What discs are those, Lyle?" Carmen asked.

I sighed. I didn't want to hurt her. "Just some videos of Al here," I said. "Nothing to worry about."

Carmen eyed me suspiciously, then turned her gaze on Farnum. He squirmed but didn't offer any further explanation.

"My point is," I continued, "Michael Angelino is a pretty efficient guy. He wouldn't waste his time warning off some lowly P.I. When he could have made me go away whenever he wanted, why would he warn me?"

Carmen got up and walked over to me. She knelt on the floor at my feet, and gently placed her head against my knee. As she reached up to take my hand, I watched something behind Farnum's eyes begin to boil.

"Maybe we don't need to understand, Lyle," Carmen said softly. "Maybe it's not too late for us to just get away from all of this."

I looked down at her. Her eyes were wide and innocent. The eyes of a child that doesn't need to know just how the world works, only that some grownup will keep her safe.

"What was that he told me?" I wondered aloud. "He said, 'she's not what she seems.' He said that he'd told you that too, Al. He also said he'd told Rovig."

"Told me what?" Farnum asked angrily.

I didn't answer. Instead, I continued to stare into Carmen's eyes. Tears swelled like shivers in those deep, brown eyes. "It was you, wasn't it?" I asked.

"I don't understand, Lyle. What are you saying?"

"You played Ted Rovig. Didn't you?"

"I…I just don't understand."

"You played him. You seduced him. The same way you got to Farnum. The same way you got to me. He was another guy you thought might be able to help you, so you gave him some version of the sob story you gave me. You let him think you wanted to break it off with Al and let him think he could help you. What did he look like when he told you? I'll bet he looked proud. I'll bet he got all puffed up telling you how he was going to discredit Farnum, how he was going to get revenge, and how he was going to make your dreams come true. Was he willing to double-cross his partners? Did he tell them about how he was cutting you in for a share of the cash he'd skimmed from your boyfriend? Or was that a secret just the two of you shared? Another one of your little secrets."

Carmen rose slowly and stepped away from me. Her

tears came quickly now. She spread her arms, her palms upturned in supplication, in a piteous gesture of helplessness. Sobs nearly choked off her words. "You think I killed Ted Rovig? You honestly believe I'm capable of that?"

I shook my head. "No. You didn't kill him. But I think I know who did. And why."

Farnum picked that moment to play the white knight. He rose from his chair shaking with anger. "I've had enough of this!" he roared. "I've had enough of you. You've no right to treat us like this. We came to you for help. Instead, you insult us. You molest us. I will not stand for this any longer. I'll...I'll—"

Farnum didn't get a chance to tell me what he was going to do. I lunged at him, my gun in my hand. Farnum saw the gun and immediately his anger fled. He threw his arms up to shield his face. He peered out at me through his upraised arms, his eyes glimmering with terror. I drew back the gun as if to strike him with the barrel, but his eyes...His eyes were those of a cornered rat caught in the beam of a flashlight. I stopped a couple of feet before him, staring at those frightened, rodent eyes. Farnum slumped back into his chair. I hovered over him for a moment. Carmen's sobs filled the room, rolling over me like ocean swells lurching toward shore.

I was still pulsing with rage and had to do something to clear myself of it. I looked around briefly, and my eyes lighted on the coffee table. I kicked at it awkwardly, barely jostling the cup and saucer that were sitting there. Unsatisfied, I snatched up the cup and stared at it, so small, so delicate in my hand. So breakable. I flung it across the room. It crashed against the fireplace. A few pieces skittered across the wood floor. That's when I heard it. It came from behind me. It was low and even and calm. It was a voice.

"Temper, temper, Mr. Dahms."

I whirled around to find Michael Angelino leaning against the wall near the hallway. There was shiny, blue gun in his hand. "Don't do anything foolish," he said. "Just place your weapon on the table and walk away."

I did as he said. Numb, I took a couple of steps back. Carmen continued to sob, standing in the middle of the room, near the coffee table, unable to look up. Farnum stayed in his chair, staring at his former employee, the fear in his eyes slowly changing over to calm acceptance. Angelino glanced at both Carmen and Farnum, then he trained his eyes on me. His cold, lifeless eyes.

It took me a while, but finally I found my voice. "She's been with you all along?"

"As much as she's been with anybody," he said.

I nodded. "Why did she drag me into this?"

"Insurance, I suppose. Carmen likes options. Lots of options. Farnum was one option. Rovig was another. I was a third. You? Well, perhaps not a particularly viable option, but desperation will make even someone as calculating as our Carmen grasp at remote possibilities."

"Why did you try to warn me off? Why not just kill me like you did Rovig?"

"I had to kill Rovig. It was business. Carmen had informed me of the way he had betrayed his trust. There was no other way. It was unfortunate, but he'd made his choice. With you, it was different. You never really had a choice. You were just a patsy."

"You could have warned Rovig. Your bosses hadn't discovered the missing money. He could have put it back. No one had ordered a hit."

Angelino paused for a moment. "Perhaps I did act somewhat rashly. Perhaps that is why I tried so hard with you. Perhaps I saw it as an opportunity to make up for the harshness I showed to Rovig."

"So, killing Rovig wasn't all business. You killed him on your own. You just couldn't help yourself."

Angelino shrugged slightly. "I was disappointed to learn of his relationship with Carmen. It would be accurate to say that his death was partly revenge, and partly a warning to Carmen not to betray me in the future."

"But your warning didn't take," I said, unable to keep a hint of smugness from my voice.

Angelino smiled thinly. "It will evidently take further warnings."

I could feel my lower lip trembling as Angelino stepped forward. He circled around in back of the chair in which Farnum was sitting, his eyes locked on mine. The echo of the shot nearly drowned out Carmen's scream. I shuddered, closed my eyes, and opened them to find Farnum crumbled forward in the chair. Angelino had shot him in the back of the head.

Carmen fell silent after a single scream. Angelino calmly walked over to her. He placed one hand on her shoulder, careful to keep me covered with the gun that he held in the other. His touch sent a shiver through Carmen's body. They were both looking at me, but the moment belonged to them.

"Now, that was business," Angelino told her. "Farnum's retirement was ordered. Dahms here will serve as a warning. I do hope he is the last person I need kill because of you."

Angelino released Carmen and started toward me. I

backed up, trying to decide if my best play would be to make for the door behind me or to try to rush Angelino. A third option occurred to me. I could just kneel down and let him cap me. It didn't matter, I thought. I knew that I was about to breathe my last.

For the moment, time stood still. But not quite still. I thought I could see Angelino's finger tightening on the trigger. I shouted and dropped to the ground. I fumbled momentarily at my ankle holster, but instantly decided that I wouldn't have time to pull the .22. Instead, I rolled toward Angelino, hoping to grab on to him and pull him off his feet. It didn't work. When I came out of the roll, Angelino was outside my grasp and I was on my back, flailing at him with both my arms and my legs. I must have looked like a beached whale desperate for the sea.

"Would you like to stand up and try that again?" Angelino asked.

I shook my head and rolled over on my belly. I was nearly to my feet when I heard the shot.

I stood. There was a puzzled expression on Angelino's face. He still held the gun, but no longer steadily. It bobbed up and down in his hand. He looked first at me, then at his chest. There was a hole in it, a small red circle on his shirt that widened rapidly as his blood burbled from him like water from an underground spring. Behind him stood Carmen, both of her hands clasping the gun I had laid on the table. Angelino tumbled to the ground.

Carmen lowered the gun. Her eyes were two dead things. "I'd like to go home now."

Chapter Twenty-six

She didn't get to go home. First, we had to wait while the local police walked around the cabin, scratching their heads and writing things in little notebooks. They made us sit opposite each other, briefly took our statements, and then warned us not to say anything else until we got to the station.

One of the cops, a skinny blond kid who looked like he'd just graduated from junior high school, kept eyeing me and fingering the revolver on his hip. He must have figured that at any moment I would make a break for the door, and he would have to cut me down in a barrage of hot lead. I hated to disappoint him, but even if I'd wanted to, I was in no shape to attempt an escape. I was too tired. So tired that my eyelids were like manhole covers that I had to struggle to keep from clanging shut.

The cops seemed a whole lot less concerned that Carmen would try to flee the scene. One after another, they approached her, made concerned noises, and nodded their heads sympathetically. One of them even went to get an afghan for her and later asked if he could fix her a cup of coffee.

Finally, they put us in the back of separate patrol cars and drove us to a small, cinder block building in the center of town that served as both the police station and the volunteer fire department. We were led to separate interview rooms for our formal statements. I told them everything I knew in the first ten minutes but got to spend the next hour and a half going over every detail.

Finally, I was led out of the room. Carmen was sitting just inside the door of an office marked "Chief of Police." I didn't get to sit in anybody's office. Instead, I was led down a long, narrow hallway to an empty jail cell. There my sitting options were limited to a squeaky cot and a toilet that was nearly black with mildew. I lay down on the cot and let fatigue overtake me.

I awoke with a start. I didn't know how long I'd been sleeping, but it hadn't been long enough. The skinny, blond cop screeched open the jail cell, drew his baton, and told me to get up. It wasn't easy. My muscles rebelled against the order to move, sloshing around inside me like Jell-O in a plastic bag. Incredibly, I made it down the hall and to a small conference room. Inside, I collapsed into a chair and had to prop my head up with my hands to look around.

A tall, older man in a cop's uniform was standing with his back to the wall. Next to him was a man with a sallow complexion in a dark gray suit and a thin blue tie. Sitting at the head of a long, rectangular table was Augie Tarkof.

Tarkof cleared his throat, glanced over at the other two men, then cast his gaze on me. "It's been a long day, Dahms," he said, "so I would appreciate it if you would spare us your usual wisecracks."

"I'm fresh out, Augie."

"Good. The Chief and I have agreed that there is no reason to hold you any longer, provided, of course, that you assure us of your cooperation. Your presence may be required in the event of an inquest, but that will be decided later. Your weapon, the one used to kill

Angelino, will remain here as evidence until such time as it may be returned to you.

I nodded.

"I want you to understand that it is only because of the generosity of the Chief here that you are being allowed to leave at all."

"I'll add him to my Christmas list."

"Shut up, Dahms."

"Who's the pasty guy in the suit, Augie?"

"That's special agent Flanagan. FBI."

"Uh huh."

"Now for the important stuff," Augie said. "You are not to speak of this incident to anyone except the proper authorities. Since this incident is peripheral to an ongoing federal investigation into organized crime, the federal authorities have jurisdiction in this matter. They will, no doubt, be contacting you shortly. I can only repeat that it would be extremely unwise for you to speak of this matter to anyone not directly involved with the handling of the case."

"What's going on, Augie?"

"What do you mean?"

"You know damn well what I mean."

Augie glanced at Flanagan, then looked at me and shrugged. "I told you that this was bigger than you."

"How much bigger?"

"All I can tell you is that federal authorities have been developing a case against Farnum and his business partners for some time. Although Farnum's operation is now shut down, his partners remain an active target for investigation. A witness has come forward that they believe will help bring those partners to justice. Our goal now is to protect that witness."

"Carmen," I said.

Augie nodded.

"She can be pretty persuasive when she wants something," I said. "I'm sure she'll tell them quite the tale in exchange for their protection."

"As long as it helps them get an indictment..." Augie said, letting his words trail off.

"Did she say anything about the money?"

"Farnum's money? The money Rovig skimmed?"

"Yeah."

Augie glanced over at Agent Flanagan who shook his head slowly and very firmly. "She said she could get it for them," Augie answered.

I chuckled mirthlessly. "It's no surprise that the money made it into her hands. But there's no way she's gonna cough it all up."

"They don't care, Dahms. They just want the indictment. Everything else is just details."

"Everybody wins," I said.

Flanagan stepped forward. "This interview is over, Detective," he declared. Glaring at Tarkof, he added, "We've no need for further information from this witness."

Tarkof smirked but said nothing.

I stood and was nearly to the door when Flanagan cleared his voice loudly. When I turned to face him, he tilted his head so he could look down his nose at me. He sniffed dramatically a couple of times and his face took on an unpleasant expression that seemed to indicate that my deodorant wasn't all that it should be.

"Be sure you speak of this to no one," he said.

"Augie here mentioned that," I said. "A couple of times."

"Specifically, then, make no attempt to contact our witness. Do I make myself clear?"

I shook my head. "The last person I want to see is Carmen," I said as I left the room.

My car had been moved to the police station and it was only a couple of miles to the interstate. But I was a long way from home, it was dark, and I was very tired. I played with the radio dial until I was able to pick up the faint signal of a Twin Cities oldies station that I could listen to all the way back to the Bijou.

After a commercial that declared that what she really wanted for Christmas was a diamond pendant from Pedrotty Jewelers—three convenient locations—the DJ played Chuck Berry's "Run Rudolph Run." I cranked up the volume to help keep me awake and watched my headlights sweep the trees that lined the road as I wound my way toward the freeway.

Christmas was little more than a week away. I had shopping to do. Monday late afternoon was the big *Bop Street* Christmas show on KFAI—the only place on the FM dial to hear Santa do the mambo—and somewhere, right then, I knew that some TV station was showing *Holiday Inn*. Christmas dinner would be at my parents' house.

I wondered if I could get Edgerton to go with me. If not Edgerton, then maybe the Milkman. I owed the Milkman something. I had to call him when I got back. The feds would be talking to Lorraine Rovig. The Milkman needed to know what was going on.

Suddenly, my headlights caught the figure of a deer bounding out onto the road from the safety of a clump of trees. The deer stopped to stare at me as I hurdled toward it. I jerked the steering wheel and hit the brakes. I spun out of control along the shoulder of the road, narrowly missing the deer.

By the time the car stopped, the deer was gone. I looked out into the darkness and saw nothing but a distant halo that marked the freeway onramp.

I hunched over the steering wheel and cried.

A word about the author...

Brian Anderson is a graduate of the University of Minnesota whose Dinkytown neighborhood provides the setting for his mystery series featuring private investigator Lyle Dahms. The Dahms novels spring from his lifelong love of mystery fiction, especially the works of Dashiell Hammett and Raymond Chandler, as well as more contemporary masters like Robert B. Parker and G.M. Ford. He is a three-time finalist in the Pacific Northwest Writers Association mystery and suspense contest.

Brian spent much of his professional career working to alleviate domestic hunger serving as the operations director of the Emergency Feeding Program of Seattle & King County as well as the manager of the Pike Market Food bank in downtown Seattle. Married with three beautiful daughters, he now lives and writes in Ocean Shores, a small city on the Washington coast.